NO LOVE FOR THE WICKED

Text copyright © 2013 Megan Powell
All rights reserved.

Printed in the United States of America.

Published by 47 North
PO Box 400818
Las Vegas, NV 89140

ISBN-13: 9781477807637
ISBN-10: 1477807632
Library of Congress Control Number: 2013935321

NO LOVE FOR THE WICKED

MEGAN POWELL

47NORTH

To my mom and dad—a true example of
unconditional love

CHAPTER 1

Six months of smoking cloves, and I still couldn't blow a smoke ring. Best I could manage was a big ball of gray puff. I held the cigarette between my berry-glossed lips, inhaled deeply, formed a little O with my mouth, and tried again. Puffball. Whatever.

A swell of techno music filled the air, then cut away as the club door across the street opened and closed. *Holy shit, it's cold*, the emerging woman thought. I rolled my eyes. What did she expect? It had been snowing for two days now. She pulled her fake-fur wrap tighter to her chest and scanned the street. No taxis. Pulled out her cell phone. Dead battery. She pushed a few buttons anyway and started walking. The click-clack of her heels feigned purpose as she made her way down the icy sidewalk. "Hey, sorry I'm later than I thought, but I'm on my way now," she said, and then paused. There was no voice coming through the other end of the phone. She was pretending. Smart girl.

Unfortunately, I wasn't the only one who saw through the ruse. The man looked respectable enough, camel trench coat over dark pressed pants and thick-soled loafers. He emerged from the shadowed entry of a neighboring club. He'd been waiting. Not for this girl in particular, but for a type. He wanted a very specific prey.

So did I.

OK, this was it. The final test. I could do this. Dropping my cigarette, I instantly became invisible. It was so easy, I smiled. I'd been able to go invisible for years, but now using my powers was like any other natural function. Breathing, blinking, turning invisible. It felt good to have this much control.

I stepped out at the same time Trench Coat Guy did. He lit a cigarette and kept his distance from the woman. She didn't sense him yet, but her defenses were still up. Her voice intentionally carried through the cold air. "Yeah, headed there now, so I should be at your place in, like, ten minutes." She laughed. "Sure. Tell you what. If I'm not there in exactly eleven minutes, call 911." Impressive.

I stayed on the opposite side of the street, a block behind the guy. I heard him chuckle behind his cigarette as she picked up her pace. He had seen her try to turn on her phone in front of the club, then watched her struggle to walk with a don't-mess-with-me attitude. He watched her now, the swivel of her hips under that tight little skirt. He had all kinds of pictures in his mind about lifting that skirt and listening to her screams.

I stumbled and closed my eyes to his thoughts. What the hell was wrong with people? Being with a man wasn't supposed to be like that. The bittersweet scent of musk and metal wafted through my senses. Theo's dark smirk flashed in my mind. Quickly, I pushed the image away. No distractions tonight. I needed to get through this and stay focused. When I opened my eyes, Trench Coat Guy was almost two blocks away. *Shit.*

The next instant I was across the street, right behind the guy as he strolled into a parking garage. The woman's voice faded as she hustled up the garage's enclosed stairwell. When the sound of a door opening echoed through the stairwell, the man started running, taking two, sometimes three steps at a time. I didn't bother keeping pace. I just met him at the door. He slowed when he reached the landing. His eyes darkened, and a smile crept across his face. My breath caught. I'd seen transformations like this before. Much, much worse than this, actually, but the effect was still the same. It was a slight shift in features—a deepening in his eyes, a curl of his lip—but it was the same as if he had pulled off a mask, removed the handsome facade to reveal the monster that really lived there. Playtime was over. He reached for the door handle. I dropped my invisible shield.

"What the fuck!" he shouted as I body slammed him face-first into the door. He was a whole foot taller than me, so I jammed my shoulder into his lower back to keep him in place. He wriggled against my hold, but I barely noticed. I had to concentrate. Turning invisible, listening to other people's thoughts—those abilities were nothing. But this newest power had taken me months to hone. If I could totally control it now, I knew I'd be ready. I curled my nails into his lower back and focused my power into my hands. The bones popped and stretched as they transformed into leathery, elongated talons. Claws. I twisted my wrist and sliced through his coat and shirt until I felt the warmth of his blood tickle my fingertips.

He saw me from the corner of his eye, and his knees buckled. I brought my face up close to his. Blood dripped onto the floor around us. His flesh and the door behind him darkened to a deep shade of pink. I paused. My eyes were turning again. Damn it, I still couldn't completely control that one.

No matter. It was an emotional thing, that's all—a warning that my pissed-off was quickly turning to real anger. I inhaled a deep, calming breath and narrowed my gaze. His pupils dilated under my compulsion. "Here's what's going to happen, Mitchy. You're going to walk out of the garage and go home to your wife. You're going to wake her up, tell her what an incredible woman she is, and then you are going to spend the rest of your miserable life making sure she never has to question your devotion to her. It's going to be a real-life happily ever after."

His mouth opened and shut without sound. I pressed my claws in deeper. I could feel the blood trickling down to my wrists now. His eyes bled to black.

"I will walk out of the garage and go home to my wife. I'm going to wake her up, tell her what an incredible woman she is, and then I'm going to spend the rest of my miserable life making sure she never has to question my devotion to her. It's going to be a real-life happily ever after."

The pink receded, and my vision returned to normal. I slowly withdrew my claws from his back. Still holding him against the door, I pressed the long, narrow palm of my hand to the deep wounds I had worked into his back. I pushed my energy into his flesh and felt the heat as his wounds knit themselves back together. Then I erased the bloodstains on our clothes. The tears on his jacket could stay—let him wonder a little.

When he was all neat and healed, I stepped back and flipped my hair. Shooting him the bright, innocent, twentysomething smile I'd been practicing in the mirror, I said, "So this is my floor. I'm parked just by the door. Thank you so much, Mitch. I just hate walking by myself at night. Oh, watch your step. It looks like someone spilled their wine."

He blinked twice, looked down at the puddle of blood at our feet. "Uh, yeah. No problem." He straightened his lapels and ran a hand through his hair. "If you don't mind, I need to get home. My wife's waiting up."

"Oh yeah, of course." I reached around him for th‹ "Thanks again, Mitch."

He nodded as I stepped past him. I had barely pulle door closed behind me before Mitch's footsteps pounded ‹ the stairs in a sprint. I looked down at my hands. Back to n mal. The only sign that any transformation had occurred was ‹ slight redness at my knuckles and cuticles. I'd done it. I'd stayed focused, completely controlled the transformation, and stopped a bad guy all at the same time. It may not have been as planned out and executed as a Network mission, and Mitch was just a run-of-the-mill serial rapist and not a supernatural terrorist with powers similar to my own, but I'd set an objective, stayed on target, and completed my assignment. Just like any other Network agent.

I was finally ready to rejoin my team.

Chapter 2

No one ever plowed the old county roads. The barren corn-fields and skeletal woods glistened in the same perfect white as the long road ahead of me. It all looked so serene. Like some icy fairy tale. Of course, when I was growing up, my family's estate had always looked like that in winter too. And God knew that place was no home to happy endings. At least not for me.

I shifted into four-wheel drive as I approached the old tractor path that cut through one of the unused cornfields and disappeared deep into the woods at the field's edge. The small farmhouse at the end of the driveway was still too far away to see, but already my spirits soared. This was home. Not the sprawling estate of limestone luxury and immaculate gardens where I'd lived for the better part of my life. This was the small, neglected farm Thirteen had given me when he'd asked me to train his Network team. There was no fear here, no pain or sadistic relatives ready to attack me at every turn. Here I had felt comfort and peace for the first time in my twenty-three years of life.

I'd found the transfer of ownership papers packed in my bags a few months back. I still needed to sign on the dotted line, but it was all mine now. And after six months away, I was back.

I slowly crept forward, my stomach growing tighter with every inch. Up ahead the motion-sensor porch lights peeked through the frosted trees. I was ready for this, I reminded myself. Not only to reconnect with the Network, but to return to this life. I'd gained so much while I was away, and not just in control over my powers. I'd socialized, lived on my own. Normal emotions and relationships weren't confusing to me as they'd once been.

Finally, I drove past the last line of trees. There it was. The wide clearing sparkled. The lingering clouds parted so the moon could spotlight the small house. Faded black shutters, cracked cement wraparound porch, stained white siding—it was beautiful.

I pulled up along the side of the house and breathed in the feeling of homecoming. I never parked in the back parking area where everyone else did. The house wouldn't be mine if I didn't have my own parking space. God, it was just like I remembered— so small I could race around the entire exterior in the blink of an eye. If I stretched my neck, I'd see a living room through the front windows, jam-packed with mismatched sofas and ottomans. And if I went to the back door...

My smile vanished. Whispered voices carried over the low growl of my idling car. There were people inside my house. I'd been distracted pulling up the drive, but with my heightened senses, I heard the murmured voices now. I cut the engine. I hadn't told anyone I was coming back—not Thirteen or Heather or...Theo. The house and the hundred-plus acres surrounding it were mine. It never occurred to me they'd continue using the place after I'd left.

I used my mental feelers to do a quick brush through the house and froze. Four people—three guys, one girl. This wasn't my old Network team. I didn't recognize a single one of them. Thirteen would have never let another task force use this place, not after he'd signed over ownership to me. So who the hell was in there?

Rage whipped through me hot and fast. Strangers in *my* house? Oh hell no. The porch lights shattered as my power stretched past the bounds of my car. I could tell from their thought patterns that the four inside were nervous but armed. Probably some local drug dealers or something—tough-minded plebes happy to have found an abandoned house to process their product. *Bastards.* In a blur, I exited the car and moved up the porch steps. They had turned off all the lights. As if I couldn't find them in the dark. Of course, random squatters wouldn't know it was someone like *me* showing up in the middle of the night. Most people had no clue that people with powers like mine even existed in the world. If they had, they probably would have hightailed it for their cars the moment I'd pulled in the drive.

My powers took care of the locks, and I pushed open the front door. The small foyer was dark, and when the door shut behind me, it became even darker. Someone hid in the shadows at my right. Two more in the kitchen ahead. I stepped forward toward the narrow kitchen. Anger simmered through me, but I kept a tight rein on my powers. I reached out to my intruders' minds once more. The click of a gun cocking sounded at my left. The fourth guy had emerged from the living room. "Stay right where you are," said a deep, accented voice behind me.

Yeah, right.

The overhead light came on with blinding brightness. I blinked the corridor into focus. A man with tight dreads and a woman with too-bright green eyes stood in the hallway before me. Both were frowning, and both had guns aimed at my head. At my left, the guy from the living room moved his cocked gun a few inches from my temple. Bad move.

My vision turned red as I moved on instinct. The cocked-gun guy went first. I broke his hand with a quick twist and took him to the ground with a heel to the knee. The guy with dreadlocks came next—a gut-kick that had him barreled over and coughing blood. The chick got off a shot, but I moved way too fast for her to get a target. I gripped her ponytail and slammed her face into the wall, dropped her to the floor. With all three moaning on the ground at my feet, I turned on Accent Guy. Shock and anger twisted behind the blank expression he tried to keep in place. My power had him pinned to the foyer wall—his shoes a good three feet off the floor—so I didn't blame him for letting a little anxiety slip past his careful guard. I sauntered toward him, stepping over one of his whimpering friends along the way.

"I'm going to give you one chance and one chance only," I said quietly. My fingers strained—the urge to shift to claws just waiting to be let go. I clasped my hands behind my back. "Who the hell are you, and what are you doing in my house?"

Accent Guy's eyes widened into bright circles, but his lips pressed together into a tight line. He wasn't going to tell me anything. Oh well. I'd warned him. Letting loose just a hint of my anger, I tore into his mind. Telepathy didn't have to be painful, but fuck him. Break into *my* house? His body convulsed violently. He screamed in pain. I flipped through his thoughts with excruciating ease.

Colin St. Pierre. Thirty-four years old. Single, but nominally interested in some woman named Danielle. He was English, Oxford educated, trained with British Special Forces for five years. I saw more military training, but no longer with Special Forces. He was in the desert, one of more than a dozen men and woman fighting with swords, guns, hand to hand. Then he was in a classroom, the same dozen people sitting in desks around him. On a drop screen at the front of the room, mug shots and criminal profiles flashed one after another.

Al-Hassan Ilmudeen: illegal arms supplier to known terrorist organization Haldan Boi. Murder, assault, rape, kidnapping, illegal weaponry. Known abilities: telekinesis, pyrokinesis.

A man entered the classroom. Bodybuilder huge, his muscles stretched the crisp pin-striped shirt that squeezed tight at the collar around his thick neck. His hair was pulled back in a long silver ponytail, and the sharpness in his eyes couldn't hide the kindness in his crinkled smile. Thirteen. My vision instantly returned to normal as I pulled back and let Colin drop to the floor with a thud.

Well, screw me. These weren't squatting drug dealers I could kill for breaking into my house. They were another Network team.

Chapter 3

I leaned back in one of the hard kitchen-table chairs, spinning my glass of whiskey between my fingers and demonstrating remarkable patience. Colin was in the great room, whispering to his chief on his cell phone. Like that would keep me from hearing both ends of the conversation. The other three agents glared at me from their different positions around the kitchen. Their minds buzzed with questions, but no one had spoken a word.

"So, Luce," I said conversationally to the woman seated across from me. At twenty-eight, she was even younger than she appeared. Her light hair was pulled back in a tight ponytail that emphasized her almond-shaped green eyes and sharp cheekbones. Add to that the military-style tank and cargo pants, and she exuded a rough persona. Just like she wanted to. "How long have you been an agent for the Network?"

She flinched. She hadn't expected me to be a mind reader as well as a kick-ass fighter. Slowly she drew the ice pack away from her broken nose. The double black eyes were painful, but she wasn't too upset. The injury was a war wound, proof of her toughness against a true supernatural threat. Maybe now she'd gain a little more respect with her male teammates. Not that I was holding my breath for a thank-you or anything. She leaned forward, curled her lip in a sneer. But before she could berate me with a series of well-thought-out quips about my deficiencies as a human, the guy leaning against the wall behind her cleared his throat. Luce's hands curled into fists. She sat back and replaced the ice pack on her face.

I cocked a brow at the guy. "You know, Darrel, I have some lozenges in my car. I could run out and grab them for you. Could really help with that throat thing you have going on." I uncrossed my legs as if getting ready to stand.

"You're not going anywhere," he snarled. I smiled. He was a lean guy, about six feet, with the creamy complexion of a mixed race. His hair was knotted in tight dreads, and his jaw was set. He was a tough one, controlled. But I'd got him to break their little code of silence. It was a petty victory, I know, but a victory none-theless. And Darrel cursed himself for falling for it. I leaned back again, took another drink.

"How's the wrist doing, Tony?" I asked over my shoulder to the third guy sitting on the counter. He was younger than the others—just under twenty-four. And while his mind was sharp, he had the blond curls and golden tan of a West Coast surfer. I'd run into a lot of guys like him over the past months whenever I'd ventured out to a mall or passed through a college campus. I couldn't take him seriously if I wanted to. "Sorry to shatter the bones like that. It's just this thing I do whenever someone aims a gun at my head. I hope it doesn't hinder your role in your current assignment."

He didn't respond, of course, but his mind wasn't quite as disciplined as his teammates'—I saw some of the details of their current Network assignment. Like the name of their supernatural target. Weird, it wasn't anyone from my family.

Colin walked carefully back into the kitchen, tapping his cell phone against his forehead. Luce sat straighter in her seat. Tony continued to nurse his broken wrist but hopped off the counter at Colin's nod. His now bullet-free Glock clanged against the counter when he moved. Colin blew out a breath and studied my face. He reminded me so much of Jon. Clean-cut, thirtysomething, oozing natural leadership. Hell, even his hair was gelled in a similar catalog-model style.

Thinking of Jon immediately reminded me of Theo. I looked away and focused on my drink.

Colin dropped his cell phone on the table. When I glanced up, he'd put on his serious interrogator face.

"Magnolia. Like the flower. That's what you said your name was, right? What, is that supposed to be some cool single name like Beyoncé or Ke$ha? Tell me again, cool flower girl, why are you here?"

I ignored his lame attempt at intimidation and looked around the kitchen. The faded gold-and-brown wallpaper still peeled in the corners. Ugly wood paneling still covered the wall behind Darrel. There were still breaks in the wood from a little disagreement Jon and I had had last summer. I ran my hands over the oversize table. This was where Thirteen had asked me to teach his team how to kill someone with my powers. My chest ached remembering the hurt that request had caused me. The furnace kicked on and blew burned air through the vents in the ceiling. Over the sink, the yellow curtains I'd once bought to pretty up the place wavered.

"This is my home," I said softly. Damn it, even I could hear the longing in my voice.

"No," Colin replied. "This house is owned by a private organization, one you seem to know quite a bit about."

"The house is owned by me. And of course I know about the Network. I work for them."

"So says you—an obvious supernatural threat. Why would someone with your abilities work with an agency whose sole purpose is to police and contain individuals considered a supernatural risk? It would be like fighting against your own kind."

He had no idea.

"Who are you really working for?"

I rolled my eyes.

"OK, then," he said, changing tactics. "If you really work for the Network, then who is your team leader?"

I gave him a look. "Network members are anonymous except to those they immediately work with. I could list out my entire team and you wouldn't know a single name to confirm or deny." A near-silent beep sounded from the small bedroom at the back of the house. I shrugged. "But maybe the guy pulling in the driveway will have a higher clearance level than you. Who knows?"

Colin nodded to Darrel, sending him to check out the front window. "It's FedEx," Darrel announced, returning to the kitchen and shooting me a tight, satisfied grin. "He's pulling around the back."

"Little late for deliveries, isn't it?" I asked. All four of them watched me closely, waiting for the sweat of anticipation to bead on my face. It was such a cute, stereotypical cop-movie moment. I almost felt bad for letting them down. The car outside shut off. Snow crunched under heavy footsteps as the driver made his way around to the front porch. His thoughts were clipped. No wasted emotion, just straight here and now. It was strange to sense so much method and so little feeling. Yet vaguely familiar. When the front door opened, I actually found myself feeling a little of that anticipation they were hoping for.

Colin met the man before he entered the kitchen. "Thanks for coming," he murmured. "She's in here." They walked back in together. The guy was enormous. Solid muscle. Six seven, six eight—he had to walk a little sideways to fit his wide shoulders through the narrow hall. His straight black hair hung to his shoulders, casting shadows on his already-dark, stubbled jaw. He looked down on me, his face equal parts masculine lines and blank expression. I heard Luce's breath catch in appreciation. I totally agreed. But his thoughts had my guard up instantly: *Magnolia Kelch. Youngest offspring of Magnus Kelch, CEO Kelch Incorporated. Previous informant under Network chief Thirteen. Known preternatural powers include telekinesis, telepathy, supernatural speed, supernatural strength, and regeneration.*

"Are you sure that's all?" I asked drily and let my eyes glow a moment with a touch of power. His expression didn't change, but a mental wall slammed shut in his mind. I had met him only one time before, when he'd delivered a package to Thirteen during a team meeting last summer. His mental walls were as solid now as they had been then. I could still get through if I wanted to, but now wasn't the time. "Hello again, Jesse," I said tightly. "Or is it FedEx now?"

He didn't speak. He just pulled a cell phone from his back pocket, punched in a number, and held it to his ear. When the call was answered, he didn't wait for a hello. "She's back," he said in a gravelly voice.

There was a long pause. "Where?" a deep voice asked softly on the other end. I froze with my drink halfway to my mouth. Thirteen.

"South-side farmhouse. St. Pierre's team is using the place." His wide lips twitched. "They're holding her here."

"No one's hurt, are they?" Thirteen asked quickly. I swallowed my drink in a gulp and slammed the glass on the table.

"Oh! Like I can't go anywhere without hurting someone? Thanks a lot, Thirteen!" I shouted loud enough to be sure he heard.

"One broken nose, a shattered wrist, multiple contusions, and one possible internal bleeding," Jesse replied stoically.

I poured myself another shot. "Thanks a lot," I muttered under my breath.

Darrel drew close to Colin and whispered in his ear. "Thirteen? As in senior chief of red-level threats?"

"Shut up," Colin murmured, measuring me with new interest.

Jesse slapped his phone shut and pushed it back into his pocket. He turned to Colin.

"You had no clearance to use this residence."

"We needed a secure location," Colin argued. "This HQ hasn't been reported as in use for months. As team leader I'm authorized to set up base in any available Network location deemed reasonable."

"Not this location. Your team is relocating to a west-side safe house. The address will be forwarded to your phone in a moment." Colin's phone vibrated. Jesse turned back to me. "FedEx is my Network contact name. It was good to see you again, Magnolia." Then he turned and walked out the front door.

Mr. Personality, that one. Good thing he was hot.

For a long moment no one spoke. "What the hell?" Tony erupted. "We're just supposed to pack up and relocate? That's bullshit!"

"Be quiet," Colin ordered. Oh, I had definitely piqued his interest—not only because I was a supernatural, but because I knew a Network bigwig he'd only ever seen in training. Did I have some kind of leverage against Thirteen? Was I his lover? How did I know FedEx, when he'd only just been given access to the task force liaison with this most recent assignment?

I waited for him to ask any one of the questions swimming in his head, but instead he just barked orders to his team. "Gather your files. I'll forward the new HQ location, and we will reconvene at oh-six-hundred. Until then, get some rest. It's been a long night."

With that he ran a tired hand through his hair and returned to the great room. One by one the others gathered what papers and folders they had lying around, eyeing me curiously as they prepared to leave. I finished off my drink and went automatically to the broken cabinet over the refrigerator to get another bottle of Beam. I had to dust off the glass, but the contents were just fine. When I sat back down, Luce was staring at me.

"It's mine," I said, answering her unspoken question. "I put it there months ago for safekeeping. Want a drink?"

"I'm about to drive," she pointed out.

"So that's a no, then?"

She shook her head in mild disgust and followed Tony and Colin out the front door. Darrel shot me a lingering glare, then followed.

"It was a pleasure meeting you!" I called out. "Maybe we will all work together sometime!" A car door slammed in response. I frowned into my drink. As much control as I'd gained over my powers, my emotions were still too close to the surface. Strangers in my house? Instant rage. Thirteen assuming I'd injured Colin's team? Immediate hurt. I'd been back for less than an hour, and already the emotions running through me were more intense than anything I'd felt in the six months I'd been away.

It made me wonder, how much more would I feel now that I'd come home?

CHAPTER 4

The good thing about Colin's team invading my house was the food they left in the fridge. I'd planned on running to the mini-market a couple of miles down the county road, but now I could spend my morning unpacking. And cleaning. The pile of dishes in the sink told me they must have met here for planning sessions and recon meetings pretty regularly. But they couldn't have spent any more time here than necessary, because the place was absolutely filthy.

The scent of mothballs and burned air coated everything from the sofas to the walls. I started in the small single bedroom, sweeping cobwebs from the ceiling. Nothing had been moved since I'd left. My department store quilts still covered the lumpy queen-size mattress; plastic crates I'd stacked to make a mock dresser still lined the wall under the metal-framed window; the completely out of place high-tech security system still remained hidden under loose files and cardboard boxes. The heater kicked on just as I dusted off the vent on the ceiling. Stale, dirty air blew right in my face, sending me into a bitch of a coughing fit.

I managed to get through all the dusting and was back on the ceiling, regluing the wallpaper border in the kitchen, when the quiet beep of the alarm announced a visitor. Instantly I reached out to the driver. No way I'd be caught off guard again.

I couldn't help the small twist of disappointment when I confirmed the driver wasn't Theo. Before I'd left, the connection between us had been stronger than any other power I'd ever experienced. But that connection was emotional. As excited as I was to see him again, I knew that my emotions weren't as under control as my powers were. How that would affect our connection, I had no idea.

The car's door shut quietly in the back parking area. An odd nervousness settled in my stomach. It wasn't Theo, but it certainly wasn't a stranger. I wiped my hands off on my sweatpants. From the cabinet over the stove, I grabbed a couple of juice glasses and poured out a finger of whiskey in each. Heavy footsteps hurried to the porch.

"It's open," I called out before Thirteen could knock. Quietly, he opened the front door. I didn't listen to his thoughts— his mental walls were too strong for me to subtly browse anyway. He angled his way into the kitchen and stood in the doorway. Everything I'd missed about him was there. His strong hands that dwarfed my face whenever he cupped my chin. His crinkly smile and long gray hair that always needed cutting. His enormous stature that towered over everyone around him. The innate authority he wore like a thick overcoat. If he didn't say something soon, I'd have to read his thoughts just to keep from biting my nails.

"You've grown," he said softly.

"What? No, I haven't." I glanced down at myself. I looked exactly the same. My thick brown hair might have been a few inches longer, falling nearly to my waist now, but that was the only difference I could see. My legs were still too long for my five-foot-six height and still met with lean hips and tight tummy. My chest was just as generous as ever, turning more heads than I ever wanted. I adjusted my posture and scowled at him. "Why would you think that?"

A small smile tugged at his lips, softening his serious features. Against my will, tears burned the corners of my eyes.

"I wasn't referring to your appearance." He sighed. "Oh, Magnolia, how I have missed you."

That was all it took. I leaped across the room and barreled into his chest. His arms wrapped around me in a tight bear hug that would have bruised anyone else. Thirteen's scent of Old Spice and herbal tea filled my senses. This was the father I should have had. And my true welcome home.

He chuckled deep in his chest and set me back. His face was a mixture of surprise and amusement. "See?" he said. "When would you have ever voluntarily embraced another person before?"

I turned my back to him as heat flooded my face. Damn it, he was right. I would have never hugged someone before. Not even him. It was just seeing him after all this time—seeing that the unconditional affection he felt for me was still there—it was too much to hold back.

I shrugged and added ice to the whiskey glasses. "I guess I was just happy to see a familiar face. Especially after my not-so-welcome-home party last night. What are Colin and his team doing in Indiana anyway? I didn't get everything from their thoughts, but that pyrotech art smuggler they're tracking is from South Africa. If my father or uncles wanted to buy some priceless piece of crap, they'd use one of their mindless minions to go get it, not bring some dealer home to the estate."

"There are supernatural threats other than the Kelch family, Magnolia. The Network tracks every one of them."

"Maybe so, but no way anyone else with powers would dare come into our home state for any length of time. Not without invitation."

He adjusted the cuff of his shirt. "Are you sure about that?"

I snorted. "Don't pretend the Network isn't aware of my family's reputation."

"We are. I just wasn't certain that you knew your family's notoriety in the supernatural community. Having been confined to the estate the majority of your life, I assumed you hadn't encountered others with preternatural gifts."

His words warmed my heart. He'd always thought of me as gifted, even when, at times, my powers seemed more a curse than anything else.

"Father and Uncle Max didn't just bring business competitors and political adversaries to the estate. Lots of people with supernatural abilities were brought home over the years. Some actually worked with Father on different side projects for Kelch Inc.—usually the deeply buried ones. But most of the time, when someone came in, it was because they'd made the mistake of thinking they were stronger or more powerful than us. I don't have to tell you how Father reacts when he thinks someone's powers might be a match for his own." I took a long swallow of my whiskey as my bones ached in remembered tortures.

Thirteen frowned. I continued explaining. "The year before I escaped, Father brought a telepath to the estate. It had been years since I'd been around a supernatural I wasn't related to, but I felt his power immediately."

"I thought you only felt your family's power."

"Anyone with supernatural abilities can feel it when we're around someone else with powers. It's just easier for me to recognize my family's energy because I'm so familiar with it."

"So if I took you to a Network holding cell right now, you'd be able to tell me the powers of each person under investigation?"

The idea of the Network holding supernatural people prisoner made my mouth go dry.

"Er, no. Not really. It's more like when we were investigating the break-in at Banks's house last year—I knew power had been used, but I couldn't tell who exactly had used it or what they had done. Anyway, this man at the estate had heard all kinds of horror stories about what happened to people with power who crossed paths with our family. For whatever reason, the guy was feeling brave. He stopped for some lunch at one of the delis near Kelch Inc.'s headquarters. Father might never have felt him if he'd eaten somewhere else. As it was, when Father's driver took him past the deli—the street only a few feet away from the deli's entrance—Father sensed the man's power. He went inside, found the man among the crowd, and picked him up. The man's bravado didn't last past the estate's main-house foyer. But his screams echoed even into the north barn, where I was being held."

Thirteen sucked in his breath. He hated it when I talked about my life on the estate. I moved on quickly.

"So like I said, no way another person with power would come near here without it involving my family. Is Uncle Max doing a political thing, establishing a relationship with an African ambassador or something?"

Thirteen took my offered glass of whiskey. "Well, now that depends. Colin and his team are Network agents. Their activities are privy only to those within the Network." He eyed me carefully. "Are you a part of the Network, Magnolia?"

I studied my glass. "You said I was. If I wanted to be."

"Yes, but typically we do not allow our agents to leave their base of operation for unspecified months at a time with no communication to their division chief."

The subtle edge behind his calm words gave me pause. "I had to leave, Thirteen—you know that. It had nothing to do with you or the Network or the team. There was just too much going on. I mean, you saw what happened, what I turned into. How could I be around everyone else after that?"

I looked down at my hands. Such slight, feminine things that could turn so terrifying and grotesque. And they weren't the only part of me that could transform. I remembered that night with Markus, how my face had contorted into such a monstrous sight, with glowing red eyes and a mouthful of sharp teeth. Thank God I had control over that now.

"Your team knew from the beginning that you had preternatural abilities."

"It wasn't the same, and you know it." I cleared my throat to keep my voice from wavering. "I killed my own brother."

"You saved the lives of several Network agents, including mine."

"I became something else. I was transformed into some kind of beast and ripped Markus's throat out with my teeth. Everyone on the team thought I was a monster."

"No," Thirteen said, setting his untouched whiskey on the table. "No one thought that about you." I gave him a dry look. "They were intimidated by the level of power that you wielded, but that was all. If you had stayed long enough to hear their thoughts, you would have known that."

He was wrong. I had heard their thoughts. "I had no choice."

Thirteen peered down at me, his lips in a tight line. "You had a choice to remain in contact. You chose not to."

The urge to look away nearly undid me, but I forced myself to hold his gaze. "I needed time, Thirteen. To understand what was happening to me. The powers inside me have changed since I escaped from the estate. Some have gotten stronger. Some I never even realized I had before. I knew the changes were happening while I was training the team last year, and I thought I could handle it. But when I turned into that…thing, I knew I needed to get control over myself, and I couldn't do it here."

"Why not here?" he said sharply. For the first time, I saw the hurt behind his commanding blue eyes. "I could have helped you. The Network has resources that could explain why your powers were acting up."

"No, they don't have resources for this, Thirteen. Not when it comes to *my* powers. You might have been able to help me deal if it had been one of those traits that all people with supernatural powers share, but it wasn't the extra strength and speed that I needed to worry about. I'm not like the other people the Network monitors. You know that. Hell, I'm not even like the other people in my family. I don't have just one ability, like Uncle Max's telepathy or Father's telekinesis. I can do everything they can do and more. It was the more that I needed to get control over."

"And did you get the control you felt you needed?"

I poured another finger of whiskey. "I wouldn't have come back unless I had."

He nodded, but I knew he wasn't satisfied. Unfortunately, I didn't know what else to say.

"Well, whatever your reasons for leaving," he said finally, "I'm glad you've decided to return."

I let out a long breath and felt like a balloon deflating. He wasn't really mad at me. I felt like I'd just lost fifteen pounds in thirty seconds.

"It was time," I said. "And like I said before, I have total control over that whole claw-and-beast thing now. No transforming unless I want to."

Thirteen's expression went carefully blank. "And have you? Wanted to, that is?"

I thought about the predators I'd tracked while honing that particular ability. The rush I felt after each surge of transforming power. "I have control over it. That's all that matters."

He eyed me a moment longer, then picked up his whiskey again. "So now that you've returned, what are your plans? If you don't mind me asking." There was still a carefulness to his words that made me want to kick myself for not checking in before now.

"Well, I figured, you know, that I could, like…help. Again." His expression stayed blank. "I know your task force doesn't really need any more training to fight my family's powers, but you said I was a part of the team—that I'd always be a part of the team."

"Are you certain that's what you want? If I recall, joining the front lines in the fight to bring your father and uncles to justice wasn't always an ambition you wanted to pursue. And if what you say about their reactions to other supernaturals is true, rejoining your team means taking a greater risk than simply exposing your continued existence."

I took another long drink. Power grew warm beneath my skin. I thought of the years I'd spent at the mercy of my sadistic father. The pain. The blood. The experiments and unending hatred. My family might have brought horror to their adversaries, but that was nothing compared to what had been done to me. How many times had Father killed me, only to have my powers bring me back? How many times had my brothers stalked me or watched in excitement as Father and Uncle Max tried out a new method of torture for their enemies on me?

"I'm not scared of them anymore," I said. With deliberate control, I flexed my power until it was a warm hum of energy in the air around us. Thirteen lifted his arm, watched all the hairs stand on end.

"Returning to your team is about more than just control over your powers." Thirteen lowered his arm to his side. "A team has to trust each other to accomplish their missions. You left. You'll have to prove to them that they can trust you again."

I almost laughed. "They never trusted me."

"Trust is a two-way street."

I rolled my eyes. "OK, how about this: if we can make it through an entire meeting without Shane or Charles attacking me, or Marie accusing me of plotting against the Network on behalf of my family, I'll consider trusting more of them than just Heather." And Theo. I trusted Theo maybe even more than I trusted Thirteen. I didn't think Thirteen needed to know that right now.

Finally, he let out a quiet sigh. "Go get cleaned up."

I threw back the rest of my whiskey and bounded back to my room with an excited spring in my step. Thirty seconds later we were headed out the door.

CHAPTER 5

"Where are we going anyway? Your offices are off I-70." I squinted down the highway and then looked at Thirteen in the driver's seat for an answer.

"Kelch Incorporated's headquarters are expanding—a result of your father's most recent pharmaceutical acquisition. Several of the buildings surrounding the Kelch Inc. compound have had to redistrict. The Network moved our local offices to the Chase Tower."

Ah yes, Father's ever-increasing economic empire. Kelch Incorporated was a world leader in pharmaceutical research and development, military-grade weaponry, and over-the-counter consumer products. The family's net worth reached far into the eleven-digit range on legitimate business alone. Add in the less-than-legal business, and that amount tripled. Secret supernatural power was easier to hide when you overflowed with more of the mainstream powers like business and politics.

We exited from the highway and were immediately in the heart of Indianapolis. I'd seen several cities in the last couple of months: Chicago, New York, Boston, Saint Louis. Nothing compared to Indy. It had the skyscrapers, the street vendors, the business suits rushing here and there. But it also had a quaintness that the bigger cities lacked. People drove their own cars here, confident they'd find a parking spot. If you got confused on the one-way streets, you rolled down your window and called out to someone passing by, and that person would point the way without hesitation. People were nice here.

How in the world my family ended up in a city like this, I had no idea.

We pulled into the underground garage and parked in a reserved spot. I followed Thirteen to the bank of elevators, rode up to the main level, then walked with him past the sea of tile and glass that made up the building's main lobby. We hopped on another elevator—a much nicer one decorated with the same deep green as the lobby. When we reached our floor, we stepped out into a standard hallway. No artwork, no nameplates, no signs directing guests to various business suites. Just one set of double doors with no handles.

"Not very welcoming," I pointed out.

"It's not supposed to be." He typed in a code on the keypad next to the door. I expected a click releasing the locks, but instead the keypad flipped open. Thirteen bent over, putting his face directly in front of the open pad. A red laser ran over his face, forehead to neck. The doors opened automatically.

"Impressive," I said. "Your old offices didn't have any security like that."

He gave me a sideways glance. "I never took you to our old offices."

I shrugged. We both knew I had tailed him constantly in those early days of our acquaintance. And why wouldn't I? I'd only known him as an enemy of my father. Why would I trust a guy who was supposed to hate me?

Fortunately for both of us, he didn't hate me. Turned out that as much as I was in need of a surrogate father, he had been in need of a daughter. At least with me, he knew that there would never be a time when he could lose me to the supernatural threats of his enemies. He hadn't been so lucky with the child he'd lost.

The doors closed behind us with a silent click. "We're going straight through to the back office," he said, leading the way.

The majority of the work space we passed was one big bull pen. Dry-erase boards set up in various desk groups displayed names and timelines with arrows indicating relationships or connections. Agents I'd never seen talked on phones or buried their noses in laptops. No one paid us any attention as we made our way to the far end of the room.

"How can all these people work together like this?" I asked. "I thought Network agents were anonymous to each other unless working directly on an assigned team."

"These aren't field agents," he explained. "They're support. When an agent is having an issue with their assignment—the target is closing in on them, they require specific equipment or authorization, or the target they're tracking has abilities the agent was unaware of—they call in to the support center. It takes a different kind of training to work in Network support. Right in here."

It was a corner office, of course, with a wide, proud desk and windows that overlooked the State Soldiers' and Sailors' Monument. Right now, enormous Christmas lights streamed down from the top of the memorial all the way to the street. At sunset, the city would light the colorful strands, making a giant Christmas tree, while carols played through the sidewalk speakers. I had seen the tree lit on TV once when I was young. Father's temper had been running high, so he hadn't bothered waiting until we were in one of the barns. He'd started beating me right there in his study.

The guards found me in one of the more frequently used guest rooms. It had been risky for me to hide there, but it was the best place to eavesdrop on Malcolm and Markus's tutoring session. Father never allowed me any kind of real education, so if I wanted to learn anything more than what I picked up through my mind reading, I had to listen in on my brothers' lessons. The vents to this guest room connected directly to those in my brothers' library. Risky or not, it was the best place to take notes. Of course, it was also one of the first places the guards looked whenever Father summoned me.

When we reached Father's study, the guards didn't hesitate to toss me inside the elaborate office-like room and quickly leave, bolting the doors shut behind me. I knew instantly that this father-daughter session would be a bad one—his frustration over a failed business deal screamed in his thoughts. He'd hated me since the moment I was born, when he'd realized that the strength of my power surpassed anything he'd ever felt. Tonight, he needed to work out his anger, and what better way to do that than to beat senseless the only person who could take whatever damage he inflicted and still wake up the next morning ready for more? Me.

The first hit came before I could brace myself. Blood poured into my mouth as the side of my face shattered. The pain was excruciating, but I didn't care. This was just an anger session, where Father would beat me until I was a broken mess on his floor. I'd rather be Father's punching bag a million times over than the guinea pig in one of his many experiments.

It wasn't too long before he complained that his fists weren't creating enough damage; I wasn't bleeding as much as he preferred. So he brought out the antique engraved blades he kept locked away in his office safe. An hour later, I pretended to be unconscious and peeked through swollen eyes to the big-screen TV built into the wall behind Father's desk. Blood had pooled around my head; the side of my face was gone from the slicing cuts of Father's razors. But from what I could make out, the monument lights had looked really pretty on the TV.

Maybe I'd get the chance to see them for real sometime.

"No one responded to you," Thirteen said, pulling me back to the present.

I turned to face him. He stood by the door, watching me. "The agents out in the bull pen," he continued. "Not a single one noticed you any more than they would have any other young, attractive woman. How is that possible?"

I knew what he was referring to, and I smiled a little in pride. "I can hold it back now. The sensual allure that radiates off me, it's another aspect of my power that I've learned to control. It's not hard—kind of like holding back a yawn—but I've found it's easier to deal with people if I tone it down a bit."

Thirteen's eyes glistened, and I could feel that he was impressed. My smile widened.

He drew my attention to the opposite side of the room. "They've been questioning him for over two hours. I'd hoped they'd made more progress than this."

I stepped up beside him. The wall was actually the window side of a two-way mirror. The room next door was an interior conference room—no windows, only straining fluorescent lights. At the end of a long table, a middle-aged man sat sweating in his seat. He wore a uniform of some sort and had unbuttoned his collar. He tugged at it as if it still wasn't loose enough. I'd never seen the man before. But the two men facing him sent my heart thumping.

"It's Jon and Charles!" I exclaimed, then slapped my hand over my mouth.

"It's OK," Thirteen assured me. "They can't hear you."

Jon Heldamo, my former teammate, stood at casual attention. His light-brown hair was trimmed and gelled perfectly. He wore a sports jacket and khaki pants that I knew weren't required but were just his style. If Jon was here, chances were that Theo was somewhere close by. My body grew tingly as I reached out to the rest of the building. Fifty-two floors, a couple thousand people, but no Theo. *Damn.*

As Jon spoke, he strolled behind the empty conference chairs, moving with the arrogant authority of a natural leader. He stopped a few seats away from the man being questioned and put his hands on the back of the chair where Charles Hilliby sat glaring.

I stifled a cringe at the sight of Charles and his buzz-cut hair. Wearing heavy cargo pants and a tight black turtleneck, he looked every bit the angry ex-soldier I remembered him to be.

"Who are they questioning?" I asked.

"He's a pilot," Thirteen explained. "For the last two months he has been flying your father and Senator Kelch to various locations throughout Eastern Europe. Chang broke the encryption on the travel logs from the private airport they used, so we have times of departure and arrival but no recorded destinations. Captain Bennett here logged in as pilot for every flight. We believe the brothers have been making regular visits to somewhere outside Romania, but we need the pilot to confirm. Unfortunately, he seems to have absolutely no memory of ever flying your family anywhere."

Charles pounded his fist on the conference room table, making Captain Bennett jump in his seat. The captain ran his hands over his face, then held out his palms as if pleading. It was no use. They could beat him with questions all day long—hell, they could beat him with sticks all day long—it wasn't going to change the fact that Uncle Max had erased the man's mind with his supernatural persuasion.

"What do you usually do with victims of aggressive telepathy?" I asked, trying to sound official. This was the most exposure to inside Network workings that Thirteen had ever allowed me. I didn't want to blow it by sounding unprofessional.

"There is no 'usually' with this kind of power," Thirteen replied. "If you recall, we were unaware that this level of mental manipulation even existed until you pointed it out to us. We have been able to recover some memories of a few minor informants using a sensitized serum that your teammate Cordele Bleu has developed. But when someone has experienced the level of specified neurological damage that this pilot has, it has little to no effect."

"Hmm," I responded with a nod.

His gaze shifted down to mine. "Would you like to help them?"

"Really? Like go in there and ask the guy questions?"

"I was thinking more of utilizing your gifts from here. Assist Captain Bennett with his recollection of events."

A sharp pang of remembered betrayal tightened my gut. I knew that being part of Thirteen's team would include being used for my supernatural gifts. It was part of the reason I'd worked all these months to gain such perfect control. But there was still a little piece inside me that wanted him to see me as just another key member of the team—not a secret tool to be called on to make their jobs easier.

It didn't matter. I wanted to work with Thirteen and the guys on my old team. Now I was getting the chance.

"OK," I said, stepping closer to the glass. Thirteen flipped a switch on the wall, and Jon's voice filled the room. I could already hear every word, but this way Thirteen could listen in as well.

"…to a destination somewhere along Russia's western border. This is fact, Captain. We have records, satellite feed, flight logs—you flew that plane."

Bennett held his head in his hands, his fingers curling into his messy gray hair. "I didn't. I swear to you. I don't know what you're talking about!"

I pushed into his mind. Poor guy—Uncle Max had really done a number on him. He barely knew his address, let alone where he'd flown in the last month. I scanned past the mental scars and holes and found what it was they were looking for.

"It was a city," Bennett said suddenly, surprising himself. "Bohlren. A small dirt airstrip. I thought we were landing on the water at first, but then suddenly there were guide lights. A wide river. And buildings."

Charles quickly got over his shock at Bennett's sudden revelation and scribbled furiously on the pad of paper in front of him. Jon looked over his shoulder to the two-way mirror. "You flew to a city called Bohlren. A city on a big river. Who was on the plane with you?"

Bennett frowned as he tried to hold on to his train of thought. "I—I'm not sure. A guy, I think. Yeah, definitely a guy."

"What did he look like?"

Bennett rubbed his forehead. "I don't know. Tall? Maybe. I don't know. Look, I don't know why I'm remembering any of this anyway. Did you drug me or something?"

"We didn't drug you," Charles growled.

"Because until this moment right now, I would have sworn on a stack of Bibles that I've never flown outside the continental US. But I have. I remember it now."

"Yeah," Jon said and turned to face us in the two-way mirror again. "That is strange. But now that you do remember, let's see if we can dig a little deeper."

I pulled back as Jon began his next round of questions. "Getting a description is going to hurt him," I explained. "I can pull it out of him in a mindsweep, but chances are he'll probably hemorrhage."

"No," Thirteen said. "We already know who was on the plane. That's enough for our purposes. Jon and Charles should be able to fill in some of the holes in the logbooks with what you've brought out of him." He turned to me, his face set in a practiced blank that told me something important was brewing in his mind.

"Thank you," he said after a long moment. "Once again, you've offered aid to our team in a way that no one else has the capability of providing." He held out his hand. "I would like to formally offer you a position as a task force agent within the International Network of Special Defense."

I narrowed my eyes at him. "So this was a test. Is that it?"

"It was a test, yes, but not how you think. Our agents go through years of education and training to acquire a pittance of the knowledge you possess on supernatural strength and ability. The few moments you've experienced where you've had to make the choice to put the goals and safety of the team ahead of your own ego and insecurities, you've never let me down. If you work with the Network, I will ask you to use your gifts on assignments, in interrogation, while retrieving target information, or however else the situation may call for. And I will ask you to provide intimate information about your father, uncles, and surviving brother. I will ask these things and expect you to comply."

My stomach quivered at the bluntness of his words. But I understood what he was saying. And why. It had been a misunderstanding of expectations that had led to intense feelings of distrust between us the last time around. Neither of us wanted to go through that again.

"I can do this. I *want* to do this."

He slid his big hands down my arms, held out his hand once again. "Then, Magnolia Kelch, welcome to the Network."

CHAPTER 6

Thirteen treated me to the Thirsty Turtle Bar and Grill for a late lunch. We walked in and I immediately scanned the minds of the crowd. Something felt off. Maybe it was knowing that my father was only a few miles away, but my paranoia had seriously spiked since we'd left Thirteen's offices. Fortunately, no one seemed to be paying us any attention—or thought.

"Where's Miller?" I asked as we slipped into a booth. I'd scanned the entire building, including the secret conference room deep beneath the Turtle's basement, and hadn't found a single sign of the gruff bartender.

"Miller doesn't run the Thirsty Turtle for the Network anymore," Thirteen explained. "He was reassigned a few months ago." The pang of frustration surprised me. So much was different now. New agents, new offices, no Miller to growl at me about my drinking. When I'd lived on my family's estate, it had been a torturous hell, but at least it had been a consistent torturous hell.

I'd been in the real world for nearly a year now, and it seemed as if nothing stayed as it was for more than a few moments.

Thirteen and I split a breaded tenderloin the size of small hubcap while I entertained him with stories of my travels. His eyebrows drew together when I told him about some of the unsavory people whose plans I'd thwarted. "I had to practice to make sure I was in control of my powers," I explained with a shrug. "Wasn't like I really hurt anybody. I mean, if I did hurt someone, I healed them right after."

"I'm sure you did," he murmured. "And did you enjoy it? Not the stalking, necessarily, but being out there on your own?"

I thought about going to the movies for the first time, going to a mall and shopping like all the other twentysomething girls out there—the freedom of being normal that I'd never experienced until those months away.

"Yeah," I said softly. "I liked it. But there were too many unknowns. I know you said that my father and Uncle Max haven't made any moves like they know I'm still alive. But when they found Markus, whatever excuses they gave to the media, they had to know that something powerful killed him. A normal person couldn't have torn him to shreds like that."

Thirteen spoke hesitantly. "I understand you believe your uncle Mallroy saw you during the rescue mission last summer."

"How did you—" *Right. Theo.*

"All estate security disks were confiscated during the FBI investigation. We've replayed the escape over and over, and while there was footage of your uncle standing on the ledge of the estate's wall, oddly waving to the prisoners as we drove away, there was nothing that indicated that he saw you past your invisible shield. You didn't show up on the disks at all."

I'd basically convinced myself of the same thing. But it still didn't ease the odd feeling that something felt off.

"I'm full," I announced, my appetite suddenly gone. "We should go if we're going to meet everyone at Jon's house." After another moment, Thirteen called for the check.

* * *

We pulled into one of the hundreds of cookie-cutter neighborhoods that had taken over the suburbs like a plague. The homes were pretty enough, with brightly colored siding and neatly trimmed yards. Pear trees so young they still had their support ties lined the sidewalks every few feet. We passed three versions of the same house before parking in front of a newer two-story on the edge of a cul-de-sac. Two cars already filled the tight driveway. I didn't recognize either vehicle, but chances were I'd recognize the owners. Theo wasn't here yet.

"How long have Heather and Jon lived together?" I asked as we climbed out of the car. Snow had started to fall again, making the brightly lit house with a Christmas tree in the front window look like something off a holiday card. There was even a little snowman standing guard in the front yard. A chill of anticipation slowed my pace. This was it. I was going to see my team again. I couldn't tell if the butterflies in my stomach were from excitement or nerves.

"I believe she moved into his apartment while he recovered from his shoulder wound in July," Thirteen said. "His physical therapy was rather extensive, and she stayed with him to help. They moved to this home a few weeks before Thanksgiving."

I held back a few steps as my legs grew heavy. It had been so easy to walk into all those unfamiliar clubs and restaurants and coffee shops. Benign strangers in faraway cities didn't mean anything to me. But these people knew me. They knew the humiliating pain of my past. My powerful "otherness." They had seen what I turned into when I let my powers take over. What would they think when I walked through that door? Would it matter that I'd saved some of their lives, or would they be scared of me now because they knew exactly what I was capable of?

Thirteen paused at the front door. He looked at me over his shoulder. "Ready?"

My throat tightened. Damn it, I hated this anxiety. I took a deep breath and nodded once. Thirteen knocked twice on the door. My heart pounded as light footsteps hurried over laminate floors inside. The door swung open and revealed a pretty blonde with sharp eyes and dark roots. She wore a brown turtleneck that went well with her light skin tone and jeans over a lean and fit body. The bulge of a weapon harness left the line of her side slightly off. She shifted her gaze in my direction, and the welcoming smile faded. Her mouth fell open.

"Hey, Cordele," I said lamely.

With an audible snap, she shut her mouth. Her thoughts flashed with a myriad of images before going into a concentrated rendition of the alphabet song. Interesting. Her mental focus hadn't been that strong before. I tilted my head and studied her closer. Why wouldn't she want me to see what she was thinking?

"Oh my God!" she exclaimed suddenly and sprang forward. Instantly I shifted out of the way. She stumbled down the front steps into the snow. I frowned as she turned back to me with an annoyed smirk. "I was trying to give you a hug, Magnolia. Not attack you." She dusted the snow from her hair and brushed past me back up to the front door. "I see your personal relations skills haven't improved while you were away."

She left the door open for us to follow. I looked to Thirteen. "How was I supposed to know she was giving me a hug? She's never hugged me before—never even thought about it. She just came at me." And with her thoughts focused the way they were,

I'd had no clue what she'd intended. He gave me a sympathetic shrug, then waved for me to go first. "At least I didn't defend myself," I murmured.

I felt Thirteen's smile as he walked behind me into the home's patch of an entryway. "That is a good thing," he said and placed a hand on my back to guide me inside.

The small entry was separated from a pleasant front sitting room by a narrow half wall. We followed the voices past the front room and into an open area that combined a good-size kitchen, dining area, and living area in one space. Cordele headed to the L-shaped couch against the wall. "You guys aren't going to believe this," she said with a shake of her hair. Before the two men facing the TV had a chance to respond, a glass shattered in the kitchen. I spun into a crouch automatically, power ready. Of course, there was no need.

"Magnolia?" Heather whispered from the opposite side of a peninsula counter. "You're back?" She walked around the kitchen counter carefully, her wide eyes never leaving me. Her hair was shorter than I remembered, curling around her ears in a cute blunt cut. Unlike Cordele's, her blonde was natural. Her white, fuzzy sweater and cream khakis reminded me of a schoolteacher. But it was her thoughts that grabbed my attention. Apparently, I wasn't the only one who was stronger now than she'd been a few months ago. Heather's empathetic impulses were nearly to the point of aggressive. I felt a hesitancy as she approached, and for a moment I couldn't tell if the feeling was coming from me or from her.

"Hey, Heather," I said.

Every eye in the room was on us. I shifted my weight on instinct, keeping the others in my line of sight. Heather sniffed; her eyes welled with tears. Slowly, as if approaching a beaten animal, she spread out her arms and stepped into me. Instantly, I stiffened. But unlike Cordele's shock-and-awe approach to affection, this hug was…perfect. I closed my eyes and let the relief in her thoughts wash over me.

For several moments, I let her hold me. Her thoughts spun with questions. Where had I been? Was I back for good? She thought I looked different but not in a bad way. When she finally stepped back, her genuine happiness at my return overshadowed all her questions. "I missed you," she said with a small smile.

My chest swelled, and I felt tears pool in my eyes. I could be stabbed, burned, beaten, and broken and wouldn't shed a tear. One day with Thirteen and Heather, and I was blubbering like an idiot.

Across the room, Jon cleared his throat. Thirteen had joined him, along with Cordele and Shane, in the living room. "Guess I know why Bennett had a sudden burst of memory in interview today," Jon said. "So, Magnolia, are you back for good, or is this just a rest stop before you get back to running away some more?"

I felt the slap of his words, and power surged inside me. Heather snatched her hands from my shoulders as if burned. I turned slowly to face Jon. He, Cordele, and Shane adjusted their stances. It made me smile. Good, they were still smart.

"Magnolia has accepted my offer to officially join the Network as an agent member of our task force," Thirteen explained. "She is here to stay."

Jon lifted his brows. Shane scoffed and crossed his thick arms over his chest. "She hasn't even gone through classroom training," he argued. "She can't join the task force officially until she's certified."

I met Shane's glare and saw the simmering hurt and rage that festered there. His sandy hair had gotten darker in the winter months. His wide, muscular frame was more cowboy than soldier. Sharp, deep eyes, strong, blond-stubbled chin—I knew for a fact that the other girls on the team found him quietly attractive. But he wanted me. Always had, even though we both knew it would never happen. Seeing me now, all that resentment came pouring back into him.

"Magnolia will not be required to gain certification in classroom training," Thirteen said with some impatience.

"She shouldn't have to," Cordele added. "I mean, she's the one who trained us on powers that we didn't even know existed. If we wait for her to get certified, we might miss out on the chance to move on the brothers before they solidify their operation in Eastern Europe."

I lifted a brow. First she'd tried to hug me, and now she was defending my assignment to the team. I glanced again into Cordele's thoughts and saw a specific image of my brother Markus ordering her torture. Then me, standing before him, blocking her and the others from his assault. Cordele met my gaze and nodded. She'd shown me that image deliberately, letting me know that whatever else she might be thinking, she knew just how dedicated to the Network I was. A warm feeling of solidarity spread through me, making it easier to face the others.

Jon eyed me carefully in the silence that followed. They were waiting for his reaction. He'd cringed a bit at Cordele's slip about their current assignment, but then he'd remembered how Bennett's memory had come flooding back. *That has to be her doing,* he thought. And if that was the case, I already knew what they were trying to do.

"Bohlren," I said, answering Jon's unspoken question. "I've never been there and have no idea what significance it holds for my father and uncle." I let the electric gleam I was feeling shine in my eyes. "But I can help you find out."

A slow grin lifted his lips. "Magnolia... Welcome back."

CHAPTER 7

By the time the Chinese food arrived, most of the rest of the team had joined us. Jon had sent out a text message letting everyone know the good news of my return, so when Charles and Marie Hilliby walked through the front door, they didn't freak out and try to kill me on the spot. They wanted to, but they managed to restrain themselves. Charles had figured out that it had been me "helping" Bennett with his memory that morning, but it didn't matter. I'd broken, healed, burned, and reburned his hands more times than either of us wanted to remember. He'd hold tight to his grudge for as long as possible. I couldn't blame him. I was surprised, however, by the lack of emotion coming off Marie. The petite Latina fashionista with her Chanel sweater and leather knee-high boots had always been a bitch to the nth degree when it came to me. She barely spared me a thought or glance as the meeting got under way.

"We know that Senator Kelch has been meeting with ambassadors from several nations formerly of the Eastern Bloc," Jon began. "We've recorded meetings with diplomats from the Russian Federation, Belarus, and Ukraine. Only in the last three visits has the senator included his brother Magnus in the meetings." His eyes fell on me automatically at the mention of my father. I didn't flinch, but the urge was there.

"Kelch Inc. wants to secure a power base in Russia," Cordele continued. "Senator Kelch met publicly with Federal Assembly member Ronal Spielrien under the guise of gaining support for additional aid to the US and Russian military units in the Middle East. Privately, he also met with Deputy Prime Minister Sasha Fedorov. Fedorov is a heavyweight in the rebuild of the Russian economy. Jon's Captain Bennett was first recorded as piloting to Eastern Europe around the time of this private meeting. Our belief is that Senator Kelch called in little brother Magnus to set the groundwork for Kelch Inc. building up an industry base there in the Russian Federation."

"But that was just the first meeting," Shane cut in. He sat directly across from me on a recliner, so he actually had to make an effort not to look in my direction. "After the Fedorov meeting, Bennett flew the brothers together for private meetings in Belarus and in Ukraine three and four weeks later. We only have supposition right now as to who attended those private meetings. But no matter who they met with, it just doesn't seem worth the time and energy to establish an industrial base in all three neighboring nations when each one could barely provide the economical backbone to fuel a Kelch Inc. product market."

OK, I thought I was following pretty well. They needed to know who my father and Uncle Max were seeing at these secret meetings so they could stop whatever nefarious plot they were most likely forming. And the whole thing about setting up a Kelch Inc. plant in one of these countries—Father needed the multibillion-dollar company and its vast lines of products and military weapons contracts to keep up his legitimate global power base. The company was also the perfect front for all of Uncle Max's arms and drug deals with foreign terrorist nations. Not to mention, the more recognizable power the family had, the more they could focus on strengthening their supernatural power levels, which was always the underlying goal in everything they did.

"But what if Magnus has developed something that would appeal specifically to the Eastern European market?" Heather added. She made a note to research further the current specific needs of the nations in question. She sat on the love seat right next to me. I got the vibe that she'd cling to me at the first sign that I was trying to leave before the meeting was over. Maybe Thirteen wasn't the only one I should have called while I was away.

"The product isn't as important as the contract they'll force the Russian government to sign," Charles said, sitting forward. "Or the Belarusian government or Ukrainian government. We've seen the specifics of Kelch Inc.'s contracts with foreign nations in the past. The senator will play it up as providing a much-needed economical boost when in reality they'll turn the country's workers into slaves—insane hours with little to no pay for the development of some weapon or ammo that they'll just end up shipping to one of their country's enemies."

"Even more," Marie added, sitting forward to match her husband, "Kelch Inc. industry in any one of those countries will establish a fiscal leverage against the governments that the senator can then use for his political agenda. Everything is about power with the Kelches. We can't ever forget that." She glared at me. As if anyone could miss the subtext of her words. I just ignored her—that always pissed her off more than actually responding to her little jibes.

"Chang," Thirteen said in that soft, commanding voice of his, "what have you been able to find in your deeper searches into Magnus's logs?"

I turned my attention to the wiry tech and had to admire his continued sense of style. Skintight black jeans, black T-shirt with a cartoon of a bunny flipping the bird, and laceless Chuck Taylors that matched perfectly the neon blue of his hair. He jumped when I looked his way. He'd been staring at me. Again.

"I, er." He cleared his throat. "I have the dates of the meetings, and now that we broke Bennett, I've been able to fill in a couple of the holes in the itinerary. But as far as meeting minutes or potential product line, I still can't get past the firewalls." He paused. "You look different," he blurted out at me like an accusation.

"My hair's two inches longer," I replied drily.

"That's not it," he argued. His eyes searched my face, then slowly did a nice, insulting body scan.

"Hey!" I shouted, making him jump again. "Do you mind?" I'd actually been enjoying the meeting until now. The last time I worked with the team, my brother Markus had been targeting the Network themselves—taking out as many agents as possible to impress dear old Dad. This time I got to work with them on a real, normal assignment. I didn't want to screw it up by standing out now.

"He's right, though," Marie added. "You aren't all, you know, like you used to be." I cocked a knowing brow at her and enjoyed the pissed-off blush that spread across her face.

"I can pull it back now," I explained after she squirmed in her seat a few seconds more. "The sensual draw that comes from, well, being me—I can suppress it now." I shrugged. "It made leaving the house a little easier not having to worry about people going comatose from passing me on the street."

"I mean, you're still"—Chang waved his hands uselessly in my direction—"you know, like, beyond hot. But I'm not getting all whacked out like before. It's, like, cool."

I smiled despite myself. "Thanks."

I gasped as a sudden and almost violent surge of sexual need sliced through me like a blade. My head fell back, and my eyes shut tight. The pulse of energy grew stronger, hotter. "Oh my God," Marie whispered on a moan, and I knew they all felt it as well.

"Magnolia." Thirteen's voice was sharp, grabbed my attention. His eyes were frighteningly wide. "Whatever you are doing, please stop it. Now!" The lightbulb in the lamp beside him shattered.

I breathed in pants, tried to steady myself. This energy came from me—I could feel it spreading out from within me—but I couldn't control it like my other powers. Damn it, I'd worked too hard these past months to gain complete command of my abilities. Why the hell was this happening now? I could feel the need of every person in the room fueling the need inside me. And the power. I held up my arm. Every hair stood on end. Glowing. Power so great it literally radiated from me and filled the room. Only one other time in my life had this level of pure, golden energy flowed through me, out of me, with such potent force. Even as I thought it, the bittersweet smell of musk and metal wafted through the air. I knew what was happening, and I closed my eyes, fighting to hold back the pulsing power inside me.

Theo had just arrived.

* * *

It took more effort than I wanted to admit to stifle the glowing energy pouring out of me. Not because it was hard to do, but because my natural—or rather supernatural—reaction was to give in. It actually felt wrong to pull it all back.

Heather breathed heavily beside me. "Why did you do that?"

"I didn't mean to. It's just that…I was surprised. It won't happen again."

"Surprised by what?" Shane was exasperated. He rubbed his hands over his thighs, trying to wipe away the residual effects. Beside him, Charles petted Marie like he couldn't stop touching her. The doorbell rang. No one moved. I couldn't meet anyone's eye. It rang again. I felt Jon's stare as he left the room to answer. I looked at Heather. Her thoughts were full of knowing. Of the group in the room, she knew the most about Theo's and my connection—her empathetic abilities kind of made it hard to hide.

Jon walked back into the room with Theo trailing behind. He stepped into the room, and our eyes locked. Everyone else faded into the background.

This must be what angels looked like. The fallen ones, at least. A whole head taller than me, his square jawline was dark with unshaved growth. His hair was cut short in back but longer in front, so the black strands fell over his eyes. So many times I'd dreamed of sinking into those chocolate eyes. His lips parted, and I felt them on mine again. My first real kiss. My only real kiss. His callused hands had been so soft on my arms, my back, in my hair. Someone moaned.

Pull it back, Mag. His thoughts whispered through my mind. My cheeks burned at the intimacy.

I didn't realize you could still do that, I thought back, my mental voice surprisingly steady.

Yeah, I'm sure there's a lot you didn't realize when you decided to leave for months on end. His words were clipped, brought up my guard. But then his voice softened. *We need to talk, Mag.* I looked deep into his eyes and suddenly realized that I couldn't read his thoughts. We could talk in each other's heads—our own personal telepathy—but his unconscious thoughts were closed off from me. I pushed a little, not enough for him to feel it, but just a little to know what he was thinking. There was nothing. No mental walls blocking me out. Just nothing.

I instantly panicked. No one's thoughts had ever been inaccessible to me. Not Uncle Max's, whose mental powers were stronger than anything I'd ever seen. Not my father's or even my other uncle, Mallroy's—not that I'd ever been anxious to go there, but still, I always could if I wanted to. This was like some sort of black hole. I pushed harder, deeper into his mind. There had to be something. A hand rested on my arm. I jumped and jerked from Heather's grip. She lifted her hands in surrender.

"You're hurting him, Magnolia," she said calmly. I turned back to Theo. Sure enough he'd shifted his stance, bracing himself. Sweat beaded at the collar of his gray henley. I stopped immediately. His shoulders sagged in relief.

"I'm sorry," I said quickly. "I'm...sorry."

Shit! It was like the emotions I felt around these people were ten times stronger than any other feelings I had. And they affected everything about me.

Heather hesitantly touched my arm again. "Maybe we could go pick up some drinks," she suggested to Thirteen. "We only have a couple beers left, thanks to you boys hanging out here every night off. Magnolia and I will just run over to the Hoosier Daddy and grab a case or two. And you like Kendall-Jackson chardonnay, right, Marie?" She tugged at my arm, and this time I didn't pull away. "Is it OK if we take a quick break?"

Thirteen's eyes had gone dark, dangerous. He eyed Theo like an unwelcome insect that needed to be squashed. "Yes, Heather, I think that is an excellent idea." He pulled his keys from his back pocket and dragged his gaze from Theo to me. Instantly his face softened. "Take my car." He tossed me the keys. "Be careful."

I nodded and let Heather guide me through the room. My eyes kept going back to Theo. As we passed him, an urge to touch him flared inside me. His eyes widened, and he took a forced step back, careful not to brush up against me. When we finally left the room, he and Thirteen were locked in a silent staring contest.

As soon as we stepped out into the cold air, the heat of the moment washed away. I took several deep breaths, looked up to the cloudy sky. The intensity of our connection was more overwhelming than ever. Even now, all I wanted to do was go back in there and be near him again.

Heather stood silently by Thirteen's SUV. When my nerves finally settled and I was sure I was back under control, I unlocked the car and we both climbed in. She waited until I pulled out of the drive before turning in her seat to face me.

"You want to tell me what the heck just happened in there? Or would you prefer I pretend you didn't almost drive us all to an orgy the minute Theo walked back into your life?"

CHAPTER 8

The rest of the meeting was pretty uneventful. The tension had remained, everyone waiting for me to blast them with some intense power again, but I had been in much better control after my little beer run with Heather. Of course, it also helped that Theo had participated mostly from a bar stool in the kitchen.

Soon, Mag, his thoughts had whispered to me as I'd left Jon and Heather's house with Thirteen. I'd smiled the entire drive home.

That night, alone in my farmhouse, I dreamed that I sat on a small island of golden sand in the middle of a large lake of blood. This place was real, even though I only ever visited in my dreams. This was the bloody place inside me where all the dark Kelch power existed. It had grown since my escape, but the blood no longer tried to take me over. We had an understanding now. The blood was rage, hatred, and all the ravenous, violent urges that were such a significant part of me. But, unlike the rest of my family, I could control this part of myself without letting it consume me.

At least most of the time.

I played my fingertips along the surface of the blood and stared down at my reflection. The image staring back at me shared my long dark hair and distinctive eyes, but she wasn't really me. She was my twin. The one who had died on the day of our birth. She had had no powers—I'd consumed every supernatural ability we would have shared in the womb—but when Father sensed the level of power inside me, he hadn't taken the chance that my twin wouldn't one day develop similar powers of her own. He'd ordered us both killed. She died and I lived. I saw her every now and then in this bloody place. Always staring up at me from the blood, always smiling with an innocence I'd never had.

"Your island is getting larger," a deep voice said from behind me, letting me know I'd conjured another presence in my dream. "It's a reflection of a different kind of power inside you. One that gains strength by the minute."

I looked around the dream's landscape. The voice was right. The golden sand of my island stretched far to the horizon now, a sharp contrast to the bloody lake and pink sky surrounding it.

A man stepped into view, and I tried not to flinch as I looked up to meet his gaze. He was tall, towering over me in his three-piece suit that looked like something out of another time. His hair was slicked back, regal looking. The high cheekbones and dark slashes of eyebrows looked foreign and familiar all at the same time. He was my family—every member combined into one. Or rather, he was the embodiment of who I saw my family to be. He had Father's sharp jawline, Uncle Max's intelligent blue eyes, Uncle Mallroy's thick, untamable hair, Malcolm's arrogant posture, and Markus's uncertain smile.

A few months ago, when he'd first appeared, I'd thought his presence was a result of some new power my father or uncles had developed: that they had figured out I was still alive and were worming into my mind to track me down. Deep down, though, I'd known that not even Uncle Max could enter someone's mind enough to carry on conversations with them in their dreams. It was through those conversations that I'd realized this dream man had to have come from me. I saw my family in him, but he was interested in me, talked to me. He'd never tried to hurt me in my dreams, even when we'd disagreed. After a while, I'd realized that this man was the part of me that wouldn't let go of the fantasy of having a nice, normal relationship with my family.

It pissed me off that a part of me still held on to that pointless hope.

"You're all dressed up," I said, taking in his appearance. "Like when Father would have one of his business parties."

Across the crimson lake, the landscape changed as a memory came alive in the dream. *Wide double doors of the estate's front entrance rose. A line of glossy limousines pulled up the stone drive. Men and women stepped out, wearing top hats and tuxedos and long flowing dresses. They paused to look up at the sparkling white of the limestone mansion, pointing with delight at the etched windows and wide, ivy-covered columns that stretched the entire four stories. I followed their stares to a third-floor terrace. Pushing the plush curtains aside, I saw inside the suite. There I was, a statue in front of a full-length mirror. The dress was silver this time, with tiny beads that shimmered like water as I moved. Tonight all the men would look at me, lust for me. The women would hate me. I couldn't pull back the sensuality yet. I didn't know how. After all, I was only fifteen.*

Father appeared in the doorway. Instantly, I stopped breathing. People always thought him handsome in a dangerous sort of way. With chiseled features and dark hair and eyes. The gray at his temples only emphasized the aristocratic breeding that he so surely carried. He was wearing one of his tuxedos and looked like a picture out of a magazine. Only instead of a camera-ready smile, his face was distorted with disgust. He looked me up and down. "Is it ready yet?" He wasn't referring to the dress.

The seamstress sweated bullets as she tied off the final strand of beads to my hem. She was foreign, illegal, and barely spoke English—Uncle Max's idea. No one was going to miss her when the night was over. She nodded enthusiastically, then stepped back, offering me for inspection. He came to me, and I forced my power down. I was getting stronger. And the more fear, the more rage I felt, the more my power grew. I couldn't let him know that, though. It would be much too dangerous.

Father circled around me as footsteps tiptoed down the hallway outside the room. My stomach wanted to roll. Malcolm and Markus poked their heads in the doorway just as Father shoved his hand down the front of my dress. As he gruffly adjusted my breasts, I knew he'd leave bruises on the flesh under the material. He always did. Markus wore a thinner version of Malcolm's tux. Nearly twenty now, he was filling out nicely in the shoulders and chest, but he was still a couple of years away from Malcolm's athletic build. Both had brushed back their hair, ready to play their roles as doting sons for the press that Uncle Max insisted on inviting to these events.

Markus blushed when Father's fingers momentarily exposed my nipples. Malcolm grinned. He said we can watch, *his thoughts sneered as he raked me with his gaze. His dark-blond hair was trimmed to just above his collar. I focused there instead of meeting his eyes.* If we're quiet and impress Father's guests with the polite conversations that we've been practicing, we get to watch what he does to you. Afterward. *Markus let a low giggle escape and slapped a hand over his mouth before Father could tell him to shut up.*

"It was the only entertainment they ever had," I said softly, watching their eager eyes through the blood of my dream. "Watching Father punish me—it was what they lived for. They shared his inherent perverse and violent nature. And after those parties, when he would use the whips with the barbs to tear my dress away until I was naked and bloody—it was like a super-special treat for them."

The blood in the lake started to wave. My twin still smiled up at me, but the man hovering beside me frowned. "Why are you getting agitated?"

The blood settled a bit as the mansion faded back into the scenery. "I'm sorry," I said. "Remembering pisses me off, and seeing you makes me remember."

He considered me for a moment, then waved a hand through the air. "I do not wish to speak of this anymore. I came to visit you." I rolled my eyes. Even in my dreams my family's arrogance knew no bounds. "Tell me about this golden power you have growing inside you, Magnolia. You know from where it has come, do you not? Why it is growing stronger?" He talked like Uncle Mallroy sometimes, like he didn't speak out loud enough to know vernacular English.

"Yes," I answered. "I know where this power comes from."

Across the sky Theo's image appeared. He leaned back against a motorcycle, a tight frown darkening his face. It was exactly the way he'd looked the day I'd left. But unlike other times I'd dreamed of his image, he looked much clearer now. He stood golden and bright against the pink sky.

"It is part of the *more* inside me," I explained. "I never realized it was there while I was living on the estate—Father always made sure my powers were as repressed as possible. But now I know better. I am capable of so much more than just hate and rage and pain. I can trust and be trusted. Maybe I can even love." Theo's image cocked a half grin at me that I remembered so well, one I was eager to see again.

I turned to the man I'd conjured, the embodiment of the hold my family still had over me. "This golden place is made up of so much more than any of you could ever imagine."

The dream man frowned. "What do you mean, 'any of you'?"

"You," I said and waved in his direction. "My family. All of you. I was always the strongest—all of you always knew that. But now the power in me is more than just our bloodline."

For a long moment, I enjoyed staring out at the image of Theo. Soon, he had said, and I couldn't wait. My fingers played in the blood, tickling my twin's fingertips and making her smile even wider. When the dream man remained silent, I turned to him again. His expression had dropped, startling me. He looked as if he were stunned.

"You think I am from you," the man whispered, his voice barely audible. "You think you have imagined me as some representation of your family, the way you've imagined a vision of your dead twin sister and the man you pine for. You think I am nothing more than another part of your dream."

The blood in the lake started to quiver as an uneasy feeling settled over the landscape. "Of course you are from me. None of my relatives has the power to enter my dreams like this."

His eyes flashed red, and I gasped. No one in my family had ever done anything like that. Only I had that power. He turned his gaze to my hands. They had completely changed, turned into long leathery claws. I hadn't even felt the shift.

With a tight smile, the man said, "Wake up, Magnolia."

Instantly, I came awake, gasping for air.

Chapter 9

My hands fisted into the sheets as the remnants of my dream still shook me. I was scared to look, but slowly I glanced down. My hands were normal. They hadn't shifted at all. Thank God. It really had just been a dream.

The man from my dreams flashed in my mind, and I automatically reached out with my senses to see if he was really there. Of course, there was nothing. But now I wondered if he really was just a part of my subconscious. The way he'd told me to wake up—it felt as if his words had actually pulled me away from the dream. I'd never done that to myself before. The thought made me shiver.

I lay back down and cuddled my quilts tight to my chest. Just a dream. The man's eyes had flashed red because he was a part of me, that's all. I lifted my hand again. There was the smallest glow to my skin now, visible even in the darkness.

* * *

In the morning I sat on one of the mismatched ottomans in the little farmhouse's living room and powered up my Network-issued laptop. Computers weren't exactly my forte—considering my lack of formal education, I figured it was pretty impressive I knew half of what I did. But after spending a couple of weeks hanging in a Wi-Fi café in Cincinnati, I'd grown pretty comfortable with the Internet. Geeky minds were so easy to access.

For all the place's shortcomings (even with the furnace at full blast, I had to wrap myself in blankets just to keep my skin from goose-bumping), the farmhouse had great broadband Internet service. Must be all the high-tech security stuff hidden under the boxes in the little bedroom. The moment I signed into the secured intranet line Chang had set up, the whole screen went black.

"Good morning, Agent Magnolia One, Red-Level Task Force," an electronic female voice greeted me.

"Er, hi."

It didn't answer. Chang had had to program my last name as One because, apparently, the system had an autodestruct mechanism that would be triggered if anyone with the surname Kelch tried to log in. Whatever.

The computer hummed for a few seconds, then connected me to a remote desktop that looked exactly like the one in Thirteen's office. I cracked my fingers, pulled the quilt tighter around my shoulders, and got to work. My very first e-mail was from Thirteen. I had an assignment. Not a turn-invisible-and-use-my-supernatural-strength-to-break-into-a-target's-home type of assignment. But a normal, could-have-been-assigned-to-anyone assignment.

And how cool was that?

My job was research. Specifically, I was to find out everything I could about a small city named Bohlren located somewhere in Eastern Europe on a river. This would be cake. I pulled up Google Maps and started my search.

Twenty minutes later I was done. Bohlren didn't exist. That's all there was to it. It wasn't on Google Maps anywhere, and according to one of the Cincinnati coffee geeks, *everything* was on Google Maps. Obviously this place didn't exist. Frustrated, I got up to add some more whiskey to my coffee. It was after noon. I checked my phone, but there were no missed calls. Theo's thoughts last night had whispered that we'd talk soon. So where was he?

The quiet alarm beeped. A quarter mile away, a car turned in to my icy dirt driveway. It paused just past the fencerow and just idled there. I reached out to the driver's thoughts. Well, well, this was an interesting surprise.

I leaned back on the kitchen counter, sipped my whiskey. They idled at the road for almost seven minutes. Then with a murmured *Fuck it*, they pulled up the drive to the house. I made sure the door was cracked open when they stepped onto the porch.

"Come on in," I called out. They hesitated. Slowly the door opened. Luce entered the kitchen first, Tony a few steps behind. "Welcome back," I greeted them. "Want a drink? Oh, wait, you're driving. What about you, skater dude? You old enough to drink?"

"Are you?" he replied quickly. I just smiled.

"How's the nose?" I asked, wincing at the bandages across Luce's black-and-blue face. "Looks painful."

She narrowed her eyes a little. At least I think she did. Hard to tell with all that gauze and swelling. "Magnolia?" she said drily. "Just a single name like Beyoncé or Ke$ha?"

"Those were Colin's words, not mine."

"Your father is Magnus Kelch. *You* are a Kelch."

I took a drink and studied my glass. "Your point?"

She leaned back on her boot heels, thoughtful. Tony pushed off the wall he'd been leaning against and strolled around the kitchen. His untied hiking boots squeaked on the hardwood floors. He had tucked his baggy cargo pants into the boots and left his thick orange coat unzipped. He looked at the walls and peeked into the living room as if my mere presence would somehow shift the house in some strange, supernatural way. The laptop on the ottoman snapped shut. Tony jumped. I smiled as I poured more whiskey into my glass.

Luce's thoughts grabbed my attention. "I'm impressed," I admitted and looked her over with new respect. "You've tailed me since yesterday? Thirteen didn't even catch a whiff of it. I had a few moments of paranoia, but nothing that set me off. Impressive." And distressing. If these guys could put a tail on me without me catching it, my father could track me no problem. I'd been sloppy, too relaxed. That needed to change.

"We don't move on our target for another couple days," she said. "And you're dangerous. Even someone who doesn't know about the supernaturals of the world could sense that."

"So you two took it upon yourselves to follow me. And Thirteen." She averted her eyes. "Yeah, probably not such a great idea to set a tail on a Network chief like that, huh? Does Colin know you're here?"

"He's the one who sent us," Tony answered from behind me. He'd taken a post at my back. Not that it would help him if they tried to jump me, but I had to respect the thought. "The Network has never employed supernaturals before. Er, at least not that we know of. And you can get in our heads. We needed to be sure you were really with the Network."

"Jesse's word wasn't enough?" I asked over my shoulder.

"Who's Jesse?" Luce frowned.

"I mean FedEx. He knew who I was."

They exchanged a look. They didn't trust Jesse either. Interesting. "So now that you've followed me around and listened in on Thirteen's and my conversations—two things that I can assure you won't be happening again—what's the plan?"

Luce wandered the kitchen. Her internal debate was fascinating. Colin's order was for the two of them to find out if I was a legitimate member of the Network. If I was, then they were to see if I could be authorized to assist in apprehending their target. Luce knew I was legit, but she wasn't convinced I could be trusted. Follow orders or follow instinct. What was a good little soldier to do?

"What were you going to do if you discovered I'd been lying?"

Tony's thoughts went through an elaborate scene where they overpowered me and turned me over to the Network, the two of them receiving all kinds of accolades. I spewed out my whiskey across the table, accidently drenching the bandages on Luce's face. "I'm sorry," I said quickly, trying to contain my laughter. "Here, let me get that." I grabbed some paper towels off the counter and passed them to her. The gauze was ruined. She went to the sink and started peeling off the bandages. "There's some first aid stuff in the bathroom."

"I know where it is," she snapped and stomped off down the little hall. The door slammed behind her. I wiped up the table and looked to Tony. "Well?"

"We want your assistance," he said after a moment of deliberation. "New information has come to light on our current target, and we need additional team members to guarantee the takedown. Colin doesn't want to risk going over budget by increasing the team's head count by three or four like we need."

"But if it's just one supernatural team member with the eyes and ears of three or four normal agents, that wouldn't stretch the budget at all." I finished off my whiskey and pretended to weigh my options. Truthfully, though, I couldn't wait to help with their target. They'd need me there, in on the takedown. Not staring at a computer screen, flipping through page after page of research crap.

"Do you think your team chief would approve the cross-team assistance?" Luce called out from the bathroom.

Thirteen liked to keep a close eye on me. He trusted me, sure, but if I went on an assignment that he wasn't directly involved in, it might be pushing the risk level past his comfort zone.

"I'm sure he won't have a problem," I said. "My team's current mission is weeks away from moving forward, so I'm basically in standstill mode anyway."

"Good." Luce slipped back into the kitchen sans bandages. Her nose looked purple. "We're reconvening at the west-side safe house tonight at eighteen hundred hours to finalize plans and go over the new information. I'll tell Colin to expect you." She gave me one last hard look, then headed for the door.

Tony paused long enough to give me an appreciative once-over. "Gotta admit, I'm looking forward to seeing what you can do." He strode toward the front door, then stopped again. "Not that you'll tell me or anything, but I'm curious. Just how many supernaturals you got on your Network team?"

"You're right," I said. "I'm not telling you."

His eyes were sharp. "I just asked because at your meeting last night another guy showed up, a late arrival. I could have sworn I caught a feeling of power the moment he stepped into the house."

I swallowed the rest of my whiskey in a long, slow gulp. Theo's powers were strong enough now; I could imagine someone who knew what to look for feeling his energy.

When I remained silent, Tony nodded and shot me a tight half smile. "Yeah, that's what I figured." Then he walked out and closed the door behind him.

CHAPTER 10

The next day, Heather and Cordele showed up early on my door-step with plans to go shopping. Apparently I wasn't the only one who got bored with research. I'd never really done the whole "girl-friends" thing before, but since my cell phone had remained silent all night—Theo hadn't even bothered to send me a text—I had to admit that I looked forward to getting out of the house. Downtown was too far away, and the closest mall was overrun with holiday shoppers taking advantage of the last weeks of Christmas sales. So in an attempt to avoid all that, we just went to the nearest Target.

"It's weird not having everyone drool all over you anymore," Cordele said casually while inspecting a new bath mat.

I flipped through some shower curtains. I'd been showering with just an open stall because the last shower liner had molded while I was away. I should probably grab some thicker curtains for the bedroom too. And maybe some lamps. And groceries, definitely groceries. God, I loved Target—it had everything!

"I mean, it's cool," she continued. "It must be horrible having every person you pass want to jump your bones." I ignored the hint of jealous sarcasm she didn't realize she was throwing. "But it must take a lot of control to suppress something that's a natural part of you like that. Your powers must be getting really strong."

I froze with two toilet covers in my hands. She didn't look at me, but there was a nervous tightness in her face as she continued to flip through the same bath mats she'd been flipping through since we'd come down this aisle. I looked in her thoughts. Bath mats, bath mats, bath mats—her focus was way too intentional.

"My powers are what they've always been," I said carefully.

She nodded quickly, studying the pattern on the mat in her hand. "Oh, of course. I mean, you've always been more power-ful than anyone we've ever heard of. Did Thirteen tell you about the truth serum I developed for interviews? I would have never thought to combine the doses like that if you hadn't shown us how you can use your telepathy aggressively. There's a lot we could learn from you."

I relaxed a bit. I'd forgotten that Cordele had moved into the R & D end of things. No wonder she was so interested in my power level. I'm sure I'd make an excellent lab rat. Not that that would ever happen—I'd kill everyone in the Network, including Thirteen, before I let someone lock me in a cage and study me. But at least I could understand the why behind her interest.

"They have Merona tank tops on sale," Heather said, appearing at the end of the aisle. She had a cart half-full of clothes and shoes.

"Why would we buy tank tops when it's thirty degrees out-side?" Cordele asked.

"Because they're only fifteen dollars and they never shrink."

"Seriously?" Cordele pushed past me. "I'll meet you over there."

"You want some?" Heather asked me.

"Er, that's OK." I had enough clothes for now. And truth be told, while I was fine buying discounted lamps and bath mats, I wouldn't put that cheap-ass fabric on me if she paid me to. One of the residual effects of growing up on the estate: everything I'd ever worn had been top-of-the-line or custom-made. Not because Father cared about what I wore, but because that was all that was ever purchased. Nothing but the best for anyone with the name Kelch. That my clothes were burned or shredded off me every night during Father's sessions had been a moot point.

I tossed my bathroom stuff in the cart with Heather's things and started to the next aisle. After a few steps, I realized she wasn't following me. "You OK?" I asked, looking back at her.

"I was about to ask you the same thing," she said with a frown. "What were you and Cordele talking about? You seemed tense when I showed up."

Ah yes, an empath at work.

"She was interested in my powers. How strong they are now compared to before I left."

Heather nodded. "Yeah, she talked about you a lot while you were away."

"Really."

"You saved her life twice last summer: once on the assignment with your uncle's guard, and then again when you rescued her and the others from your brother Markus. She wants to get to know you better now that you're back, but she just doesn't know how."

I considered that for a moment. Becoming friends with Heather had been easy. She was so open and kind, it had been impossible not to like her. Cordele was different. Her thoughts weren't open at all, and her attempts at chitchat seemed like forced conversation.

Heather inched the cart up next to me. "Have you talked with Theo yet?"

Instantly power sizzled beneath my skin. It had only been a day and a half, but still. I'd expected him to call or text me or something.

"No. I haven't had time."

She gave me an arch look. I started walking at a clipped pace. She kept up, pushing her shopping cart quickly. "We'll talk soon," I said. "I just don't know when I'm going to see him outside of a meeting."

I could see her argument forming: I should just call him and get it over with. Fortunately, when I ignored her, she decided to let it drop. For now anyway.

We had walked all the way to the electronics section of the store. A wall of TVs showed the local news in various degrees of HD. I headed to iPod accessories. Over my shoulder, Heather moved to one of the wider TVs and turned up the volume.

"With the call center expansion, Kelch Inc. is looking to bring another three thousand jobs to the greater Indianapolis area. Governor Bader was enthusiastic in his press conference yesterday afternoon, explaining that the addition will help bring the state's unemployment rating to a twenty-year low. When asked if the north-side expansion can be seen as a stepping-stone to further growth, CEO Magnus Kelch was unavailable for comment."

The newscaster moved on, and Heather turned the volume back down. "How come your father never speaks to the press? Senator Kelch gives press conferences every other day practically. It would make sense that Magnus would want some of the limelight as well."

"Father hates people," I said bluntly, browsing the available iPod docks so I wouldn't have to look at her. "Sees them as sheep. They're good for working the various jobs at Kelch Inc., but why should our family, with all of our powers and intelligence, waste time speaking to them any more than necessary? Normal people are totally beneath us. Uncle Max hates them too, but he needs voters. His telepathy is powerful enough that he can coerce an audience pretty easily. So he does what's necessary. If he didn't need them to maintain his position, he'd never acknowledge them at all."

"It's all about power with your family, isn't it?"

I felt the hum of energy tickling inside me, waiting for the rush of release. "Power is everything," I said softly. Then I shook myself. "Come on." I nodded back toward home goods. "I forgot to get curtains."

CHAPTER 11

The snow had taken the past few days off, giving the sun a few teasing moments to show its colors. When Heather turned onto my driveway, the dirt road had turned to slush and mud. For once, I was grateful I wasn't the one driving. We got to the tree line, and instantly my guard went up. People were in my house again. I touched the intruders' minds as we pulled around to the back of the house. Jon, Thirteen, Chang, Shane...

I stopped breathing. Theo. His presence was like a beacon, drawing me in.

Tempering the urge to leap out of the car and find him immediately, I led the way to the front porch and held the door open for Heather and Cordele. "I'll be there in a second," I said and shut the door behind them as they took their bags inside. I placed my own bags on the cleared-off stoop and walked around to the side of the house. The smell of cloves hung thick in the air, making my body tingle. Standing a ways from the house, staring into the nearby woods, he'd put up the collar of his heavy navy peacoat. Dark hair fell in waves around his strong face. His long legs were covered in black jeans tucked into thick-soled Doc Martens. I took a steadying breath.

"I felt you coming," he said softly as I approached. God, I loved his gravelly voice. "Before you even hit the driveway, I knew you were on your way here." He blew out three perfect smoke rings. *Show-off.*

He glanced down at me with subtle surprise. "I can show you how to blow them. It's not that hard."

Every muscle I had instantly tightened. "I didn't say anything."

He scowled and looked back out over the woods. "It comes and goes. For months now. Ever since that day we"—*made out, dry humped, almost went all the way*—"got close, I've felt it. I can hear people's thoughts. Not the way I can with you, but like listening in. It doesn't happen all the time, but sometimes. And some days, I can bench-press ten times what I normally can. Or run a freaking five-minute mile." He ran a hand through his hair. "I have all these fucked-up dreams about you, and when I wake up, I'm glowing. Glowing, Mag." He turned his scowl on me. "What the hell did you do to me?"

I flinched. Everything came back to me in a rush. I'd been drawn to Theo from the first moment I'd laid eyes on him. No, before that—the first time I'd felt him enter the Thirsty Turtle. I couldn't explain it. I was attracted to him—I mean, who wouldn't be? But it was so much more than that. It was a pull, a need to be near him. He'd felt it too. And as frustrating and confusing and terrifying as it had been for me, it had been more so for him. Because the connection between us was real, a separate entity apart from either one of us. And when we were together, it grew.

I stared at my feet because I couldn't look at him. "I'm sorry. I never meant for any of this to happen. I don't know why…or how…"

His fingers were warm against my skin as he lifted my face. His eyes were soft. Melted chocolate. "I don't blame you, Mag."

"But you just said—you said, what the hell did I do to you? I didn't mean to do anything to you."

"I didn't say that."

"Yes, you did."

"I thought it, maybe for a second, but, Mag, I didn't mean it. Not like that."

I closed my eyes and inhaled deeply. We'd had this conversation before. When all our walls had been down, when we'd been at our most intimate, I'd seen what he really thought of me. I was a monster. A Kelch. Evil. And he'd hated the feelings he'd had for me. I'd pushed it away and tried to convince myself that his errant thoughts didn't really matter.

"But I couldn't get into your head the other night," I said, forcing myself back to the conversation. "Not even a little. It was like, you remember how when we were…you know…on the couch?" Heat flashed in his eyes; his gaze went to my mouth.

"Yeah, I remember."

"Well." I had to swallow twice. "That time it was like we shared the same thoughts—there were no barriers at all. I could see everything inside you."

"And I saw everything inside you." His gaze traveled over my face, soaking it in.

"The other night at Jon and Heather's, it was the complete opposite. There was nothing but barriers. I couldn't hear anything in your head at all. It was all a complete blank."

His hand had been caressing my face. Now his fingers tightened in my hair. "This is what I'm talking about. One minute I have every power in the world. I can hear bugs in the dirt like they were bulldozers. I can lift a car over my head. Apparently I can also block your telepathy. Then the next minute, it's gone."

I turned my face into his palm automatically as his other hand skimmed along my sleeve. Like now that we'd made the contact, we couldn't help ourselves. His frustration, humming in the air between us, slowly dissolved into something warmer.

I've missed you so much. Was that his thought or mine?

With a concentrated effort, I stepped back. We both gasped at the break of contact, but there was more to say and it needed to be said before we gave in to everything coming alive between us.

"It's stronger now that you're back," he said, rubbing his sternum. He tried to hide the returning frustration in his voice but didn't quite manage.

I steeled myself and made sure he saw my determination. "This connection isn't the only thing that's stronger now. I'll figure this out, Theo. I promise. And once I do, if you want to be free of me, you will be. Forever."

His eyes widened. "No, Mag, that's not what I want. I mean, I want to understand this connection between us, and this power that's inside me now, but I don't want to lose you. Not again."

He took my hand and stepped in close. A heat stirred low inside me.

"I have so much control now," I said breathlessly. "I can handle all of my powers, even the new ones. But this—"

"This isn't a power that is yours alone," he said softly. "This is our power. The things I can do now—yeah, it was easier blaming you while you were gone, convincing myself that you had done something to me. But this power didn't exist until we got close."

The heat inside me swelled. "No, it didn't. I've never felt anything else like it."

"So it's the two of us, then."

I reached up and slid a hand inside his coat, resting my palm on his chest. He pulled me closer so that our bodies touched. His scent filled me as everything around us brightened. The snow, the dark woods, the gray sky—the landscape glowed with a subtle golden light, brightening more and more as Theo leaned down.

Our power, his thoughts breathed. *Together.*

Our noses brushed. I held my breath. He sighed into my open mouth just before his lips—

Thirteen cleared his throat. I jumped and spun toward the back of the house. They were all standing there: Thirteen, Jon, Heather, Shane, Chang, Cordele—hell, even Charles and Marie had shown up. My whole freaking team had just snuck up on us, and I hadn't even felt them there. Talk about ruining the moment. And what if they had been an enemy? I'd been so distracted by the feel of Theo, I'd been completely oblivious to the rest of the world around me. Definitely not good.

"It's time to get this meeting started," Thirteen said, his eyes boring into Theo. I glanced over my shoulder to see Theo tap another clove from his pack, light it. He matched Thirteen's glare with his own.

"No problem," Theo said. "We were just coming in." Then he placed his hand on the small of my back and guided me toward the house. Thirteen's mental walls were up, but I'd seen enough rage in my life to recognize the feel of it. Something was happening between the two of them. Before I could say anything, though, Thirteen turned on his heel and led the group of silent eavesdroppers back into the house.

Oh yeah, this meeting was going to be productive. With everyone focused on Theo's and my little exchange, they would have no problems sticking to the agenda. No problem at all.

CHAPTER 12

"Break out the formal wear, folks. We're going to a party."

Chang's hair was green today, and as he rubbed his hands together, he looked like some greedy little leprechaun. I handed Thirteen a tall glass of orange juice and sat cross-legged on one of the ottomans. Theo took a seat beside Cordele on the sofa behind me, his legs brushing my back. He had started out on the couch by the window, just like I'd started out on the chair by the kitchen. But the pull was just too strong now. After a few minutes of awkward shifting, we exchanged a glance and just gave in. Tension filled the room no matter where we sat anyway.

"OK," Chang started. "So basically the senator's computer tells us nothing. He has a flat system that's hardly protected at all. The government blocks are a joke. He has a little more protection than most Washington guys, but still, getting the deets on the guy's itinerary was like total cream. Little bro Magnus, on the other hand, has a killer system stacked with the latest and greatest in techno security. We're talking ghosted transmissions, layered encryptions that Stephen Hawking would piss himself over, and fail-safes—oh, baby, this is a freaking bomb ready to blow. It's a thing of beauty. It truly is."

I held back a chuckle as he took a moment out of respect for the system. I wished I could have figured out earlier how to control my supernatural sex appeal. It would have been cool to hang out with a noncomatose Chang before now.

He cleared his throat. "So anyway, genius tech that I am, I was able to narrow down the system that's housing the details to Magnus and the senator's mysterious trips overseas. I've got fifteen dates where everything in the system goes on lockdown. I can't even get a freaking time stamp on the log-in. Since these dates coincide with what you guys got from Bennett's travel logs as well as with the senator's itinerary, I figure Magnus's system is the key to our meeting details."

"That's good," Jon said, leaning forward. "What's it going to take to get through the security and into the data?"

"That's the thing," Chang said. "The data system is housed in Magnus's personal computer. I need to be in front of the actual PC to get anything out of it. I can get the info—no worries about that. I mean, it's going to be tricky." He rubbed his hands together again, an eager glint lighting up his eyes. "But oh, baby, I'll totally get through."

Charles rolled his eyes. "So bottom line, you have to be sitting in front of the actual PC—Magnus Kelch's personal computer—to get at the data. And you expect that to happen how?"

"With these." Cordele tossed a heavy envelope on the empty ottoman in front of Charles. As he lifted the thick vellum, I saw in Cordele's mind what the envelope contained. My stomach sank. Theo shifted in his seat behind me. Heather moved forward beside Jon, her eyes worried.

Charles pulled out the invitation, and Marie read it over his shoulder. "The esteemed board of directors, along with Chief Executive Officer Magnus Kelch, invite you and a guest to the Twenty-Fifth Annual Kelch Incorporated Winter Gala." She turned the envelope upside down and poured out the remaining contents. "There're five invitations here."

"The Winter Gala is the big annual party where all the Kelch Inc. executives pat each other on the back for all the good they're doing in the world," Shane explained, narrowing his eyes on me. "They give speeches about their drug research and medical breakthroughs, about what new and improved detergent they've come up with to revolutionize the way we clean our houses. Of course, no one bothers to mention the gunrunners and drug lords that also make up a large portion of the annual report's bottom line." He looked away from me as if I were the one killing people all over the world. *Whatever.*

"In the past, the Winter Gala has been held at the estate," Cordele explained. "This year, because of the big quarter-century thing, they're holding it at the new addition of the Kelch Inc. compound up on the north side. It's supposed to serve as both a holiday celebration and the official kickoff for the new call center opening right after the New Year."

I focused completely on Cordele and her thoughts, not letting a single memory of my own slip to the surface. She concentrated on the decorative details of the invitation in her hand, as if she didn't want her own thoughts straying too far either.

"And wouldn't you know it," Chang said, all sly smiles, "Magnus has taken a personal interest in the new center, temporarily moving his offices on-site."

"So this is what we were thinking," Cordele began; then she laid out a tentative scheme for infiltrating the gala. For the next hour or so, people went back and forth on the details: who should go inside, ways to slip into the private office suites, exit strategies once Chang got the info he needed. They probably said a whole bunch more, but I couldn't pay attention any longer. I closed my eyes. My skin had gone icy cold. When I brought my whiskey to my mouth, my hand trembled.

I was going undercover to the party. To one of my *father's* parties. A couple of people still argued my involvement at that level, but Jon's and Thirteen's minds were set. Father would feel a supernatural presence when I arrived, but the family didn't know I was alive. No one would suspect that the power they sensed was from me. The team would use it as a distraction, build it into their plan. They were infiltrating Father's personal space in a way never attempted before. It was simply too important not to have their most powerful resource on-site.

God, I wanted to throw up.

"I'm still looking for Bohlren," I said, surprising Jon. My eyes stayed closed as I fought back the cruel memories just waiting to roll over me. That didn't mean I wasn't paying attention, though. Well, kind of paying attention.

"Oh, you mean you're actually listening and not dozing off over there. You know we're laying out the details for a plan to gain access to your father's offices here. You're role is going to be key. It would be nice if you were a little more engaged."

I opened my eyes and glared at him. "I've never been to his offices. I have no idea what to expect from his security. Until last year the only place I'd ever been was my family's estate—or have you forgotten that? I'll find out where in the world Bohlren is, and I'll get you and whoever you assign to go with you through the gala's security. And I'll make sure everyone on the team gets out of there in one piece, even if that means killing every other person there. Is that what you want to hear? Is that *engaged* enough for you?"

He ground his teeth. Jon wanted to trust me; he really did. But looking at me right now, all he saw was his best friend and the pain I had caused him by leaving last summer. Images of Theo's frustration and confusion pounded into my head. Add that to the terror and dread swirling in my gut at being near my father again, and I basically felt like an energy bomb waiting to go off. I needed another drink.

"Fine," Jon said finally. "The gala's less than two weeks away. We need facility blueprints, established network lines, and a solid bead on their security. Charles, Chang, Shane—that's you. Heather, Marie—we need guest lists, agenda, anything and everything on what's going to happen at that party. Cordele, Magnolia—stay on the research. The more we know about those trips overseas beforehand, the better." He paused and looked to Thirteen.

The big man was leaning back in a comfy chair by the fireplace, still nursing the glass of OJ I'd given him an hour before. He hadn't said a word the entire meeting. Now his voice was soft. "Jon, Theo, Shane, Cordele, and Magnolia will join Chang at the gala. Charles, Marie, and Heather will set up a contact base within a hundred yards of the new call center. You will need to determine the best location for the base and request any necessary surveillance equipment within the next twenty-four hours." He pushed to his feet and continued speaking as he walked into the kitchen. "You will meet again next Thursday evening to lay out the information gathered and finalize your plans. The gala will be held the following Saturday, so you will have plenty of time to fill in any missing pieces and request any additional equipment you feel you may need." He rinsed out his glass, placed it in the sink, and stood framed by the wide entrance that separated the kitchen from the living room. "Your designated identities will be delivered during your Thursday meeting. I will take care of establishing your covers."

"We each have established covers already—" Jon started, but Thirteen cut him off with a wave.

"New covers will be created for this event. Your portfolios will be delivered Thursday. I expect a copy of your objective, agenda, and designation by oh-seven-hundred. Magnolia, may I speak with you a moment?" Then he turned and walked down the hallway from the kitchen and out the back door.

I pushed myself up and followed with heavy feet. Either we were going to talk about the implications of my attending a party thrown by my father, or he was going to reprimand me for doing something wrong. Either way, I grabbed the bottle of Beam as I made my way through the kitchen.

CHAPTER 13

Thirteen stood on one of the wide stepping-stones that trailed from the back of the farmhouse around to the front porch. He looked at me as I came down the rear cement steps, his expression unreadable. I wrapped my arms around myself.

"I'm closing in on locating Bohlren," I lied, stepping into the yard. "I'm pretty sure it's south of Ukraine. I just need to pin it down."

His expression didn't change. OK, maybe my lack of progress wasn't the reason for this little convo like I'd hoped. I peeked in his thoughts for a clue but came up blank. His mental walls were solid today, and I wasn't going to hurt him just to find out what his deal was.

"I'll be fine going to the gala, Thirteen," I said, trying again. "I've been to enough of Father's parties to know what to expect." My whole body trembled in a violent shiver before I could stop myself. I just ignored it. "And I'm totally listening to Jon—I really was paying attention in there. When he takes over the team for good, I'll listen to him as well as I listen to you."

His mouth twitched. "Because you listen to me so well?"

I kicked at the slushy ground. "I listen," I muttered.

He waited until I looked up again. "I received an e-mail from Colin St. Pierre this morning expressing his gratitude for my approving your cross-team work on his current assignment. He is an ambitious team leader and was eager to get his name in front of me. Please remind me, when exactly did I approve your involvement with his team?"

Oh shit.

"I, er, I was going to tell you—ask you, I mean... It's just..." My words fell away. I'd heard the expression *tongue-tied* before, but never realized the term described the feeling so literally.

"I offered you a position as a full task force agent without the formal classroom requirement because of your special circumstances. However, I realize now that the courses outlining Network procedure and protocol were a key part of the orientation that you were permitted to bypass. That is about to be rectified." He pulled a thick manila folder from the back of his waistband. Had he been sitting in that big squishy chair with that thing shoved in his back that whole time? How uncomfortable.

"This is the introduction manual outlining Network policy and procedures. You will read this cover to cover and complete the test at the end of the manual. You can e-mail the completed exam to the support center e-mail address provided for processing." My face must have shown my shock because his jaw tightened as he continued. "You will not participate in any Network assignments until that test is processed."

"What? But I have to be at the airport with Colin and his team tomorrow morning!"

"Then you better get reading." He crossed his arms over his chest.

I took a deep, calming breath. When I was sure my voice would be level, I said, "OK, I'll read your manual and I'll take your test. But I am going to the airport with Colin's team tomorrow. I gave them my word, and their plan won't work without me. They won't have another shot at their target like this, and even though the power these art-smuggler guys have isn't anything compared to my family's, I can't imagine you want them to get away just because I didn't fill out a fucking questionnaire before their plane landed."

His body stayed tense for a long moment; his mental walls shimmered. Regret. He was second-guessing making my involvement in the Network official. My anger deflated fast. Guilt was the last thing I needed right now. I snagged the manual and flipped through the pages. I was a fast study, but this was going to take all night to get through. "So do I copy you on the test when I e-mail it in?"

"That would be fine, yes. And it would expedite the processing as well."

I kept my eyes on the manual. "I'm going to be a good agent, Thirteen. I'm going to be the best you've ever had."

When I looked up again, he smiled, that sad smile that was just for me. An image of his daughter passed through his thoughts. She'd been twelve when she was killed by one of Thirteen's enemies. He often thought of her whenever I did something that pleased him. It never hurt my feelings—just the opposite, actually. I knew I was forgiven whenever I made him think of her. I smiled up at him, and his eyes softened even more.

"You will be a wonderful agent, Magnolia. In fact—"

A loud burst of laughter echoed from inside the house, followed by a deep masculine curse. Then several other voices joined in the laughter. Theo's chuckle was a strong rumble that I felt over all the others. I looked back at Thirteen, and his grin had vanished.

"You need to remove yourself from Theo, Magnolia."

I raised an eyebrow. "I don't think I know what you mean."

"Yes. You do. And you need to avoid getting close to him. I already spoke with him about it, and I know—"

Heat flared inside me. "You spoke to him? About me?"

He shifted his weight, and for a moment chagrin flashed through his thoughts. "A relationship with him would be inappropriate. He understands that."

"What the hell are you talking about? What about Jon and Heather? Or Charles and Marie? How come those relationships aren't inappropriate?"

"He's thirty-four years old, Magnolia. You're twenty-three. To take advantage of your naïveté would—"

"*Naïveté?* Are you insane? When he was doing Jell-O shots at Notre Dame, I'd already been tortured to death six times! How can you possibly think that I'm naive about anything?"

He winced at the reminder of my life before my escape. "I'm not talking about your powers, Magnolia, or your ability to deal with physical pain. Or even how you are more than capable of handling any life-or-death situation thrown your way. I'm talking about your emotional maturity. Your, er, sexual maturity." For the first time since, well, ever, I saw a hint of blush on Thirteen's cheeks.

My own face grew hot, and I suddenly found the slush on my boots totally fascinating. God, he really did not want to hear this, and I really did not want to say the words. But I cleared my throat anyway and said, "I have more sexual experience than you may realize, Thirteen. And not just from all of the thoughts of people who lusted after me—although I have to admit, I learned a lot from the minds of Father's disgusting business associates." I shivered at the memories. Then the shame washed over me as it always did when I remembered these particular experiences. My voice was rough when I said, "My brother Malcolm, some-times one of the estate guards when Father's experiments left me unconscious, they would... Well, I have experience in that area. Just so you know." Maybe not full sex, but Malcolm had done his best to grope and touch and prod whenever the chance had come up. I figured Thirteen didn't need to know all the gory details.

When he remained silent, I looked up. The horror on his face made me recoil. He shook himself quickly. "Whatever experi-ences you've been forced to endure, they are not what a true rela-tionship is about." He was red again. "The physical and emotional ramifications of your developing a crush on someone like Theo are something you simply are not ready for."

I gaped at him. *A crush? A fucking crush?* I knew he'd felt the power that surged when Theo and I saw each other at Jon's. Why was he denying the level of our connection now?

The back door swung open before I had a chance to respond. "We're heading out," Jon called across the lawn. I wanted to ask what had happened that had been so funny, but I was still struck dumb. *A crush.* In Thirteen's thoughts, his daughter's face flashed again. A child, twelve years old. If a part of him still saw me like that, maybe it was time to reconsider the benefits of our father-daughter dynamic.

Thirteen straightened his coat. "Support functions twenty-four hours a day. Get that exam to them before oh-two-hundred hours, and they will have it processed and back to me in time for you to receive official approval for Colin's mission tomorrow morning."

He tried to give me a small smile, but I ignored him. Obviously I didn't have time to deal with his denial of who I really was. He walked past me to the front of the house, and I heaved the brick-size manual in through the back door. Might as well start another pot of coffee—I was going to be up for a while.

CHAPTER 14

I'd stopped adding whiskey to my coffee hours ago. It didn't help. I dragged my gaze to the fork-and-spoon clock over the kitchen sink: 1:47. God, this was worse than research. There was more than just the test at the end of the manual—there were quizzes after every section. And only half of what the tests covered was actually worth knowing. I mean, seriously, did it really matter that there were different expense forms for overseas assignments and regular assignments?

Some of the history stuff was interesting, though. For example, the Network had been around a hell of a lot longer than I'd ever suspected. Almost a century. The name of the organization had changed close to a dozen times, but it always included the words *the Network*. It had started as a small assembly under the direction of a certain enthusiastic congressman. As the group had grown, and the organization's needs expanded, private investors with personal interests had stepped forward to fund whatever was needed to do the job. I guess if I was a railroad tycoon in the thirties and had been kidnapped by a bunch of guys with telekinetic powers, I too would have been eager to give a bunch of money to the people who could ensure that it would never happen again. With that base money, they'd been able to invest privately until their budget was well into the nine-figure range. Not bad for an agency that technically didn't exist.

I answered the last question on the last test and hit the Send button on e-mail. One fifty-seven. Thank God that was over. And no worries about whether I actually got the questions right or not—supernatural memory is great for rattling off inconsequential facts.

Colin's team was meeting off the Sam Jones Expressway at eight a.m. If I fell asleep right now, I'd get a good four and half hours in before I had to get ready for the meeting. I poured a bedtime whiskey, drank it in one gulp, and crawled under the pile of quilts on my bed. I was out the minute my head hit the pillow.

* * *

I knew he was there. His presence had woken me the moment his car hit the driveway. The sweet scent of musk and metal preceded his soft steps to the back door. I'd opened the locks with my powers and waited. My eyes still closed, I felt him in my room.

A hot finger brushed along my cheek, traced my lips. My skin tingled everywhere he touched me. The bed dipped.

I couldn't stay away any longer. Theo's thoughts whispered through my mind. I felt his face nuzzle my hair. And I sighed. It was as if every moment since my return had been leading up to this.

You shouldn't stay away, I thought back to him. *It's our power, remember? The two of us.*

Then I looked up and met his eyes. Melted chocolate—the kind that turned darker under heat. A wave of need pulsed through the room as his heartbeat thrummed in sync with mine. We moved together, our lips sealing as if they should have never been apart. His arms wrapped around me as my hands knotted in his hair. This wasn't a dream or a fantasy. I felt everything about him. His blood pumping through his veins, the sheets tangled under his legs. But his thoughts stayed closed off. While his powers were sporadic, he grew stronger with me in his arms. He could hold his mental walls in place and feed on the energy that spun faster between us.

I was glad for his strength—I didn't want an errant thought to ruin this moment.

He lifted my shirt over my head and quickly covered me with my quilt, keeping away the chill. My heart pounded. I'd never been so aware of my body before. He sat back and kicked off his shoes. My mouth went dry.

His heavy coat came next, tossed over a chair in the corner. Then he tugged off his shirt. When he turned back to me, the dark intent in his eye was clear. I wore only my panties under the quilt, but in a few moments more, I'd be completely naked.

The panic came quickly. I crossed my arms over my stomach and shivered violently. Naked meant torture. Humiliation. He stretched out beside me, and I automatically flinched away. I wanted this, wanted him. In my mind I knew that. But a lifetime of instincts had reared up inside me. I couldn't help but fear the pain that had always come when I was at my most vulnerable.

"Open your eyes, Mag." I hadn't even realized I'd closed them. He pulled back the quilt, and a chill blew across my stomach. *No!* I turned away quickly, instinct screaming at me to run. He grabbed me at the waist; the power between us surged as he held me to the bed.

"No, Mag, look at me. It's me here with you now. Me touching you. No pain, no embarrassment. Just me."

I held on to the melting chocolate of his eyes. Like a lifeline, he grounded me. No pain here. No blood or shame. Only Theo. With his fingertip, he traced a line between my breasts. "Look," he murmured.

Along my skin where his finger touched me, a thin glowing line appeared. He drew the glow farther, down to my stomach. The line stayed. The lingering panic eased. This wasn't my father stripping me for one of his experiments. And the power rising between us wasn't something to push back.

Theo traced a heart around my belly button, and, softly, I giggled. God, that felt good. I reached up and brushed back the hair from his face. The heat in his eyes turned serious. I pulled him to me. A soft, sweet kiss.

"Are you sure?" he asked in that gravelly voice.

"I know who you are, Theo. I want to know what this power is capable of. What *we* are capable of."

He narrowed his eyes. "So you're only interested in the power, then?"

I couldn't help but smile. That had been my worry the first time we'd felt the connection between us—that he was only using me for my power. "No," I said. "I'm interested in what I've been interested in since the first moment I saw you. You."

Panic gone, I was ready to revel in our connection. Dark hair sprinkled over his chest, narrowing as it trailed down to his waist. My hands moved over the tattoos covering his pecs and back. I wanted to see all of them—the ones I'd dreamed about for the past several months and the ones I had yet to see. Bare chest to bare chest, we groaned as we came together. Our tongues sent flames through to one another's hearts. I felt him chuckle with delight at the strength of my desire.

He went for my panties, slipping his fingers under the waist-band. I opened my eyes and sucked in a breath. We were glowing. Light poured out from us, brightening the room as if the sun had risen to midday eight hours early.

He slid off my panties, keeping his eyes locked on mine, reas-suring me against the panic just waiting to flare again. His fingers tickled in slow caresses along the outside of my leg. He kicked off his pants and lay over me, using his thick arms to lift his upper body while his lower half still remained just a hairbreadth from touching me.

I wanted nothing to ruin this moment. But there was some-thing he needed to know.

I always fought them off, I thought quickly. *As hard as my brothers and Father's guards tried, as many times as they came after me, I never let them have me. Not completely.* I let down my mental walls only a peek. Just enough to show him what was only fair for him to know.

His gaze traveled over me with gentle eyes. Glowing, radiat-ing power. He looked more like a fallen angel than ever before. Softly, he smoothed a hand down my hair.

"I want you, Mag. That no one else has ever had you only makes me want you more." He brushed his face against mine, nuzzling, breathing me in. "Tell me what to do, Mag. Show me what you want me to do here." His mouth was on mine again. Energy hummed inside me, through me. So warm, so powerful. How much more would it be if we were joined completely?

I pulled back. Holding his gaze, I ran my hands along the length of one of his tattoos, moving from his strong biceps down to his wrist. Then I guided his hands around to my back, sliding his fingers to squeeze my bare ass. His lips covered mine with a demand that stole my breath. I knew that this moment would change everything.

Then my alarm clock blared like a foghorn in the night.

I jumped as he growled and kicked my clock against the wall. He came back to my throat, nipping, sucking, making me ache. I pushed back on his shoulders. "Theo. Theo, wait. We have to stop."

He growled again. "Like hell we have to stop."

As if proving his point, he gripped my ass tighter and pulled me onto his lap. I gasped as, for the first time, I felt his naked body under me. I threw my head back in response. The glow surrounding us surged brighter, nearly blinding as he guided my movements over him, rubbing me perfectly along his length, bringing me higher, tighter.

From the floor the alarm blared again.

"What the fuck!" he snarled and threw the book I'd been reading the night before at the clock, silencing it with a sad, broken whine. I struggled for breath and put my hands on his chest to hold him back.

"No. I mean it—we have to stop. I have to go. I have to be at the airport in like an hour and a half."

His hands were on my breasts, kneading, teasing. He watched my lips. "We don't have a meeting at the airport. We don't have a meeting at all today. All we have to do is stay right here." He leaned forward toward my neck once more, but this time I held him back. It took nearly everything I had.

"Theo, I mean it. I don't want to rush this. It's too important. But I have to go."

We were both breathing heavy, but my words finally sank in. He paused and narrowed his eyes. "Why are you going to the airport? Where are you going?"

A flash of panic shot through him, and his mental walls wavered. All the frustration and confusion he'd felt when I'd left before would be nothing compared to his devastation if I left him again.

"I'm not going anywhere," I said quickly, cupping his face in my hands. "I'm here to stay, Theo. I swear it."

He rolled me back onto the bed. "Then what's going on?"

"I have another assignment. With another team. Our target arrives this morning." I took a deep breath to steady myself as much as possible.

His frown turned dangerous. I felt a push against my mind and realized a second too late what he was trying to do. The rage was immediate.

"Don't you even fucking think about it! You want to know something from me, you ask me. Just because the bond between us gives you glimpses into my mind doesn't mean you can try to get in my head anytime you want. It's not going to happen, and someone's going to end up hurt. And guess what? It's not going to be me."

"Is that a threat? We're lying here naked and glowing, and you're fucking threatening me?"

"Don't even put this back on me. You're the one who just tried to get in my head."

He shoved my leg from his lap and got to his feet. "Yeah, I'm trying to get in your head because you don't fucking tell me anything. All those months away, did you even think once about calling, letting me know you're still alive? You came back, and I had to find out from Thirteen. You're working with another team and don't even bother telling me, or anyone else for that matter. What if you need backup? The people on Thirteen's team were chosen because we're the best. What if another team fucks up and you get exposed? Jesus, Mag, of course I'm trying to get in your head. How the hell else am I supposed to know what's going on with you?" He yanked on his pants.

The quick shift of emotions was shocking. The heat of desire so easily turned to anger. I didn't know what to do. Power sizzled all around us, golden and hot, but I could feel my sudden anger churning that dark place inside me. I didn't want to go there. Not now.

He tugged on his shirt and stopped. Both hands fisted in his hair, and he took several steadying breaths. The link between us strummed tightly. As his deep breathing calmed him, so it also calmed me. Anger slowly fading, I pulled the quilt over me, missing the heat of his body.

He dropped his hands to his sides. For a long moment, we simply stared at each other.

I didn't know what to do, I thought finally. For some reason, I couldn't find the words to say them out loud. *I knew what I felt for you, and I knew the connection between us was stronger than anything I'd ever known, but no one had ever cared for me the way you did. I didn't know what to do.*

His jaw flexed. "Is that why you left? You were scared of what was happening between us?"

I sat up, holding the quilt to my chest. *No.* I still couldn't find my actual voice. *No, I didn't want to leave you. It felt like I was leaving a piece of myself behind. I had to get control of my powers—that's all.*

He took a deep, lung-filling breath, then turned to pull on his boots and grab his coat. My heart pounded. I knew I had to get going, but was this it? Had I blown it? The connection between us was still there, the power still a live presence around us. But his grid had shut down; his expression was a complete blank.

Ready to go, he sat heavily on the bed beside me. I took his hand in mine automatically. He didn't pull away, but rather rubbed his fingers along my knuckles.

"I saw a glimpse of your assignment," he said, looking at our joined hands. "Before you shut me out of your head, I saw a little of your other team. St. Pierre is a kiss-ass, but he's a decent agent.

Double-check his contingency strategies, though. Make sure he's got you covered. And, Mag, if you get even a hint that something is going wrong, you call me. Got it?"

I nodded. "I can handle myself, Theo."

"I know you can," he said, still staring at our hands. A moment longer passed and he pushed off the bed. I felt his absence instantly. The power inside me jolted as if punched. At the door he paused. Without turning back to face me, he said, "Be careful, Mag." He cleared his throat. "It would be great if you'd call me after you get back, just to let me know you're home again."

"I will," I said, and a sudden image of him returning to the farmhouse later in the afternoon came alive in my mind. We could pick up where we'd left off, take our time and really explore...

"Be sure to tell Luce hi for me," he said suddenly, cutting off my train of thought. "It's been a while, but I'm sure she'll remember."

Then without waiting for my response, he was out the back door and in his car.

Wait, what?

The alarm clock went off again, only this time it was a weak, sickly buzz. I found the thing upside down against the wall and set it back on the nightstand to turn off the alarm.

My body moved awkwardly; the unsated desire that had stirred so strongly still resisted settling down. It didn't matter. I had a job to do. I grabbed the clothes I'd laid out the night before and headed to the bathroom. Theo and everything that had just happened between us needed to be set aside for the moment. I was an agent now. Time to focus.

Twenty minutes later, I drove down the driveway, away from the morning sunlight. I was headed to my first real mission as a real Network agent. I'd be in on the action as we took down a foreign supernatural threat that had absolutely nothing to do with me or anyone in my family. I was just another agent with a role to play. No matter what else was going on with me right now, I should be thrilled about that.

But what the fuck did Theo ever do with Luce that she was so damn sure to remember?

Chapter 15

The Indianapolis International Airport was the pretty painted toe-nail on the city's callused left foot. The new terminal hub was only a few years old, so the glass and chrome still glistened like a beacon in the middle of nowhere. Inside, the restaurants and stores were clean and the layout easy to follow. I met Colin and Tony at the Starbucks just before the security check at Terminal A.

Crowded places like this used to be agony for me. All those thoughts swirling around, all the heated lust and near-comatose stares. Alcohol helped keep the mental voices in line, but shutting out other people's thoughts was a skill I'd really had to practice. When I stayed with Thirteen right after my escape, he'd taken me out to restaurants and for walks through downtown to let me practice being around benign groups of strangers. It took months to get used to it all. I'd practically attacked every person who looked my way those first few trips out. But looking back, those little chaperoned excursions had been invaluable. If Thirteen hadn't taken the time to help me acclimate, I couldn't imagine where I might have ended up.

Tony looked up as I approached, giving me a subtle once-over. I'd worn tight skinny jeans under knee-high lace-up UGGs. My long-sleeved turtleneck was covered with a soft fox-fur vest, and my long hair was pulled back in a ponytail. Tony smiled a little and whispered to Colin that I was there.

When Colin turned to face me, I stumbled, laughing. Tony wore the perfect snowboarder-chic attire I'd expect the guy to wear. But Colin was dressed almost exactly the same way: baggy pants tucked into thick snow boots, puffy blue coat over an untucked henley. He even had goggles pushed up to his forehead and his usually gelled hair in a shaggy mess.

"I didn't realize you were planning on skiing the runways, Colin," I said, nodding to the goggles.

He pulled them off in a quick move as Tony stifled a laugh. "I told him it was too much."

"Whatever," Colin grumbled. "Did you receive my communication with the portfolio attachment?"

"You mean the e-mail with the surveillance photos? Yeah, I got it. So what's the deal? Are we just going for Dr. Everett, or is his new partner joining him?" The whole reason they'd brought me on was because they'd received word that their target's partner was also arriving on this flight. If things had changed and Everett was flying alone, chances were I wouldn't be needed. My skin tightened at the idea of missing out on my first active mission.

"Just Everett," Colin said, adding sugar to his coffee. "The second image was the partner, Ken Hall. I sent you a photo as a matter of procedure, but we received confirmation this morning that our guy is flying solo, after all."

I hesitated by the table. So should I just hang around then or what?

"The plan doesn't change, though," Colin said, and I stood a little straighter. "You'll still be on point at the terminal. Send word to baggage claim as soon as you confirm the target's arrival, then again once he's headed out of your area. Tony will have the next checkpoint. Then Darrel and I will apprehend in baggage claim."

I let out a sigh of relief and took a seat at their table. Good, I was still part of the game plan. We were at a high table away from the other latte drinkers and with a perfect view of the terminal exit. When the arriving plane let out its passengers, they'd have no choice but to walk right past us.

"We also confirmed," Tony added, "that the packages being transported were checked and will have to be picked up in the special items area of baggage claim." He blew on his hot chocolate. "We knew the guy was smuggling some kind of priceless artifacts, but apparently he's disguising the stuff in manual-labor farm equipment. Our London counterpart saw Everett changing planes at Heathrow—he said that the crates the guy's shipping are huge."

"Did you ever confirm who Dr. Everett is selling the smuggled artifacts to?" I asked.

"We have the drop point about a mile south of the stadium downtown," Colin explained. "The buyer's name is Michael Kane, but we're pretty sure that's an alias. Our tech guy is tracking it, so we should have a real name by the time we have Everett in custody."

"So we don't worry about the buyer, then?" I asked.

"Our FBI contact is on standby," Colin said. "Our only concern is the supernatural threat. Once we have Everett, the FBI will take over the stolen goods and the apprehension of the buyer." He looked at his watch. His shoe tapped against the chair leg. "This mission will be successful—I have every confidence in that. But if somehow Everett manages to slip past us, we'll have to move fast. The drop is scheduled for less than two hours from now, and then Everett's scheduled to depart on the one o'clock flight back to London."

In and out. It was smart. This way he limited the risk of my father or uncle becoming aware of his presence.

Tony sipped his hot chocolate. "We have all the scenarios and contingency plans. But they won't be necessary. We got this, Colin. Our guy's going down."

I smiled at Tony's cockiness. This was much more like what I'd expected when it came to normal Network agent duties: staking out a known supernatural bad guy, ready to take him down. According to Colin's information, Everett was a pyrotech. He'd smuggle stolen artwork for a client, then set fire to the drop point after the client collected, erasing any evidence of their interaction. It would feel good taking him into Network custody.

Tony slid a steaming foam cup my way. "Didn't know what you drank, so I just got you a basic mocha."

That he'd thought to get me anything really touched me. "This is great. Thank you." Automatically I pulled off the coffee's lid and took out the flask from my pocket. I poured a couple of shots into the drink and said, "So is Luce all set on the flight deck?" That had been her planned first position, and for some reason knowing where she was felt strangely important this morning.

"Er, yeah, she's on the flight deck until the plane lands," Colin said carefully.

"Geez, girl," Tony said with a soft laugh. "What kind of alcoholic are you?"

I froze putting the cap on my flask. Marie had asked me that same question once. With her, the words had been filled with so much disgust I hadn't bothered answering. But this time, Tony just seemed curious. I checked his thoughts to be sure. Yep, just curious.

"Uh, well, the buzz helps with my telepathy. Kind of turns the volume down on everyone unless I want to hear them."

Tony nodded. "Yeah, I guess that makes sense. Ever tried weed?"

"Er, no. I've been drugged enough in my life not to want to do it voluntarily."

"Why would someone drug you?"

It was such a casual conversation. With my other team, everyone had walked on eggshells around my past. But Tony just asked what he thought—no judgment, just curiosity. It was really kind of…cool.

"Well, my father, actually. I was always kind of the guinea pig when it came to new drugs his company wanted to make. Or if he wanted to sell something illegal, he'd need to know how much to dilute the source for it to have the right effect but still be cost-effective. The drugs never lasted long in my system, but it was enough for him to figure out what he needed."

Tony frowned. "Man, that's harsh. My buddy Reece once thought he was just getting some good dope when really the dealer laced it with mescaline. Totally fucked him up for, like, days. Guy went completely straight after that. I couldn't imagine being given new stuff over and over." He gave a respectful nod. "You're a strong chick, you know that?"

I smiled. "Yeah, I know."

"Of course, the Network doesn't sanction recreational drug use," Colin added, giving Tony a pointed stare. Tony just rolled his eyes and drank his hot chocolate. Colin straightened his coat sleeves, then said, "So, Magnolia, from what I understand, you've worked with the Network for just under a year now. How did that happen?"

Yeah, right. Unlike Tony, Colin had agenda written all over him. I sipped my mocha and thought of how to answer. Thankfully, I didn't have to.

"The plane's landed," I announced quietly.

"What?" Colin frowned. "No, it hasn't—" His cell phone buzzed. A text message from Luce. He narrowed his eyes at me. "Let's get in our places."

We all pulled out our cell phones and made sure they were set for walkie-talkie function. Tony tossed back the rest of his drink, knocked his fist on the table, then ambled his way toward his position just past the men's room. Colin was suddenly nervous. He looked at me, and I could feel the repressed need to bite his nails. "You sure you know what to do?"

I sipped my mocha. "I'm sure. And hey, if somehow the guy does get past you, I'll just zap him with my freeze ray until you can throw on the cuffs." I wiggled my fingers at him, and he gnashed his teeth together. I sighed. "Colin, it'll be fine. You've organized an excellent takedown here. You'll get him—I'm sure of it."

For some reason that put him at ease. After a couple of easy breaths, he slapped on the goofiest smile I'd ever seen, but it looked perfect with the snowboarder outfit he wore. With a shake of his shaggy hair, he pulled on his thick gloves, bumped his fist on the table just like Tony had, then pointed at me and winked. "Later, snow chick." Then he headed to the ticket kiosk, ready to set his plan in motion.

I really liked these guys. They wondered about me, but they didn't treat me like a freak or like someone who needed to be watched, like my other team had when we'd first been introduced. These guys knew I was a real agent and trusted me to do my job. It was cool. Maybe after today, I could talk to Thirteen about doing more assignments with them.

I finished off my mocha and strolled over to stand among the throngs of people waiting for the exiting passengers. Children jumped up and down; people stretched their necks, trying to get that first glimpse of whoever they were waiting for. A couple of people held signs with different names on them. One family had about five generations all huddled together, ready to welcome even more of their extended relatives.

I did a double take. My heart stopped as my stomach sank to the floor. I'd overlooked him at first, just another face in the crowd. He held a sign, but I couldn't see it to read it. The family of twenty-plus relatives separated us, but through the bodies I saw his expensive dark suit, his perfectly brushed-back silver hair. He was a normal, nondescript, nothing person. But just seeing him made me want to run away and never look back.

The crowd grew excited. The passengers were coming. Heart pounding, I stepped back, tried to blend with the crowd. As the family in front of me moved forward, I peeked into his thoughts at the same moment I caught a glimpse of his sign: EVERETT. *Holy shit.* Our target was being picked up by Uncle Max's personal driver.

CHAPTER 16

My first instinct was to disappear. It would have been different if it had been one of Uncle Max's guards. Those guys were little more than drug-addled gorillas. But Sharon Illyses had never been a drug-addled anything. He was a sadist, a man loyal to my family with a kind of reverence that made my stomach churn. He'd never needed to be drugged to help in Father's or Uncle Max's torture sessions. He'd bled me over and over just for the thrill of pleasing my family.

He would recognize me the moment he saw me.

Power shimmered under my skin. I was just about to turn invisible when a group of men suddenly bumped into me. Then a passing woman smiled my way. "Nice boots," she said as she walked by.

I couldn't disappear here. People would notice. Even more, I had a job to do.

The thought steadied my resolve and pushed aside my panic. Network agents didn't run and hide from their targets. I could do this. With one eye on Sharon and the other on the passengers coming toward us, I pulled out my cell phone and clicked the Talk button.

"We have a problem. Everett has a driver waiting for him." No point freaking everyone out with who the driver was. They'd find out that good news soon enough.

"No names over the link!" Colin managed to shout at me in a hushed voice. "There's no driver scheduled. A rental car in the target's name is to be picked up in baggage claim. Confirm."

"I don't care about a rental being scheduled. I'm telling you there's a driver here for our guy."

"The manifest lists another passenger with the name Everest. It's probably for that person," Luce said in a "duh" sort of way. I ground my teeth.

"I'm telling you it's for our guy."

"You need to confirm," Colin ordered. A snarl growled in my throat, but I held it back. The target was there. He wore a crisp European-cut suit that was obviously a custom fit. Thinly trimmed mustache and goatee, short, styled brown hair. He had out a cell phone and was texting away with fast fingers. I focused in on him. I could feel the supernatural power humming inside him. He didn't expect a driver. His thoughts were on getting to baggage claim, getting through his meeting, and getting back to London, where his partner was waiting.

Sharon moved forward, trying to step past the Olympic-size family reunion that now blocked nearly half the walkway. Everett's face was all over his thoughts.

"Target's here," I said into the phone. "He's not expecting the driver. Shit, he's going to beat me to him." I moved quickly but at normal human speed, keeping my back to the approaching Sharon. Everett ran right into me, stomping on my foot with his wing tips.

"What the—"

"Oh!" I cried. "Oh, my foot!" I grabbed on to his shoulder and hopped in place, clutching my boot in exaggerated agony.

He put his arms on mine to steady me. "Oh my, are you all right? I didn't see you there." His voice was thickly accented, but I didn't know from where. I knew the moment he felt my power—his hands began to warm against my sleeves.

People bumped and pushed at us, trying to squeeze between us and the rejoicing family. I pushed a little suggestion into his mind to calm him down and not worry about the power he felt coming off me.

"Here, come over here," he said once my persuasion had set him at ease. He guided me to the nearby bathrooms, where Tony was staked out inside. I caught a glimpse of Sharon stuck on the other side of the family reunion.

"I need to get to baggage claim," I said, tears pooling in my eyes as I limped. "I'm meeting my boyfriend, and I have to get down there. Oh, it hurts! And there's just so many people." I pushed another suggestion into his mind, then looked up at him, blinking in the most innocent way I knew how.

"I'm heading down to baggage claim as well," he said. "In fact, I believe there may be an alternative route that would allow us to avoid some of the crowd. Oh yes—there! I'm quite certain it's off that way past that pub." I looked in the direction he pointed, the way I'd suggested he find, and saw the corridor in between a sports bar and a yogurt shop. *Bingo.*

"Are you sure that will take us to baggage claim?" I asked, fluttering my eyelashes. For the first time, he really looked at me. He was a distinguished forty, thin in a way that made his cheekbones look sharp. And he was thoroughly committed to the man he was currently seeing. But when he met my eyes, I released just

NO LOVE FOR THE WICKED

a touch of my natural sensuality. His mouth opened with a small gasp; his eyes dilated.

"If you're sure," I said sweetly. "Then I'll just stay with you."

He nodded slowly. "Yes, you just stay with me."

He slid his arm around my waist and helped me limp to the narrow hallway. I glanced over my shoulder. Sharon was gone. I reached out to the minds of everyone around us. The multigenerational family was finally moving its way through the terminal. Sharon wasn't anywhere near them. He wasn't farther down the terminal. Wasn't in the men's bathroom. We were steps inside the corridor. I could hear Luce and Colin getting anxious.

"Dr. Holmes Everett. I'm sorry, sir, but I need you to come with me."

Sharon was suddenly there, catching his breath, standing in front of us. I instantly ducked my head and stared at the floor. Everett stumbled over his words. "I'm sorry, but I think you have the wrong man. I need to help this young woman get to baggage claim. Excuse us."

Everett tried to move us past him, but Sharon stepped into our path. I knew what I should do. I should just direct Sharon's thoughts, get him out of our way and out of my life. So why didn't I? I snuck a glance at him and instantly looked at the floor again. God, it was like I was that girl all over again. The victim, ruled by fear and pain. How many times had this man stood by while I'd been hung and burned? How many times had he handed my father the instruments while he experimented on ways to draw out the most pain? Anytime I'd fought back at the estate, my punishment had been a hundred times worse. If I'd released my power while I was being whipped, even if it was just in reaction to the pain, the whipping would turn into a gutting. Then Sharon would bring out the salt. I trembled before I could stop myself.

"Your client has provided transportation as well as accommodations for you and your partner at his family's personal estate, Dr. Everett," Sharon said. "If you would come with me, I'll make certain that your cargo and personal effects are appropriately collected."

I closed my eyes. Michael Kane—an obvious alias for Maxwell Kelch if you were looking for it. Oh God—if Uncle Max was bringing this guy to the estate, then he was already dead. Whatever business deal they had going, it was done. Everett would hand over the artifact thing he was smuggling, and Max would kill him. And Colin's team would be out a key target.

Heat warmed at the base of my spine. I looked up at Everett. He had gone statue-still. A driver? Accommodations? This wasn't in his plan at all.

We were just inside the corridor, enough so people walking past couldn't fall over us if they tried to keep to the terminal walls. Past Sharon, several feet down the corridor, Colin emerged. I knew the moment Everett saw him because the place where his hand rested at my lower back burned even hotter.

Great. Now I had a nervous pyro to deal with. I looked up at Colin. Fists clenched, he moved toward us quickly. Luce appeared behind him, farther down the corridor. Maybe I could move with Everett at super speed, get him away from Sharon, and—

"Oh my God. Magnolia."

I turned my gaze and found myself face-to-face with a sheet-white Sharon. His beady eyes were wide in shock; his mind raced. I was dead. They had confirmed it. The senator and Sir Magnus had seen my body, knew for certain. He had to tell them. Now, before anything else. He reached for his cell phone. I didn't think. I just reacted.

The sound of his heart pounded in my ears, in my throat, in my chest, until I could feel his pulse moving against my palm. I hadn't moved an inch or touched him at all, but I felt the weight of his heart in my hand like an invisible ball that my fingers could curl around. My hands didn't transform. I didn't need them to. I'd seen Father do this a hundred times, always when it was necessary to leave a clean death. It was just like moving anything else with my mind: closing a laptop from another room, floating my bottle of Beam from the fridge to the table. Slowly I closed my fingers around the swelling beat that I felt speeding up against my palm. Sharon gasped. The heat sizzling through Everett's hand paused. I closed my hand tighter. Sharon dropped his cell phone and gripped his hand to his chest. Everett took a step back as Colin hurried closer. I grabbed Everett's arm and kept him at my side. Luce, a few steps farther down, went for the gun at her back. The fluorescent lights overhead flickered. Sharon dropped to his knees. My fist closed, and I squeezed until my nails dug into my palm. Against the pads of my fingers, I felt the pulse of Sharon's heart as it stilled. He collapsed with a painful sigh.

"Holy Mother," Everett breathed. His arm burned where I held him. There were singe marks around his cuffs. And this guy dealt in priceless artwork? I shook my head to stay in the moment. Colin jogged the last steps to join us, thick wire cuffs ready in his hand.

"Is everything all right?" he asked, looking furiously at Sharon, Everett, and me.

I looked at Everett, but his eyes were set farther down the corridor, where Luce now had her gun in hand, ready to go. The flash of heat where I held his arm was a painful shock, but I didn't let go. He tried to pull away, but I only held on tighter.

"Don't move." Tony had come up behind us. Wearing the same thick gloves as Colin, he gripped Everett by the back of the neck and held his gun into Everett's ribs, pushing us all farther down the hallway. Everett stiffened. Flames ignited on his sleeve, singeing my turtleneck and instantly burning my hand.

"Will you stop that!" I hissed at him. He blinked and stared down at me, confused. Together we looked at where my hand had begun melting against his arm. My fingers were red and blistered. Around the edges of my palm, the skin was turning black. "Damn it, pull it back, Holmes!"

Maybe it was my use of his first name, or maybe it was watching my hand melt away in front of his eyes, but either way he sucked back the fire. Colin passed the wire cuffs to Tony, who made quick use of the cuffs to get Everett restrained. "I don't know who you people are, but you are making a terrible mistake. I am Dr. Holmes Everett of the Aunre Institute."

"You are a pyrotechnic smuggler who just set fire to one of our agents," Colin said, getting in Everett's face. "Luce, Tony, escort the good doctor to the holding car. Darrel is standing by with his cargo." Tony pushed Everett forward, the gun still at his back. When they moved, my hand peeled from Everett's arm, the skin pulling like bloody goo where it clung to his now-cooled flesh. Luce made a strangled noise.

"Dear God," Colin said, cringing. "We need to get you to a hospital." He whipped out his phone.

"Don't bother," I cut him off quickly. I studied my hand and sucked in air through my teeth when a glop of skin dropped onto my boot. "It'll heal on its own soon enough. And it doesn't really hurt anymore anyway. Kinda stings a little, you know, around the edges." I held up my hand so they could see what I was talking about. "But the part in here where the bone's exposed—he burned right through the nerves there, so I can't feel it at all anymore."

I looked up, and all four of them were gaping at me. "What?"

Colin closed his eyes and murmured something under his breath. When he opened them again, he look not at me, but at Sharon. "What the hell happened with this guy? Who is he?"

NO LOVE FOR THE WICKED

"He's dead. His heart stopped beating, so when they find him it will be ruled natural causes. But we're going to have a problem. This is the driver I told you was sent to pick up Dr. Everett."

"But there wasn't a driver," Colin argued. "He has a rental car."

We looked at Everett, who shrugged. He wasn't admitting anything. A security golf cart passed by. We moved quickly down the hallway, away from the main terminal. I glanced back long enough to glimpse Sharon's dead body one more time. Then I looked down at my hand. How many times had that man assisted in making my whole body look like this?

Yeah, not sure I could muster up too much guilt on this one.

Luce pushed open an unmarked metal door that led to an enclosed stairwell. I followed quickly as we rushed down the stairs in silence. At the garage, Luce pushed through the exit and found Darrel waiting in an oversize SUV. She climbed in the backseat and maneuvered Everett in next to her; then Tony got in to sandwich the guy. Colin shut the door and turned to me.

"We have confirmation that his partner, Ken Ward, hasn't yet left his penthouse in London's West End. The drop site is set for ten forty-five a.m. All of our intel was right on this one."

"You're right," I agreed. "Everett had no clue a car was being sent for him. That's just how his client works. No surprises and total meeting control."

Colin leaned back on his heels, his face that practiced blank that all Network leaders liked to wear. "We are still waiting confirmation on his client's alias."

I let out a breath that might have been a dark chuckle. "Yeah, well no need for that now." I winced as my melted hand started to ache. "That driver was the personal chauffeur to Senator Maxwell Kelch." Colin's mouth dropped open. "Dr. Everett's client is my uncle."

CHAPTER 17

I hadn't been home an hour before the soft beep of the alarm announced visitors. Not surprising—I'd seen Colin's worry before they'd left the airport. No doubt he'd called Thirteen the minute they'd pulled out of the garage to report my "injured in the line of duty" incident as per Network procedure. Whatever. I wrapped up my hand with some clean gauze from the first aid cupboard in the kitchen. The kit in the bathroom had wraps, tape, and anti-septic spray, but as damaged as my hand was, the soft cloth would feel best until it finished healing. Stupid deep-tissue burns. They always took so much longer to heal than regular wounds.

A car door slammed out front. Then another. I listened carefully. That wasn't Thirteen. I unlocked the front door with my thoughts and finished wrapping my hand. Tony and Colin paused long enough for a quick knock before pushing open the door.

"I figured you guys would be busy processing your new prisoner," I said, keeping my back to them as they entered the kitchen.

"How's your hand?" Colin asked from the doorway. I glanced over my shoulder. They were still in their snowboarder clothes.

"I told you it would be fine." I held up my hand so they could see the shiny flesh before I continued with the bandage. "The skin has already started growing back. It's still a little raw in some places, but it's fine. Did you really come all the way out here just to ask about my hand?"

"I've never had an agent injured on an assignment," Colin said.

"Well, don't worry. I'm not going to file for workers' comp or anything." I turned and faced them. "Was there anything else?"

"We don't care about a medical bill, Magnolia," Tony said. "We wanted to make sure you're all right."

"I'm fine."

I kept my eyes locked on Colin's. I could feel his conflict. That need to bite his nails was back with a vengeance. "Actually," he reluctantly started, "there is something else. What do you know about the man who was there to pick up Everett?"

Power grew warm in my stomach. I curled my lip and said, "That's a conversation you'll have to clear with Thirteen. My time is too valuable to waste explaining things your team should be able to figure out on their own."

"My team had correct information."

"Your team didn't even know who your target was meeting!" And, damn it, why hadn't they known? I should have been prepared for Sharon being there. I mean, my God, he saw me. *Saw* me! He'd had his finger on my uncle's speed dial. One push, and I was found out. Bile rose in my throat. That had been so close. Too close.

Tony stepped forward, subtly putting himself between us. "Let's just take it down a notch. Magnolia, you have something to drink around here, right?"

I held my scowl a moment longer, then lifted a hand and floated the bottle of Jim Beam down from its post at the top of the fridge to land softly on the table. Colin's eyes went wide; Tony lifted his eyebrows. I walked over to the cupboard and took out three glass tumblers, filled them with ice. We all took seats around the table while Tony poured.

"OK," Colin said after a quick swallow. "Obviously there's more going on with this target than we thought. We were after a known smuggler with pyrotechnic abilities and a history of arson. None of our communications hinted at Everett's current client being a Kelch." I didn't miss the shudder in his voice when he said the name.

"Everett didn't know that Uncle Max was his client. He never realized that Michael Kane was an alias, so you were a step ahead of him there. Everett also didn't know that Sharon was going to pick him up. He wasn't too thrilled when he found out, either."

"How do you know he wasn't thrilled about it?" Tony asked.

I lifted my injured hand. "Our pyro isn't the most emotionally adjusted supernatural art smuggler. When he gets nervous, he gets hot."

"OK. So about this driver—"

The alarm in the bedroom beeped. Tires squealed as a car slipped and slid all over the slushy path of my driveway. When it spun to a stop beside the house, my breath caught in my chest. A car door slammed just as the alarm beeped again. A second vehicle turned into the driveway, slightly more controlled.

Tony and Colin jumped to their feet as the front door flung open. "Mag!" Theo called out. He pounded his way into the kitchen, then abruptly stopped when he saw Colin and Tony. I rose slowly. He looked totally fierce, eyes burning behind dark wet hair that had fallen over his face. He hadn't shaved that morning, even though he'd obviously gone home to change clothes.

God, had it just been a few hours ago that I'd woken up beside him? His thoughts were blocked, but the way his chest heaved and his nostrils flared, I could tell he was reeling.

He spared Colin and Tony brief glances before raking me with his gaze. He spotted my bandaged hand, and I swore I heard him growl. "What happened?"

"It's nothing."

"Who the hell are you?" Tony asked, earning a glare. Theo moved around the table past Colin. When their eyes met, Colin set his jaw. "Mahle."

"St. Pierre." Theo sneered.

Although he'd been stalking his way around the room, when he finally got to me, he lifted my hand with surprising gentleness. My stomach fluttered as he studied the pink of my fingers. His own fingertips were like butterfly wings as he brushed over my bandages. "I felt your pain," he whispered. "I didn't know what happened, but I knew you were hurt and I had to get to you." He lifted my palm to his lips for the barest of kisses. "The healing is painful," he murmured softly, making my heart ache. He knew what the healing felt like; I'd healed his many wounds last summer after my brother's men tortured him for information.

I met his eyes, and my pulse stuttered. Everyone else in the room faded away. Seconds stretched as our hearts began beating in time to one another. Beat. Beat. Beat. My hand grew warm where he touched the bandages. I couldn't look away, and in the reflection of his dark eyes I saw the subtle glow coming off me.

The front door opened and I jumped back, pulling my hand to my chest automatically. After I'd broken the contact, an instant chill fell over me. Jon and Heather rushed into the kitchen. Jon pulled up short as he sized up Tony and Colin. Heather just pushed right past them.

"Oh, Magnolia," she said. "We were at the Turtle going over surveillance footage when Theo stopped his recap midsentence and just ran out of the room. It's because of you, isn't it? You're hurt, aren't you?" She wanted to pull me into her arms, but she knew that would make me uncomfortable. I sighed and opened my arms in invitation. She took full advantage. She threw herself into me, knocking me back a step. Theo steadied me from behind. I glanced over at Colin and Tony. Both guys were eyeing Theo and me carefully. Had they seen us glowing?

Heather held me at arm's length. "Is everything, you know, healing the way it should?"

"I'm fine," I assured her, giving her back an awkward pat. She stepped back. "My hand got burned by a pyrotechnic art smuggler. No big deal."

"Mission targets are confidential, Magnolia," Colin snapped at me.

"And mission leaders are supposed to establish contingencies that ensure the safety of their team," Theo growled back at him.

"Colin didn't do anything wrong," Tony argued, adjusting his stance to cover both Theo and Jon. "The target is in custody. Outside factors altered the execution, but the mission was successful."

"And plan details are for mission team members only," Colin said. "So if you don't mind, I'll see you to the door so I can finish debriefing my team member."

Theo fisted his hands. But before he could move, Jon said coolly, "Magnolia happens to be my team member as well. And as I was the one to sign off on her cross-team involvement, I think we'll stay until I'm satisfied with her physical well-being."

Really? Jon signed off my cross-team work? Thirteen must really be moving him through the Network ranks. Colin ground his teeth but bit his tongue. Jon was totally better at the blank expression than he was.

"Fine," Colin said finally. "Magnolia, I expect a full assessment of events as they took place by sixteen hundred hours." I looked at the clock. That gave me, like, two hours. "I'll notify you of the debriefing location after I receive your report."

He moved past Jon, Tony following right behind.

"Wait a minute," I called out. "Colin, just hold up. Jon's team is in charge of everything having to do with my family. Right, Jon?"

For a second I worried he was going to be as much a stickler about team mission confidentiality as Colin. Slowly he nodded. "That's right."

"Well, it turns out Colin's target was here to meet Uncle Max."

Jon instantly tensed. "Your target is directly linked to Senator Kelch? Why the hell weren't we informed?"

"Hey," Tony said, stepping up again. Jon had gone from practiced blank to full rage in a matter of seconds. "Our chief was given full access to all our team's information. We didn't know who the target's client was past his alias. Not that it would have changed anything in our action plan if we had, but don't go jumping down our throats when we reported at full disclosure everything we had."

Colin cursed under his breath. The room went deathly silent. "You didn't know?" Jon said, his voice frighteningly soft. "Your pyrotechnic art smuggler was arriving for a meeting with one of the most powerful supernatural terrorists in the entire world, and you didn't know?"

As I watched, Jon's face turned three shades of red, then settled on a deep purple. I took a step back. The guy looked like he might actually pop, and having witnessed exploding heads in the past, I didn't want to be in shrapnel range if he did.

Heather moved smoothly to stand between Jon and Colin. "Obviously we have some overlap in our current assignments.

How about if we just call Thirteen, get clearance to officially share information, then have a little chat on how we might be able to help each other out?"

When no one moved, Heather turned to me. "Magnolia? Why don't you get down some more glasses? I think we're all going to need a drink for this one."

CHAPTER 18

He had known that I was hurt. Theo had known, and even though he knew I could heal anything, he had come running. The warm, fuzzy feeling spreading inside me couldn't be pushed aside even if I'd wanted it to.

I took a spot at the head of the table, Tony and Colin on one side, Theo and Heather on the other. Jon sat facing me at the table's far end. Colin had stepped into the restroom while Heather called Thirteen. When he came back out, his hair was properly slicked back and his baggy long-sleeved T-shirt was tucked in. He still didn't look as put together as Jon, but it was the best he could do with what he had on.

"Thirteen has approved information sharing—" Heather began as she put away her phone.

"Great," Colin interrupted. "So tell us. What exactly are you doing to eliminate the Kelch threat? Because as far as I can tell, those bastards are getting more powerful and more evil with each passing moment. Current company notwithstanding, of course."

I coughed on my swallow. "Oh, no need to exclude me. I'm totally getting more powerful by the minute."

Colin did a quick double take, not sure he'd heard me correctly. I shot him a wide, shit-eating grin. Theo chuckled beside me and took a long swallow of whiskey from my glass. I snagged the glass back from him. His own cocky grin had me biting my lip.

"Er, if you'd let me finish," Heather continued. "Thirteen has approved information sharing with concern to *your* team's current mission. We still aren't approved to reveal details on our current active assignments."

Colin's nostrils flared. Tony slammed a fist on the table. "This is bullshit. You expect us to just hand over all our intel? This was our target and our mission—a successful mission, considering our target is now in custody."

"We have no interest in usurping authority over your target," Jon said coolly. "But you are required to give us all information you have pertaining to your target's involvement with the Kelch family."

Tony sat back and crossed his arms over his chest. Colin ground his teeth. Neither one made a move to start the ball rolling. After several long moments, I threw up my hands. "Oh, for crying out loud!" I leaned forward and got serious. "Colin's plan was good. Executable, thorough. It had nothing to do with Everett's client. Dr. Holmes Everett was the target, by the way." Colin moaned under his breath. I just ignored him and continued with the recap.

When I was done, Heather asked, "How involved is Senator Kelch's driver with the family's affairs? Is he one of the—"

"That's what I'd like to know," Colin piped in.

Jon leaned far over the table, his expression suddenly murderous. With a stiff finger pointed in Colin's face, he snarled, "You interrupt her one more time, and team leader or not, I will kick your ass into next week. Do you understand?"

Colin remained silent, his glare speaking for itself. After another tense moment, I cleared my throat.

"Er, no, Heather, he was never one of the drug-controlled guards. He may have had his mind scrambled once or twice, but for the most part, it wasn't necessary. He was sadistic himself— and therefore Uncle Max's most loyal employee." My stomach cramped in memory. I ignored it and kept my eyes on the staredown between Jon and Colin.

"So he would have known details about the senator's itineraries," Jon said, his disgust obvious. This was a big opportunity missed for Jon's team. The Network played inside the limits of the law as much as possible—especially when it came to interviewing or questioning normal humans like Sharon. But had they known Sharon was meeting a known supernatural smuggler, they would have had just cause to bring him in. They could have gotten all kinds of details about Father's and Uncle Max's overseas trips.

Pulling his gaze back toward me, Jon said, "Sharon David Illyses. He's been Senator Kelch's driver for more than a decade. How did you handle him?"

His expression softened a little when he asked. Jon had been there last year when I'd snuck into Uncle Max's congressional offices, as well as when I'd returned to the estate to bring down my brother Markus. He'd seen firsthand the toll it took on me when I came in contact with my family. In fact, I wouldn't be surprised if he still had some scars from the emotional whiplash that seeing my family had caused me.

I stared at my glass, seeing Sharon's wide eyes as he dropped his cell phone and realized what was happening. In a quick move,

I threw back the rest of my drink and met Jon's gaze. "Sharon's dead. Heart attack. There was nothing we could do."

Jon nodded in understanding. "Probably for the best."

I went to refill my glass and, damn it, my hand shook. Whiskey sloshed on the table until Theo covered my hand with his. He steadied me, then gently took the bottle from me and poured the whiskey himself.

"You OK?" Tony asked softly, leaning over to me. I gave him a weak smile.

"She's fine," Theo answered. "And you weren't so concerned about her well-being when she held on to your pyro target for you, were you? Maybe if your team leader had been more concerned about getting accurate information than about upping his take-down numbers, she wouldn't be nursing a melted hand right now."

Colin and Tony jumped to their feet. Theo and Jon quickly matched the move.

"We had more than enough information to move on our target!" Colin shouted.

"This is just like that telepathic drug dealer in Argentina," Theo spat. "You had just enough intel to take down your target, and you didn't care who got hurt when things went south."

"Don't even go there," Colin shouted back. "We're talking about this mission, this target."

"Leaders learn from their mistakes," Jon said.

"She's the one who grabbed the known pyro without any protective gloves," Tony added.

"I didn't need any gloves," I argued, but no one heard me.

Jon and Colin leaned over the table nearly nose to nose. But it was Theo lunging for Tony that knocked me out of my seat. In a move faster than I could track, he went from standing beside me to the other side of the table; his hands fisted in Tony's shirt as he slammed the younger guy against the kitchen wall.

"So it's *her* fault she got burned?" Theo growled in Tony's face. "You fucking piece of shit! You think that just because she can heal anything that happens to her, she doesn't feel the pain?" He slammed him against the wall again, denting the already-battered wood paneling.

OK. Fuck. This.

Instantly everyone froze. Heather halfway stood from her seat, her arm reaching for Jon's. Jon stood inches away from Colin's face, spittle from Colin's half-spoken words stopped mid-flight toward Jon's face. Tony was up against the wall, his feet off the ground as Theo held him in place. I pushed myself off the floor and righted my chair.

"And Thirteen thinks I'm immature," I muttered as I dusted off my jeans. I took another drink and surveyed the room. With a shake of my head, I walked over to Theo. His eyes were moving, narrowing on me as I got closer. No one else would even be able to breathe unless I released them.

"Are you going to let him go?" I asked. He growled deep in his chest. I tried not to smile, but, what can I say, the sound was so dark and masculine, it just totally turned me on. I pursed my lips. "I'm serious. Tony and Colin didn't do anything wrong. OK?" More eye narrowing. "*OK?*"

"Fine," he gritted out.

Wow. I'd expected a mental response. Not even Malcolm had been able to speak when I held him in place like that. I stepped back and released everyone from my hold. Gasps of breath exploded in the room. Theo dropped Tony, who gasped for air from the floor at our feet. Theo and I kept our eyes on each other. If his growl had turned me on, then me releasing some power totally did it for him. There was heat in his eyes now that made my lower stomach tingle.

"You're really getting stronger," I said on a breath.

"So are you," he replied in a breathy voice of his own. "You weren't able to hold a whole room like that before."

I shrugged. He grinned. Jon cleared his throat. My face heated as I returned to my seat. And grew even hotter when Theo pulled out my chair for me. I glanced down at Heather, who gave me a very clear "we're going to talk later" look as she tried to catch her own breath. I smiled at her and got a wide, coughing smile in return.

Jon straightened his rugby shirt, ran his hands through his hair, and cleared his throat again. "Don't do that again, Magnolia."

I leaned back in my seat. "Then don't act like a bunch of dicks again."

Jon simmered in his seat for a minute. He wanted to tell Thirteen how I'd had used my power on them. But that would be like tattling. And he was team leader now. He'd have to figure out how to handle me on his own. I just smiled into my drink. *Good luck with that one, Heldamo.*

"OK," he said, trying to steer things back on track. Apparently I'd be "handled" later. "We need an inventory of what cargo Everett brought in. Everything from his personal luggage and carry-ons to his artifact cargo. We need to determine why the Kelch family is purchasing smuggled artifacts from another supernatural."

"Are you serious?" I asked, whiskey halfway to my mouth. "Have you seen my family's estate? The place is packed full of priceless crap. Artwork, sculptures, hell, there are Egyptian sarcophaguses in one of the basements. Even the carpets are from some ancient castle somewhere. And I can guarantee that more than half the stuff was acquired through less-than-legal channels."

"We have no previous information of the senator working with this particular smuggler."

Now I rolled my eyes. "Jon, please. You really think anyone in my family is going to pay a smuggler when it's so much easier to just kill him off and be done with it? They hardly ever work with the same people twice—especially on the illegal stuff."

Jon gave me that one and turned to Colin. "Will you be able to get us that information, or should we set up a time to interview Everett ourselves?"

Colin was still trying to steady himself. His hands were buried in his hair, elbows on the table as he breathed in through his nose and out through his mouth. He'd never had a supernatural use her abilities on him the way I had. Twice now I'd frozen him in place, completely taking away his ability to move. It shook him. He hadn't realized the Network employed people like me. He had wanted my help on his assignment because he knew I had an in with Thirteen. But no way was he ready to be around this kind of power on a regular basis. If I was an example of what Jon's team was up against, he was grateful for the level of assignments he'd been given so far. Hell, Jon, Heather, and Theo weren't even fazed by what I'd just done to them all.

"Yeah," he said finally. "I can give you the inventory. I'll send it through Thirteen."

"That will work. Also, I'll need to be copied on the interview disks when you interrogate Everett."

Colin lifted his head. "Interrogations are confidential."

Poor Colin. Hard to be by the book when your copy happens to be missing a few chapters. As if realizing how ridiculous he sounded, Colin shook his head. "I mean, yeah, I'll get you the disks as well."

Jon nodded and got to his feet. "OK, then." He pulled out Heather's chair for her as we all stood up. Colin helped pull Tony to his feet. They both gave me a wide berth as they made their way down the front hall. Guess I could say good-bye to any more casual coffee conversations with Tony. I didn't want to feel sad about that, but I couldn't help it.

Heather touched my arm as she passed. "You need to call Cordele and tell her you're all right." When I frowned, Heather smiled. "She's been worried. Look, right now the three of us have a check-in meeting with Chang, and I don't know how long that will take."

I looked to Theo, who stood in the kitchen's doorway, waiting for Heather. "I'll come by tomorrow, though," Heather continued. "If it's OK with you, I'll just bring my laptop and do my data gathering from here."

"Yeah, sure," I said absently. "That will be fine."

She squeezed my arm gently, then followed Jon out to the car. Theo stood, arms over his chest, staring down at me. "Your hand should be healed by now."

I pulled off the bandages. Sure enough, the melted skin was all shiny pink now. "It usually takes at least a couple more hours to get to this point."

He let out a heavy breath. I knew just how he felt. The intensity of the power between us just seemed overwhelming at times. He brushed a strand of hair away from my forehead, and I closed my eyes. His fingers lingered a moment more, then he pulled away. I kept my eyes closed, savoring the feel of his touch, until I heard his car rolling down the driveway.

CHAPTER 19

The Thursday before the Kelch Inc. Winter Gala, snow started falling again. Big white fluffy snow like they show on TV Christmas specials. Our pre-gala meeting was at Heather and Jon's, and thanks to Heather bringing over her laptop and doing her research at the farmhouse, I was more than prepared.

Apparently, the Network had several intranet sites with satellite feeds and government links that would have made the Cincinnati Wi-Fi nerds totally piss themselves. Once Heather showed me how to access the sites, digging through the information had almost been fun. In fact—drumroll, please—I'd actually found the city of Bohlren. Small, essentially uncharted industrial city right off the Danube River. For once, I looked forward to one of Thirteen's planning meetings.

At least, that was what I kept telling myself.

I gripped the steering wheel tightly. Oh, who the hell was I kidding? I'd been dreading this meeting for days. We were going over the details of how to break into my father's office and steal data from his personal PC. I would be in the same building, possibly even the same room, with the man. He'd sense my power, just as Uncle Max had when I'd broken into his office last year. Then it had been motivation for me to get in and get out. Now it was another part of the plan.

To Thirteen's credit, he had given me numerous outs over the past couple of days—I was still a new agent, the risk of exposure was higher than I was comfortable with. I hadn't taken any of them. Bottom line, the risk for the rest of the team was too high not to have every available inside advantage. And there was no greater advantage than having my powers on hand.

I parked at the curb behind Thirteen's SUV. Smoke billowed from Jon and Heather's chimney. With the fresh layer of snow and Christmas candles lit in every upstairs window, the house looked extra Christmas-card-like tonight. I walked the shoveled path to the front door and felt a surprising moment of happiness—this was exactly the warm and welcoming home that Heather should live in. It was a strange security to know that some things in life were just the way they should be.

I rang the doorbell and waited as Shane came to answer. He scowled down at me on instinct, then quickly checked himself. "Hey. Come on in."

Not the most heartfelt welcome, but at least he didn't sneer. He shut the door behind me, then led the way into the great room. "Grab a chair from the table," Shane instructed and walked over to his own dining table chair positioned beside the entertainment center. Both couches were fully occupied. Thirteen stood in front of the TV and sent me a quick smile before continuing his quiet conversation with Charles.

"Heard you went playing with another team," Chang said as I sat cross-legged on my chair. "What, we aren't exciting enough for you anymore?"

"You guys are plenty exciting. They just asked for my help, and I figured it would be more interesting than research."

"So you ignored your responsibilities to your team," Shane said. "Nice."

I shook my head. Things would just never be right between him and me. Any other night, I'd simply ignore him and move on. But tonight I needed to keep my thoughts occupied. I studied him from across the room. Maybe if he fell in love with someone else— someone he actually wanted to care about—he'd be able to be in the same room as me and not have to temper the pain and resentment overflowing in his thoughts. Cordele got up and headed toward the kitchen. "I'm getting a drink. Anyone else want one?"

For the first time, I really looked at her. She had sharp, intelligent eyes that tended to harden her features. But her skin was a soft pink, her lips nice and wide. She had her hair down tonight, and, even though her roots still showed a little, the thick blonde waves fell attractively to her shoulders. She and Shane would look good together. He was huge, and her tall body would fit snugly at his shoulder. "I'll take something, Cordele," I said. "Thanks."

As she moved around the kitchen, I turned back to Shane. "Are you seeing anyone?"

His mouth dropped open. "That's none of your business."

I shrugged. Cordele set my whiskey on the end table beside me. "What about you, Cordele? Are you seeing anyone?"

I had the room's full attention now. Cordele stammered, "Uh, no. I mean, kinda. Well, no. I don't know. Why are you asking me that?"

Oooh! Two defensive responses. And Cordele was definitely blushing. Maybe they were already into each other, and I'd just never picked up on it. I peeked into her thoughts. Furiously, she calculated some elaborate chemical formula. OK, obviously she didn't want me knowing who she was thinking about. It was probably just as well. Heather was boring a hole in the side of my head, her expression screaming, *Inappropriate, Magnolia.*

"Everything is set for Saturday's gala," Thirteen announced, getting the meeting under way. Instantly I stiffened.

"Don't we need to wait for everyone else?" I asked. Surely we could put this off for a few minutes more.

"Theo is on a Network errand, and Marie is otherwise unavailable this evening."

"She's ready for Saturday, though," Charles said quickly.

"I have every faith that she is," Thirteen said softly. I looked back at Charles. The guy was totally on edge, Marie in every corner of his mind. Was she sick or something? His thoughts were all over the place.

Thirteen cleared his throat. "Surveillance stations will be set up here in a mobile unit in the south parking lot, as well as here in the Capital One building down the street." Thirteen pointed out the locations on a blueprint map spread out on the coffee table. "Chang will enter with the on-site security team here in the back of the building." He nodded to a package on the floor at Chang's feet. "Your uniform and security ID are included in your portfolio."

I looked around and noticed that everyone had a brown-wrapped package on the floor in front of them. As if anticipating my next question, Thirteen handed a soft package to Shane, who passed it over to me. Cool—my own mission stuff.

"Reception tables will be set up in these three areas, with tours of the facility taking place every thirty minutes. You will arrive in pairs. Theo and Cordele will arrive first at twenty-one hundred hours. Jon and Magnolia will arrive exactly thirty-three minutes later. Shane will already be on-site."

"Why?" I asked, shifting in my seat. No point even trying to sit still during this part of the meeting. "Why will Shane already be there?"

"I'm invited to the gala on my own," Shane answered tightly. "For the last four months, I've been working as a sales rep in Kelch's telecommunications division. I won the Gold Star sales incentive for this last quarter, and an invite to the gala was part of my award. That and a big-screen TV."

My jaw dropped. "Are you serious? You work for my father? I thought you were a farmer."

His lip curled. His hands fisted. I could feel the pent-up hate building inside him. "I was raised on a farm and still own a farm. We needed someone in Kelch Inc.'s new division, and I was qualified. You would have known all this if you'd bothered being around these last few months."

I cocked a brow at him, and he looked away. He hadn't wanted me around these past few months. In fact, he'd been relieved when I'd ended up gone for as long as I had. But at the same time, whatever was inside Theo that drew him to me was also inside Shane. He longed to be near me. A compulsion. I'd just never felt anything back. I wished the whole thing was different, but if I couldn't control the things I felt, how the hell was I supposed to control the things I didn't? I took another drink.

"As I was saying," Thirteen continued. I ground my teeth and shifted again. "Jon and Magnolia will arrive right before the scheduled montage. We can assume Magnus will feel the supernatural presence as soon as Magnolia reaches the campus grounds."

"Actually, he probably won't notice until I'm already in the building."

"Even better. But we'll stick to the schedule as if he senses your power the moment you arrive. His distraction will be our advantage, as his concierge is set to position him on the stage prior to the video montage. He'll have to stay visible to the crowd while onstage but will be preoccupied trying to pinpoint the source of power."

Thirteen looked to me, and I saw the hint of worry behind his eyes.

"He won't find me," I said. "I've been dampening my power around the guy my entire life. And with the size of the crowd expected to be there, he'd have to be right in front of me to know I was the source."

"We'll be long gone before he gets a chance to get that close." Jon nodded at me confidently. I smiled a little at his reassurance.

"In the past, the montage slide show has lasted anywhere from twelve to nineteen minutes," Heather explained. "Right afterward, Magnus will give his annual motivational speech. It will last no more than five minutes."

Thirteen added, "You will then have the length of the montage and his speech to complete your mission and exit the building."

Thirteen outlined the entire series of events that would get us into Father's offices and back to the rendezvous point several miles away. By the end of his explanations, I wasn't the only one dreading Saturday night.

Finally it was over and I could breathe again. I knew my role and what I was expected to do. Now I wouldn't have to think about it again until Saturday night. One thing had been interesting, though. While I'd fought not to picture too clearly how close I would soon be to my father again, it had become glaringly obvious that Colin's mission had been a total joke. I mean, Thirteen outlined mission details, contingency plans, operation timelines; Colin had barely prepared his team for a possible problem. I knew he wasn't anxious to work with me again anytime soon, but if the opportunity ever presented itself to help out his team, I'd definitely think twice before signing on.

The meeting was coming to an end, which meant it was time for continued research updates. I finished off the whiskey I'd been nursing during the planning session and scooted to the edge of my seat. I knew I looked all call-on-me, but I didn't care.

"Magnolia?" Thirteen said, sensing my change in demeanor. "Have you found something?"

"Bohlren is a small, impoverished city located on the bank of the Danube River," I recited perfectly. "Its primary export is textiles, but it relies heavily on local tourist income because of its museums. Temperate in climate, the city's average population is—"

"Museums?" Jon interrupted, totally denting my flow. "What kind of museums?"

"The kind that have a bunch of old stuff. Anyway, the average increase in population ranges—"

"What kind of old stuff?" Jon asked drolly. "You mentioned that they export textiles. Are we talking industrial relics, manufactured goods, native artifacts? There has to be something specific if the city depends on the museums' contents to draw tourist income."

Who cared? I'd spent more than half an hour reading everything about Bohlren. They were going to hear about it whether they wanted to or not. "I have no idea what kind of crap they have on display. Their fancy museum is only a big deal because it has stuff from Ukraine, Moldova, and Russia. I guess other museums over there are only allowed to carry stuff found in their own country. But what I was saying was that the population—"

"Why would Bohlren's museum be allowed to carry historical items from all three nations?" Cordele asked, sitting forward in her seat. Great, now she was moving in on my report time too.

"Because the city sits right on the Danube River."

"So?" Shane argued. "Tons of towns sit on the banks of the Danube."

"No, I mean it's literally *on* the river. It's like a long island or something—like Manhattan. It sits just far enough away from the east bank that it can't be considered part of Ukraine. It's not part of any of the countries. Not officially. Government-wise it follows whoever steps up to claim it, but that changes almost every year depending on which country happens to have the strongest leadership at the time. That's why the museums have the stuff they do. And that's also why the population shifts are so drastic each year. People move there for a year during leadership shifts, then move back to their mainland once another nation takes over. Only a couple thousand locals have lived there for any length of time, and they work either at one of the little ports or at the museums."

Yeah, that's right. Soak in the research, people.

"Holy shit!" Charles said. "No wonder they're so eager to get something set up there. With the government in constant flux, a Kelch manufacturing site could go for years without paying any federal taxes on goods produced there."

"And how much do you want to bet there aren't any manufacturing regulations," Jon added. "God, they could move their entire weapons production there. Turn the whole city into one production facility. They'd supply every nation in the East with military-grade artillery and make fifty times what they're making right now. Good job, Magnolia. Chang, we have to run with this."

I sat back and basked in my moment of contribution. No one had needed to be mind manipulated or turned invisible—just simple research to get the right information. I looked to Thirteen, and his knowing smile just added to my happiness.

I drank the rest of my whiskey and crunched on the ice. What a really, really good feeling this was. How long would it last?

CHAPTER 20

I'd never gone down the green corridor before. Something about it had always just felt wrong to me. But last night, for the first time, Malcolm and Markus had gathered their courage and asked to be there in the room when Father was with me, not just watching from their hiding place in the shadows. Father had said no, so they were going to find me this morning while I wasn't all the way healed yet. Malcolm wanted to do things to me on his own. He thought he was old enough now. He should be able to practice his powers on me like Father and Uncle Max did. So I'd hidden in one the guest rooms down the green hallway. They wouldn't find me. They never came down there either.

I listened carefully to the other side of the door. My tummy grumbled. If I hadn't been starving, I wouldn't leave the dark safety of this strange room. But I'd had to heal a lot last night. Now I was hungry. All was silent. It was still dark outside, and I hadn't dared to turn on the lights. As quietly as possible, I opened the bedroom door. There were no lights in the hallway, only the tall south-facing windows. When the sun came up, there wouldn't be very many shadows. I needed to get out of there while it was still dark. I stepped out of the room and stifled a groan. My legs still ached from being broken last night. Father had wanted to see which healed faster: my arms or my legs. He'd made a game of it with his guards. I was strapped down on one of his worktables; he counted to three, then everyone snapped a limb. I'd tried to hold back my power, but when the pain hit, it hurt so badly. A burst of energy had shot out of me, knocking back two of the guards and cutting the third across the face like a knife. Father had been furious. The knives had come out then.

I crept along the wall toward the servants' stair. Muffled voices came from somewhere nearby. I plastered myself against the wall. Down the hall. The opposite way. Sun started to peek its way into the sky, and for the first time, I could see that the hallway actually ended at a turn. There was another hallway down there.

I'd thought I'd seen all the wings of the main house. Having rarely slept in the same room two nights in a row, I'd been in pretty much every guest room. And even though I'd never been down this green hallway, I still knew it was there. That hallway looked really dark; there probably weren't any tall windows down there. It would be all shadows. A perfect place to hide and heal.

I ignored my hungry tummy and moved quickly, quietly, crawling along the floor. The carpet was soft and thick, with raised diamond patterns that brushed my chin as I inched along.

The closer I got to the end hallway, the heavier the feeling of dread grew. I shouldn't be there. Had Father done something to the rooms down there? No. That was silly. He wasn't a wizard; he didn't cast spells or make magic. But something was very off. I hesitated. Maybe it was my instincts. Father and Uncle Max had been worried lately that I'd start growing stronger now that I was almost a teenager. Maybe that's what was happening. A new dread sank my heart. I didn't want to get any stronger. Father already hated me so much. If I grew any more powerful, I knew the sessions would get so much worse. Maybe I could stop it. Like if I concentrated hard enough, I could keep the power inside me just where it was—

Murmured voices. I froze. Nearly to the turn of the dark hallway up ahead, I heard two distinct voices. Thought voices, not spoken voices. I could tell because thought voices didn't have the same inflection as spoken voices. Men. Guards. Why were there guards way back there?

I lay flat on the ground and scooted closer. At the wall's end, I peeked my head around the corner. Two guards sat on high-backed velvet chairs, just like the ones in the big dining room downstairs. Only these chairs were dark green to match the color of the twisty vines on the hallway's wallpaper. Between them was a set of wide wooden doors. There were no other doors in the short hallway. No windows, no settees, no tapestries. So much for finding a new hiding place.

A female shriek echoed from behind the double doors as a small burst of power whipped past me. Both guards hopped to their feet, coming to attention. My mind snapped into focus. A woman. Not a servant or a reporter, but a person who stayed here. Lived here. Her thoughts opened up for me without my even trying to read them. I'd seen thoughts like this before in the guards Father kept loyal with drugs. They usually thought in numb emotions unless something set them off. That's what she felt like now. Like something had set her off. Rage, confusion, fear. And power. It was small, but she definitely had some kind of supernatural power inside her. It was rare to feel it in someone outside my family, but now that I was right outside her room, I recognized it right away.

Something heavy slammed into the door from the inside, shaking the wood on its hinges. The guards flinched. Something was *about to happen. There was a reason for the woman's sudden out-burst, and the guards knew it. I reached out to the guards' thoughts, trying to stay in the woman's head at the same time.*

The next moment I was off the ground. Pulled up painfully by my hair, I slammed into the wall in front of me. My face smashed into the wallpaper so hard I imagined little green leaves imprinted on my cheeks. I slid to the ground and cowered against the floor-boards. The first hit was always just the beginning. Father's face contorted with frightening, seething rage. His eyes bled to black, his teeth bared as he sucked in quick, low breaths through his mouth.

"You think you're so clever," he growled in a deep, low voice. An animal's voice. I shook my head in denial even though I knew it meant nothing to him. "You know nothing!"

He lifted me off my feet and held me by the throat against the wall. His face inches from mine so I could see the bottomless pit of his eyes. No, no, not again. Not yet. Heat simmered at the base of my skull, burning inside my ears as it slowly spread. He was trying to force my thoughts. But he couldn't do that. His strength was in moving physical things with his mind, not changing other people's thoughts. Even Uncle Max couldn't get in my head. Why would Father think he'd be able to?

His fist tightened at my neck, cutting off my air supply. The female shriek cut through the air again. Father turned instantly to the door. For a moment, I was forgotten. He released me. I crumpled to the floor, heaving for air. I twisted to look at the door. Who was that woman?

Father was on top of me before the burn in my lungs even began to heal. He held me on the floor by the hair, his face more savage than I thought possible.

I didn't want to read his thoughts and tried hard to block out the images, but still I saw. Power. He always wanted more. It was why he'd had children in the first place. The more people who carried our bloodline, the more powerful he and my uncles would be. But it wasn't enough. He wanted more. So he'd started bringing other supernaturals to the estate, experimenting on them, trying to strengthen his power by harnessing their abilities. He'd take their blood and try to infuse it into his own, or he'd use his telekinesis to draw out their energies until they were completely drained of life. As he held me down, the importance of his experiments grew even clearer in his mind. One day he would succeed in killing me, and the strength of my power would be gone. He couldn't be certain how my death would affect his abilities. He needed another way to grow the Kelch power.

But it wasn't working. The woman behind the door was nearly drained, should have died weeks ago. In fact, he'd told Uncle Max that she was already dead. But he'd kept her alive. This one, this Marlena, he refused to let go.

"You will forget you ever found this place," he hissed into my face. "You will never return, never speak of it, never picture it, never think of it ever again. You think you've suffered? You do not know of suffering. But you will. If you so much as consider returning here, any reprieve you have ever experienced will vanish. Your life is nothing. Speak, and it will be nothing but suffering."

Eyes stretched wide, I nodded as best as I could with his grip so tight in my hair. I could feel blood trickle from my scalp. His face tightened. His thoughts slammed shut to me, but not before I caught one last glimpse: he was afraid his brothers would discover this secret place and the prisoner he kept here. He didn't love her—I don't think he was actually capable of an emotion like that—but he was obsessed with her. He wanted to keep her despite his brothers' demands that all the supernaturals brought here be killed after he was done experimenting on them. And now I knew.

Pain. Piercing, all-encompassing, and right in my heart. I hunched on instinct and could see the handle sticking out of my *chest. He'd stabbed me with his favorite blade—the one with the special engraving on it. Now he was twisting it into my heart. I gasped. A surge of power flew out of me. I couldn't have stopped it if I'd tried, not with this much pain cutting through me. Dark light filled the corridor. His hair blew back from the powerful impact of energy, but he held on tight to my hair and his knife. He wouldn't let go until the life in my eyes was completely gone.*

A soft whine came from behind the closed double doors. I closed my eyes. I would suffer now; I knew it. I would die and come back just as I'd done dozens of times before. Then my suffering would really begin. It didn't matter what Father said, whether I spoke or thought of this corridor again. I knew his secret now. And for that, I would pay again and again.

* * *

I took a long, slow drink of whiskey and stared out at the falling snow from the front window in the farmhouse's great room. Secrets and power. That was the essence of my father's existence. I could so easily remember the details of my torture sessions, the gut-wrenching anticipation of knowing I was about to be found in one of my hiding places or the humiliation of my father's continued hatred. Those things had been so much the norm in my life that recalling them was nothing more than a matter of fact.

But other memories remained hidden in my mind. Secrets. Like the hallway or the woman—things that I truly hadn't thought about until tonight, when I knew in the next few days I'd be approaching another guarded door that Father didn't want breached. What kinds of secrets would I stumble upon this time?

I finished off my whiskey and headed to bed. *Don't think about it.* Speculating wouldn't accomplish anything. Maybe there wouldn't be anything there anyway. Just a list of meeting minutes like Chang was hoping for.

But something inside me knew it would be more than that. Otherwise, why would the thought of sneaking up to Father's office make me feel the same bone-deep dread that I had felt so long ago that day in the green corridor?

CHAPTER 21

The golden island of my dream had grown to include trees and grasses. The bloody lake stretched farther as well, disappearing into the distance where I'd never thought to look before. I knelt down, and my twin was there, smiling up at me. I touched my fingers to the blood, and her smile widened, calming some of the uneasiness that hovered here tonight.

I had gone to bed worrying about tomorrow's mission and being near Father again, but now that I was here, dreaming, my thoughts turned to my dream man. Where was he?

"Hello, Magnolia."

I spun around and saw him approaching from farther inland. He strolled, hands in the pockets of his slacks, eyeing me cautiously.

"You are part of my dream," I said quickly. "A part of me. You are in my head because my subconscious needed an image to go along with some lingering, fucked-up need to keep ties to my family. That's all."

He hesitated. "As you said before, you are more than the others of your bloodline, Magnolia. You can recognize a lie when you hear it, no matter how much you want that lie to be truth."

The blood of the lake churned. A light breeze ruffled the trees along the shoreline.

"Who are you?" I said, ignoring the tremble of my voice.

The man smiled sadly. "No one who is going to hurt you, Magnolia."

"Then why are you here? What do you want from me?"

Waves started to crash against the shore. The breeze grew stronger and whipped my hair around my face. I glanced down, and my hands had shifted again. *Good.*

"I'm here because I recognized your power." He kept his hands in his pockets, his face calm. "I wanted to get to know you. Being near you, even in your dreams, it makes me feel…good. I like you." He was making an obvious effort to be nonthreatening. I didn't buy it.

"You look like my father and uncles. You're from them, aren't you? They've sent you to find me. Well, you can just go to hell. Because I've already done my time, and there's no way you're taking me back."

My words were slurred as my teeth grew in number. I crouched down with my clawed hands ready.

His eyes flared red like the last time. "I am not here to hurt you, Magnolia." He spoke with precise enunciation. "I am not from your father or your uncles. They don't have the power to be here with you. You know that."

"Then who are you?"

He slowly took a step forward, his red eyes locked on mine. "You said you had the ability to trust and to be trusted. Well, prove it. You and I have shared many conversations in this dream place of yours. Never once have I tried to hurt you or manipulate you in any way. I simply want to talk to you. That's all."

"You manipulated me by lying about who you really are. I thought I'd made you up."

"That was completely unintentional. I assumed you had realized from the beginning that I was alive outside your mind."

He stopped a few feet away from me. I remembered our previous encounters. He'd looked and acted so much like my family, but with an interest in me instead of hatred. Slowly I straightened. He nodded toward the bloody shoreline, where the waves had started to calm.

"I believe she's trying to tell you something," he said.

I glanced down at my reflection and saw for the first time that my twin wasn't smiling. Instantly, I dropped to my knees. "What did you do to her?"

"I've done nothing," he insisted, still staying back several feet, giving me space. "She is a part of you, and I've told you, I have no desire to hurt you in any way."

I touched my fingertips to the blood's surface. My claws vanished the moment I thought them away. My twin raised her hand as she always did, as if she could touch her fingertips to mine. But then she turned her hand so her palm was flat underneath the surface.

I recognized the scar immediately. It had been branded into my own flesh time and time again for as long as I could remember. Two Xs, one over the other, with the sides linked by a curved line, making the mark seem more like a butterfly than a brand. All of Father's older tools—the ones Grandmother had used on Father, Max, and Mallroy when they were boys—had the emblem, the maker's mark from whomever had custom-made the torture instruments before I was even born.

I looked at my twin as she lowered her hand again. "Did Father have you tortured before killing you?" I asked out loud. "Even as an infant?"

A moment passed, and her serious expression faded. She smiled again, just as I always thought she should.

I turned back to the mystery man. He was gone. I looked all around the golden landscape and out over the red lake, but he was nowhere. Turning back to my twin, I knelt down again and played my fingers back along the blood. She smiled that wide smile once more.

CHAPTER 22

"Why the hell is Cordele leaving me messages about seeing a movie?"

Heather laughed. "How many times do I have to tell you? She wants to hang out with you. It's not that big of a deal."

Pacing the living room floor, I had my cell phone in one hand and my whiskey in the other. I'd tried everything to distract myself from my dream and from the gala that was only a few hours away. Replaying Cordele's message over and over had turned into the favorite pastime of the hour. "Are you going to the movie too?"

"I wasn't invited," Heather said.

The idea of just hanging out with Cordele still didn't sit well with me. I got that she had been trying to be friendlier since I'd returned, but she'd kept her thoughts so focused on random nonsense, it didn't make sense. I mean, if she was sincere, she'd want me to see it in her thoughts. Right?

"You should do it," Heather added. "I've always gone to more movies with my girlfriends than I do with Jon. Even before we were ever boyfriend-girlfriend."

I stopped pacing. "Is that what you call him? Your boyfriend?"

She chuckled again. "I guess so. I mean, I'm thirty-one years old, so saying I have a boyfriend feels a little stupid, but it's the easiest way to describe our relationship to people. I suppose I could say significant other, but that's kind of a mouthful."

Hmm. I started pacing again. "So this Cordele movie thing—you really think I should do it?"

"I told you she wanted to get to know you better. It could be fun."

"I'll think about it."

"Are you ready for tonight?" Her voice grew softer. My stomach clenched.

"I still have a few hours before I have to get ready."

"Well, I better get going. I don't have a fancy dress to wear or anything, and I still have to get the surveillance stuff together. Try to get some rest this afternoon, OK? Tonight is going to be fine. Jon's confident, and so is Thirteen. I'll call you tomorrow, regular time."

After we hung up, I stared at the clock in the kitchen. Six more hours until the gala. I think I had enough whiskey to make it that long. Maybe.

* * *

Just breathe.

The dress was a last-season's John Richmond bought on sale, not a custom design fit to my every curve. There was no stylist pouring me into it, pinching and primping as they sweated with fear. The shoes were from some store and matched as well as could be expected when not made especially for the dress. The earrings were mine—one-carat diamonds I'd been wearing the day I'd escaped.

Just keep breathing.

My hand shook, and eyeliner smeared across my lid. Again. I grabbed some more toilet paper and wiped off the black smudge. Maybe I could get by with just the foggy eye shadow and mascara—those looked somewhat decent. No. I could do this. I looked at myself in the mirror again. This was a Network mission. Not one of Father's estate parties. I would not be bound and gagged as soon as the last guest left. I would not have to run and hide when the servers started clearing the buffet, hoping that maybe this time Father wouldn't come searching for me. This dress would not be ripped to shreds by tools tearing into my skin, searching for the most painful organ to penetrate. I would not be left in a cold anteroom somewhere away from the main house, where my screams wouldn't be heard as I bled out on a filthy floor.

The eyeliner pencil in my hand melted over my fingers as power sizzled inside me. *Damn it!* That was the second pencil I'd ruined like that. The packet came with only three of them. *OK, let's try this one more time.*

I'd gotten a halfway straight line over my left eyelid when the quiet beep of the alarm made me jump. I stretched my neck to see the clock in my bedroom: 7:50 p.m. *Crap.* I was late.

The need to rush steadied my hand, and I managed to get the rest of the liner on in one quick swoop. There. I was as party-ready as I was going to get. I'd moved to the kitchen to fill my flask when Jon knocked briskly on the front door, then strolled right in.

"Almost ready," I said over my shoulder. "Thirteen texted me to say that he, Heather, and Charles are all set in the surveillance van." I grabbed my thick silk wrap. The black-and-gray-print dress clung tightly to my bust and bodice, then flared at the hips in a soft flow to just below my ankles. The satin heels kept the hemline from brushing the floor. My hair was up in a loose twist with wispy tendrils around my face and neck. It was a look I'd worn on several occasions when Father especially wanted my neckline visible. The rabbit-fur lining of the wrap would keep my bare shoulders warm. I shrugged it on, thinking, *What the hell, Jon? Help a lady with her coat much?*

Clutch in hand, I gave him a quick once-over. "You look nice." His tux was off-the-rack but fit him well. Lean in the hips, no tails. He'd gone with a silver ascot that accented my dress rather than the standard tie. His hair was slicked back, emphasizing his strong jawline. I was about to compliment his choice of accessories when I noticed—*oh shit, he's gone glassy-eyed.* His mind had turned numb with lust as he stood frozen in the doorway, ogling me.

"God damn it!" I tried to pull back my aura more, but I was already forcing down my sensuality as far as I could get it. I pulled out my cell phone. His hand shot out and grabbed my phone before I could dial Thirteen's number.

"No," he said, blinking quickly. "I'm good. I've got it." He swallowed a couple of times. "It was just…a surprise, that's all." I gave him a measuring look. "For real," he insisted. "I'm fine."

I crossed my arms over my chest. "You might be, but what about everyone else at the party? Damn it, I told Thirteen this might happen."

"Magnolia, it's fine. Thirteen expected something like this. We're arriving late, so we'll just slide right into position for the slide show. You won't even see half of the people there. Those you do see will be too distracted by your cleavage to notice the small group of agents sneaking into the executive levels. It's the perfect way to use your powers without actually using your powers."

I should have known Thirteen had planned for something like this.

"It is going to work, Magnolia," he said. "We'll make it work. We have to get in to that PC, and this is the best chance we have. Do you want to have to turn invisible again? You want to sneak into your father's office like you did with your uncle last year, when Theo and I had to clear the building to get you out?"

"Of course not. But I can't do this if I draw the attention of every man in the place."

"You're not even going to see every man in the place." He looked me up and down, shrugged. "Maybe you could just keep the shawl thing on. That helps."

I gave him a look. He sighed. "Look, Magnolia, you're beautiful. Not because of your powers or your...aura or whatever. You're going to be noticed by the people around you. But that's OK. As long as your father isn't one of the men around you." He turned serious. "You know, we've been over every contingency possible, including your father discovering you before we're done. It all works great on paper, but I need to know, are you sure you're ready for that?"

Thirteen had asked me the same thing when he'd cornered me in Jon and Heather's driveway after Thursday night's meeting. After all, the man thought I was dead. It would be far from a happy reunion. I'd assured him I'd be fine. Father would be in his office until it was time for his speech, then onstage and in view of the crowd the entire time we were there. If everything went to plan, I would be in and out and never be anywhere near the man.

Of course, as Colin's mission proved, things rarely went to plan.

I took a swig from the whiskey bottle still on the table. "If I run into him, I'll deal with it. It won't change my responsibility to the team."

He measured me a moment longer. "OK, then, let's go."

I checked my handbag: whiskey-filled flask, lipstick, tissues, fake ID, ticket for the gala. Yep, I was ready. I locked the door behind me and was surprised to see Jon standing by his sedan, holding open the door.

"Er, thanks," I said and crawled in, careful not to snag my gown. He shut the door and walked around to his side. As he turned over the engine, he gave me a sideways glance.

"I was instructed to treat you as if this was a real date. With the respect afforded a real lady."

I smiled. "Yeah, I bet Heather gave you a nice little talking-to before you headed out tonight."

His jaw tightened. "The talking-to wasn't from Heather."

My lower tummy tingled. This time, I turned to face out the window as I allowed myself another smile.

CHAPTER 23

Father had developed his company's newest complex on a large stretch of used-to-be farmland in one of the budding suburbs north of the city. There were other office towers and outlets on the wending drive, but the manicured industrial road dead-ended at Kelch Inc. Very fitting, if you asked me. I mean, everything that crossed Father's path eventually *dead-ended*, right?

"That's the Capital One Tower," Jon pointed out as we passed a tall building on our left. The glass windows lit up like a broken checkerboard reaching to the night sky. "Thirteen and the others are in the parking garage in the back. It was the closest we could get without actually being on the Kelch compound. You know where the rendezvous location is, right? Off Washington Street? It should be a pretty smooth exit as long as we stagger our departures."

I nodded absently. My stomach was in knots. I appreciated him letting me know the whatnots of the operation, but right now I didn't care. I needed to focus.

"Here we go," he murmured. We drove up to a stationed guard post. The compound was surrounded by a gleaming ten-foot chain-link fence—not as fancy as the brick wall that circled the downtown headquarters but still pretty intimidating. My mind flashed to the white-and-black stone barricade that lined my family's estate. Cameras watched every inch of the grounds, secured to trees, hidden in the foliage. I'd had to turn completely invisible to get past the wall when I escaped. Here the cameras sat in plain view, zooming in on every guest. I ducked my head automatically and rummaged through my purse for my fake ID.

"Good evening," the guard said when Jon rolled down his window and presented our invitations. The guard scanned the vellum card with a handheld scanner, then did the same with our IDs. I should have known Father's security would be tighter than the freaking Pentagon.

Jon moved forward when directed. "You OK?" he asked softly.

"Fine. Great." He glanced my way. The parking lot lights reflected off the side of his face. "Be careful," I said. "You can see your wire when the light catches it."

He ran a few fingers through his hair, adjusting the nearly invisible cord of his earphone. "Better?"

"Yeah." I pulled down the mirror to check my face and make sure my own earphones weren't visible. Everything was in place. Now if I could just stop feeling like I'd throw up any second.

When he cut the engine, I took a moment to steady myself. I looked up at the shiny new building before us. There was a sidewalk that led from the parking lot to the main entrance. We'd have to walk nearly a quarter mile, past two brightly lit fountains and up two flights of concrete stairs, to get to the row of glass doors that opened to the lobby. Every light in the building seemed to be on, making the entire place glow like some sort of capitalist beacon.

"Quite a testament, huh?" Jon said, staring up at the building with narrowed eyes. "Like lie enough, cheat enough, and kill enough, and you too could run a corporate palace of your own."

I sniffed a laugh. "Don't forget about the power thing. You have to have supernatural abilities and a complete lack of moral code as well."

He smiled tightly. "Right. How could I forget that?"

We got out of the car, and my feet felt like lead. *Don't think about it. Just stick to the mission. Focus.*

Jon offered me his arm, and we started our walk toward the fountains. The sidewalks were packed with late arrivals hustling in their fancy dresses and churchgoing suits. The average executive didn't exactly have a variety of tuxedos or ball gowns hanging in his or her closet. I could feel the excitement of the people around us. This was nothing more than a party to them, a rare and fun occasion to get dressed up and celebrate the efforts of the past year. They had no clue that all the work they did—whether it was answering customer complaints over the phone, or selling a new product line, or coming up with some new medication or new kind of dish soap—was nothing more than a means to secure Father's economic power. Oh sure, they might notice that Bob, the onetime VP of marketing, suddenly wasn't with the company anymore. But it would never occur to them that Bob had been gutted out in the estate's north barn because he'd asked too many questions about overseas shipments.

We got halfway up the front steps when the air changed. My feet stopped moving. Something felt wrong. I reached out with my senses, and the power inside me suddenly jumped. Like someone had hit my supernatural side with defibrillators, bringing that dark, bloody place inside me to new life. *Oh God.* Strength in the bloodlines—how could I have not expected this? The closer I got to him, the stronger my dark powers grew. I was a fool for coming here.

Thick and cold, power vibrated everywhere. My body trembled. I fought to continue pushing back my power, and it grew hot inside me. My vision began to shift; a light-pink hue tinted the glass doors in front of us. For the first time in months, that bloody place inside me was in the presence of the same darkness. All the rage and pain and hate rose instantly to meet the new power head-on.

Jon took my free hand in his to move me along, then quickly jerked away as if burned. "Shit," he hissed. "What the hell?" He stared down at me, and when I turned to him, he was pink and turning darker. His eyes grew wide. "You need to calm down, Magnolia. Right now. For Christ's sake, get control of yourself."

My anger spiked before I could push it back, my vision darkening to nearly red. "Don't you fucking talk to me about control," I growled.

He stepped back and shifted his stance, got ready to defend himself. In my ear, murmured voices from the surveillance station grew frantic. I couldn't hear any of them over the throbbing of hate and rage pounding in my ears. They were all so fucking clueless. They thought they could lead a team against my family? *My* family? They were nothing. I could kill Jon and everyone else here with a mere thought, and they wanted to pit themselves against the supernatural force that spawned me? I laughed. A dark, terrifying sound that I didn't even recognize.

It was the laugh that brought me back.

Oh God, no. I was stronger than this, more in control than this. I closed my eyes tightly and willed my powers back. But when I opened my eyes again, my vision stayed dark, everything almost crimson now. Jon looked to where my hands were fisted at my sides. My fingers popped and curled on their own. They hadn't shifted yet, but I felt the itch of my nails growing longer.

And that part growing inside me welcomed the change.

"You folks are cutting it close." A low, serious voice carried from the open lobby doors. "The presentation and slide show are about to begin."

I whirled my head with a snarl. And stopped. Theo. He stood framed by the glowing light of the main lobby, the scent of a freshly lit clove wafting around him. I couldn't really see him past the glare of the lobby lights, but I knew his eyes were sharp and locked on to me like a laser. It was all I needed. The power of my family had been stronger than any supernatural I'd ever heard of. But it was nothing compared to the connection I had with Theo.

Look at me, Mag. His voice whispered through my head. *Nothing else. Just me.*

Our connection had called out to him. Just like when I'd been hurt. He'd sensed my moment of panic, the surge of power that came with it, and he couldn't help but come to me. I blinked and rubbed my eyes. Finally, the red began to fade. It was Theo who was clear. Beautiful. With the light at his back, he glowed golden. A bright light in the sea of red. We held each other's eyes, my breathing slowing to match his. In and out. In and out. Together, our connection pushed the powerful rage back to that place inside me where I had total control.

Go back to Thirteen, Theo's thoughts demanded as he moved closer. *We can do this without you, Mag. Go back.*

He wanted to touch me. I could feel his desire as strong as mine. In his perfectly fitted tux, his dark hair brushed back, emphasizing the strong jaw. All I wanted to do was crawl inside him until we couldn't tell where one ended and the other began.

Thank God my mind was clear enough now not to give in to that feeling and tackle him to the sidewalk right there.

Jon murmured into his earpiece, and I pulled him to a stop. "No, Jon. Don't abort because of me. I can do this."

I took a deep breath. My power was raw, but I'd managed to dampen it again. I flexed my fingers, and they were completely normal. I was back in control. And now I knew what to expect. With a subtle push, I stretched my power out, reaching out to the monstrous energy that had slammed into me when we'd hit the front steps. Father was frantic. My power surge hadn't gone unnoticed, but it was muted now. He couldn't tell from which direction the power had come, just that it had appeared somewhere on the grounds. He would have to search for the source of it, just as we'd planned.

"I'm good, Jon," I said, confident now. "Let's do this."

He narrowed his eyes at me. After a long moment, he said, "OK, we're a go."

Voices through the earpiece sighed in relief and began their play-by-play once again. With renewed focus, I let Jon guide me through the building's front doors. I looked up at Theo when he held the door for us. *I've got this.*

His thoughts growled. *You don't have to do this.*

Yeah, actually, I do. I reached out to touch his arm, then hesitated. I was in control, but touching Theo might send my powers off the charts again.

He stepped back, understanding that distance was best. *I'm here the moment you need me.*

I was wrong, I thought back. *It's not just me. We've got this.*

He smiled a cocky half grin that I couldn't help but return. Then, with a quick nod to Jon, he turned on his heel and disappeared into the reception area, moving into his first position. Guards moved purposefully through the lobby, looking hard for anything out of place—Father's doing, I was sure. He was searching for the source of the power he'd felt, already distracted enough to call his security guards away from their designated positions. Jon nodded to a pair of them as he moved me deftly through a second set of doors at the opposite end of where Theo had disappeared.

We stepped into the enormous reception room, packed with people talking, laughing, and eating. Over it all there hung a force in the air that no one could feel except me. Cold and heavy. I breathed it in and held a tight rein on my own power, still aching to rise and meet it.

A focused slice of Father's power passed over me, searching. I just smiled. *Not this time, old man.*

CHAPTER 24

Over two thousand people filled the enormous reception area. The floor we walked in on was one level above the main floor, overlooking the reception. Thirteen had loved that part of the layout. It meant I'd be able to see the entire room from my designated post without being down in the mix with the masses. The room's ceiling stretched five stories high. At each level, a glass-railed balcony allowed guests to see hints of the various color schemes on the different floors. Tasteful, oversize artwork had been expertly arranged to give the whole area a feel of wealth and success. It was an absolutely incredible room, and it filled my mouth with disgust.

"I'm going to head over to the bar before the presentations start," Jon said casually. "Would you like anything?"

"Vodka tonic. Please."

His brow lifted infinitesimally in surprise. As if I didn't know how to keep a cover. He slid his hand down my shoulder, then turned and began his slow walk across the length of the room, setting into motion the first part of our evening's plan.

OK, here we go.

Chang had confirmed that Father was being escorted from his offices to the reception area and would be taking his place onstage in a matter of moments. My next partner was moving into position, ready to lead me to the executive elevators for our plan's next steps. I concentrated on three things simultaneously: First, I scanned the minds of everyone in the room, looking for the slightest hint that someone might suspect what we were about to do. No problems there—everyone was totally clueless. Second, I pinpointed the whereabouts of my fellow agents, making sure everyone was in place. So far, so good. Finally, I continued holding back my power to a level that Father's seeking energy couldn't recognize. I'd already felt the icy brush of his power slide over me twice more since entering the room.

The chandelier lights dimmed, then brightened. Dimmed again, brightened again. The montage slide show was about to start. I scanned the room again quickly. Jon leaned against the far bar directly in front of where Chang was stationed as security. Theo and Cordele were already gone, moved on to position two. All I had to do now was wait for my designated partner to escort me to upstairs and—

"Hello there, beautiful." Shane's voice was a tight murmur in my ear. "What do you say we get out of here before the boring part starts? Have a little party of our own?"

His hand brushed the tendrils of hair away from my neck. His fingers trembled as they caressed my collarbone. I closed my eyes as his ache sliced through me. Thirteen was the one who had decided how we would be paired up to move from position one to position two. For some unfathomable reason, he had chosen Shane and me to be partnered, to sneak away once the montage started. The man must be insane.

I made a point of pretending to look around for Jon. I mean, if I was going to play the role of two-timing girlfriend, the least I could do was be a discreet two-timing girlfriend. I turned in to Shane, rested my hands on his chest, and slowly smiled. His heart stammered, and for a moment his eyes went dull. I dug my nails into his shirt until he blinked himself back into focus.

"Sure, baby," I purred, just loud enough for the nearby eavesdroppers to have a listen. "Got somewhere in mind?"

His lips twitched in a sorry attempt at a smile. He had to swallow twice to get out his lines. "I have a passkey to some of the work areas," he finally managed. "Ones that aren't on the tours."

I trailed my finger along his bottom lip, cursing the way he so obviously loved and hated the sensation. A man passing by snickered, his thoughts blaring images of what he imagined Shane and I would be doing in the next couple of minutes.

"A passkey? So you must be pretty important, huh?"

He snaked his shaking arm around my waist. "Gold Star important, baby." Sweat beaded on his face as he glanced around, making a show of being sneaky. The guy who had just walked by met up with his two friends. All three of them held up their glasses in a toast to Shane as he directed me toward a private elevator near the lobby doors. I should give them each an aneurysm. We stepped into the elevator, and a cold brush of Father's power touched me again. I shivered.

When the doors slid shut, I turned to Shane. "OK, so when we get upstairs—"

I hadn't even seen it coming. One moment I stood in the middle of the elevator, ready to confirm our secondary escape route, the next I was plastered against the wall, Shane's heavy body pressed into mine. His mouth crushed my lips. With both hands, he gripped my hips and ground himself into me.

Holy shit! For a moment, I was completely stunned. I'd been so focused on holding back my power, getting my scripted lines correct, and trying to keep track of Father's searching energy, I hadn't even realized the depth of my partner's instability.

With a push against his shoulders, I flung Shane away from me, slamming him into the opposite elevator wall. The cables above us shook, but the elevator didn't stop. "What the hell is wrong with you?"

He slumped against the wall, head down, hands on knees. He panted as if he'd just sprinted a mile. After a moment, he lifted his head and glared at me. "I hate you so much," he gritted out.

A stab of sympathy stuttered through my heart. I knew he couldn't control how he felt about me. And tonight everything seemed magnified because of my proximity to Father. Shane had known that our touching and flirting was just part of the cover, but tonight it had just been too much.

"I know you hate me, Shane. I get that. But you are stronger than this. And we have a job to do. So either suck it up or get the fuck out of here!"

Voices buzzed through my earpiece again. I was just causing all kinds of fun back at the surveillance stations tonight. The elevator doors opened, and a hot blast of power swept through the car and into my bones. For a moment I thought for sure Father had found me. I spun with my power ready to defend.

Theo. Shit.

He didn't even spare me a glance. He just pounced. Moving faster than any normal human should, he fell on Shane. Fists pummeled; teeth gnashed. Footsteps pounded toward us. Jon and the others. I blocked the doors from shutting with my foot, then stretched over and grabbed the back of Theo's tux coat and yanked hard, ripping the coat at the seams. I stumbled back and then went in again, grabbing hold of both his shoulders. I gasped at the sudden shock of our contact but finally managed to pull him off Shane. Dear God, was all his power from our connection, or was there something else going on with Theo that I didn't know about?

"What the hell is wrong with you people?" Jon hissed when he got to the elevator doors. Cordele stood at his shoulder. I'd only seen her from across the reception downstairs, but she looked really lovely. A fitted green sequin gown, her blonde hair back in a tight wrap. She'd even touched up her roots. She quickly moved past Theo to help Shane get to his feet. I held Theo against the wall, my back to his chest, my arms splayed out to keep him back. When Shane stumbled past into the corridor, Theo growled low in his throat, sending an instant shiver down my spine. I leaned back into him automatically. Would that noise ever *not* turn me on? His hand slid around my waist, holding me to him. For a moment, I let myself enjoy the feel of him against me. The warmth, the rightness. Then the space around us began to brighten. *Crap.* Our glowing with power was so not what this situation needed right now. I took a deep breath. My muscles actually cramped as I fought hard to hold back everything inside me.

"You two get out here," Jon gritted out at us. "Now."

We all stood in a huddled group in the middle of a darkly tiled lobby. Silver-and-glass chandeliers dimly lit a sitting area of leather and velour settees. Chang had already disengaged the motion sensors on the floor as well as the elevator locks. And just as Thirteen had planned, the guards that should have been posted just here were off somewhere else, following Father's frantic orders to find anyone who didn't seem to belong.

"Now listen up and listen good." Jon was seriously pissed. "We've lost precious minutes and have to move fast. Security has already recognized the cameras being off at the exit points.

Cordele scoped out two guards at the CEO suite, but expect more to come quickly. Theo, Shane, head out to your stations and be prepared for approaching security. Cord, secure the exit point. Everyone think they can *handle* that?"

Nods all around. "Good. Let's go."

We broke apart. The minute Theo's arm slipped away, an emptiness washed over me that made me stumble. Our contact had made the energy inside me heat up, my control stronger than ever. Now that he was gone, Father's icy energy was quick to take its place. Our touch had given my power the amp-up that Father had needed to pinpoint my location. Here. There. His power was all around me. It was all I felt now.

"Oh God," I said and paused to catch my breath. He'd found me.

"What's wrong?" Jon whispered urgently, Chang right at his hip.

"Nothing, I'm fine." Father was still giving his speech, but he was wrapping it up quickly. We didn't have time to spare. "Just keep going." Jon took me at my word, and we ran down the hall to the CEO offices.

Father's suite stretched the entire width of the building. Two sets of thick red-stained double doors stood about twenty feet apart, each leading to a different area of his office. At each set of doors, two guards stood at attention. Jon cursed under his breath. Cordele's info on the number of guards had been wrong by half.

We were hidden behind a curved tile wall. Jon turned to me. I didn't wait for his order. We were out of time. I reached out to the guards' minds and instantly shut them down. Father had been drugging them, so it was easy. They fell to their knees, then planted their faces on the floor.

"Dude," Chang said in awe.

We moved forward quickly, Jon scowling at me. "You were supposed to send them away. Distract them. Not knock them unconscious."

"Whatever, just move."

We hustled into Father's office. I shut the door and locked it, but it didn't matter. Father's power pulsed all around me now, trying to probe into my brain, discover my identity. I closed my eyes, concentrated on breathing. He would come now. I would have to see him. The instinctual panic that Father brought out of me threatened to rise. I needed to get out of here. Now.

"Are you done yet?" I hissed to Chang.

His fingers flew over Father's laptop as he bounced in his seat. Under his breath he murmured things like "Fricking beautiful," "Masterpiece," "Oh no you don't," and other nonsensical bullshit.

"He's almost got it," Jon said as Chang slid a small flash drive into the PC's side.

That's when I heard them. We'd taken too long. The montage slide show was over. Father's speech was done. Security guards were racing up the stairs. Police had been called and were on their way. Leading the charge, more anxious than any of them to find out who had dared bring power into his world, was my father.

Let the cowering begin.

CHAPTER 25

I didn't tell Jon what I was doing. Didn't inform the surveillance stations of what was headed our way. I just reacted. I knew the moment Father stepped from the elevator onto our floor. Where his power had been poking at me for the past several minutes, suddenly it slammed into me like a sledgehammer. I stumbled against the wall, my breath knocked out of me. Jon rushed over just as Chang jumped from Father's desk. "Got it!"

I met Jon's wide, frantic eyes. "Don't speak," I whispered. His brows scrunched low. He opened his mouth to argue, but I never gave him the chance. He vanished.

Chang stumbled over a chair with a curse. "What the—"

Don't speak. Your voices will give you away. I spoke directly into their minds. And not just Jon and Chang, but Shane, Theo, and Cordele as well. I'd turned us all invisible at the same time. *If you need to say something, think it and I'll get it out to everyone.*

What the hell's going on, Magnolia? Jon thought. *This isn't part of the plan.*

Outside the office door, guards' shouts echoed. My father barked commands. Keys jingled against the locks. *Father pinpointed my power. They're here.*

Lots of silent curses on that one. I grabbed Jon's and Chang's arms and pulled them against the wall. It was easy to find them, since their thoughts were screaming at me. *Chang, shut up! You're the one who thought it would be cool if everyone just turned invisible and broke in here. Don't freak out now.* In the distance, someone started fighting. Cordele. *Guards are blocking our secondary exit. Cordele is keeping them back, but more keep coming.*

Send Shane and Theo in to help her. We need that exit clear, Jon ordered, completely unfazed. We'd been through this before, Jon and I. The door to Father's office flew open and guards swarmed in, guns raised, scopes ready. These weren't the security guys from the party downstairs. Dressed in all-black fatigues, these were like the guards on the estate: elite-trained and utterly loyal to Father. Their minds were sharp, focused, and emotionless. Buzzing from some kind of new drug that I didn't recognize. They weren't here to contain an intruder. They were here to kill.

Chang whined softly at my back, and I realized I'd shocked his arm where I held him tightly to the wall. My power was still as dampened as I could keep it, but energy was slipping out. Father was just too close now. I took Chang's hand and fisted it in Jon's shirt. *Stay with Jon.*

Where are you going? Jon's mind whispered.

I'm still here. The last guard is about to come through the first set of doors. Father is right behind them. We should be able to slip past them through the second set of doors if we stick to the walls.

There was a break between guards, and I heard Jon think, *Go.* He and Chang hurried into the hallway. I kept close to Chang's back, my eyes on the floor. If I didn't look around, maybe, just maybe, I'd be able to make it to the exit without actually seeing my father. That bloody place inside me boiled at his nearness. I fisted my hands as if I were fisting my entire body, trying desperately to hold in everything that wanted out. Guards were everywhere. In a linked line, Jon led us past all of them, hugging the wall as we raced toward the very rear emergency stairwell, where Cordele and the others had knocked unconscious the guards they'd been holding off.

Is Magnus following your power? Jon asked.

Not yet, but he will. He knows the power source is here somewhere. He's searching for it at the exits.

We rounded the last corner, and I could practically see where each of them stood. All three were as invisible as us, but their thoughts were so clear and so individualized, I could almost make out the expressions on each of their faces. Cordele stood by the door, propping it open with her back and listening for more approaching guards. She'd easily taken out the door's alarm and handled the first wave of guards before Theo and Shane showed up to help. Theo and Shane stood on opposite sides of the hallway, each standing over two sleeping guards and wishing it was the other that they had just beaten into oblivion.

"We're here," I said quietly. Their sighs of relief were audible. As were the sudden shouts back at the surveillance stations. Since we were momentarily away from Father and the guards, this was the first chance I'd had to give our support team a heads-up on what I was doing. Thirteen and the others had heard only the guards' and police's points of view over their transmitters. The moment I spoke, there was a commotion of orders and demands and warnings in each of our ears.

"Everyone accounted for?" Jon asked, ignoring Thirteen's demands for information.

"We're all here," I assured him.

"Then move out."

The plan had been for only Jon and Chang to exit from here. The rest of us were supposed to redisperse back into the party downstairs, each leaving at a predetermined time to meet up with Thirteen at the rendezvous point a couple of miles away. Since that plan was totally shot, it looked like we'd all have to leave together now. Somehow I wasn't convinced all six of us would fit in the small security vehicle waiting for Jon and Chang in the back delivery lot, but there were more immediate details to worry about. Like, oh, say, not dying in this hallway.

Everyone was still invisible, and the emergency exit door swung as Jon pushed Chang forward, sending him down first with Cordele. Shane went next; the sound of his footsteps rushing down the steel steps echoed through the hall. Theo and Jon waited for me. Drips of sweat trickled down my back. It was getting more and more difficult to keep up everyone's invisible shields while holding back everything else inside me. If I could just get to the rendezvous point, I'd finally be able to let go.

Gunshots rang out. I hit the floor as bullets rained down the hallway, bouncing off the door and walls around us. Jon cried out. He was still invisible, but the hit threw him against the wall. A bloody mark suddenly appeared against the tile.

"Go! Go! Go!" Jon shouted. Theo grabbed my arm. Even invisible, he knew exactly where I was. But the moment he touched me, energy flared again, strong and intense. No way Father hadn't felt that. Just as I thought it, Father's energy slammed into me again. He'd found me, all right, and he was coming fast.

Guards poured into the hallway, firing their guns into what looked like an empty corridor. None of them moved forward, and no one questioned why Father had ordered them to shoot at nothing.

Another round of bullets buzzed past me. "Move!" Theo shouted, yanking hard on my arm.

I looked to where Jon's thoughts still vibrated. He was on the ground, moving, keeping his wound from touching any other surfaces. I reached out with my free hand, not caring what part of him I grabbed on to, and started pulling. He grunted as I clung tightly to his hair. With an awkward heave, I threw him past where I crouched at the fire exit doorway and into the stairwell. His blood splattered on the floor, and I slipped, stumbling back into the hallway.

Momentum pulled my arm from Theo's hold. I could feel him on the first steps as the door slowly started to shut. I'd barely used my power to keep it open when the entire door exploded.

Gunfire stopped as metal dust filled the hallway. I plastered myself to the wall and tried not to cough. *Theo?* I reached out with my thoughts.

He began coughing in a painful, choking gasp. His thoughts didn't answer me, but they didn't have to. He was hurt. That was all that mattered.

Everything inside me—that dark, bloody place, the golden connection with Theo—it all rose to the surface in a tidal wave, and I could feel the power's eagerness to pour out of me. The hallway burned golden. The nurtured terror inside me dissolved as I turned to see my father, standing twenty yards away at the end of the hallway, a dozen guards crouched on the ground in front of him with weapons at the ready. Soot and smoke settled around us, but his black tuxedo remained spotless. He was brutally handsome, just like I remembered, with features reminiscent of some long-ago royal line.

My invisible cover was still in place, and a strange calm washed over me. I didn't attack. I merely stopped holding back, and the swell of energy vibrating under my skin unfurled.

The guards were thrown backward, the wind knocked out of them from the force with which they hit the floor. Father stumbled back as well, but only for a moment. From surprise. Then he lashed out. The lights above me shattered. Guns in every scrambling guard's hand unloaded in my direction, even though no one had pulled a trigger. Father couldn't see me with his eyes, but he knew exactly where I was.

I guided the bullets past me easily and waited for them to change course, attack me from behind. But they simply landed on the floor behind me, pinging against the dusty tile. Was he holding back? Why? Father had never held back with me before—he'd always reveled in watching how the strength of his power deflated others.

Theo clanged against the metal railing in the stairwell. Without thought, I melted the guards' guns in their hands, burning deep into their flesh while they shouted and cried. I watched Father. He didn't even flinch. After a moment, with a wave of his hand, the guards went silent. They writhed and continued to cry out in agony, but their voices made no sound. Father narrowed his eyes in my direction, and I held my breath.

"You've succeeded in your mission, stranger." Father's voice was deep but icy. "I am intrigued."

I held tight to my stance, bracing myself for the pain.

"Granted, your mercy in merely wounding my guards and not destroying them completely displays an emotional weakness I have no use for." He lifted his hand, and, just like I'd done to Sharon back at the airport, squeezed his fingers into a fist. With a pop, all twelve guards collapsed. No more writhing in pain. Just dead.

He lowered his hand. With a tilt of his head, he considered where he felt my power. "I'll agree to a conversation," he said finally. "Small tasks could be assigned. Nothing too important, of course. Your manipulation of atoms to veil your appearance could be useful, even though your insistence on continuing your concealment reflects an understandable cowardice that will have to be dealt with."

What? Cowardice? Assignments? What the hell was he talking about?

"As a first interview, I am notably impressed. But for any real consideration, I'd need a full résumé." He waved his hand impatiently, and I winced automatically.

But nothing happened. No sudden whip of pain, no gut-wrenching feel of one of my organs erupting. Nothing.

"Well," he said. "Show yourself. I haven't got all night."

Suddenly I understood. He thought I was some random person with supernatural abilities, here to show off in order to gain his attention and win some internship of power by his side. Had others done that? I wondered if Thirteen knew.

I stared at him through the glow of my vision, and something changed inside me. Not my power or my essence, but that child inside me who was still cowering by the wall at the sound of his voice. My father was talking to me. Not shouting, not snarling. There was no hatred in his eyes right now, only impatience. He had killed his own guards to silence them so he and I could have a conversation. And he wanted to keep talking: to know my powers, assign me responsibilities, maybe even guide me to the full potential he saw in me.

I wanted to be disgusted, livid, hurt. But I couldn't. It was everything I'd ever longed for my entire life. My father didn't want to kill or torture me right now. I'd impressed him. That child inside me glowed.

I let out a shaky breath, my insides trembling. His eyes narrowed. He'd heard my sigh and recognized it as female. *Shit.* Cold slithered over me, trying to strip away my invisible cover. He'd said I'd manipulated molecules to conceal my appearance. Was that what I was doing? I always pictured it more as a shield that I created. *Whatever. Focus.* The cold of his power matched the ice in his gaze.

Then, suddenly, something occurred to him. His thoughts became crystal clear, and so loud I couldn't ignore them if I tried. His power was strengthening in my presence. Just as mine was being near him. Never had he found another supernatural that could strengthen his abilities by proximity. Only our bloodline had ever done that. But he felt stronger now. His mind flashed to all those years of failed experiments on other supernaturals. He wouldn't need to try to harness my blood or drain me of my energies—just being near me fueled his abilities. His power flexed, and he smiled at the feel of it. His powers hadn't felt this strong in over a year—not since he'd thought I'd died. He might not know who I was, but I was suddenly his number-one priority.

His power slashed at me again. "I will see who you are," he said in a chilling voice. I inched backward, my nostalgia gone. If he forced me to show myself, all his rage and violence would fall on top of me, ripping me to shreds. I had to get out of there. Get Theo out of there. No more reacting. Time to move.

Rubble lined the floor. I had to watch my step as I moved back toward the stairwell. Theo had kept mostly silent, but I felt his anxiety now as he knew I was approaching. Father stepped over his fallen guards, his eyes fixed on where he couldn't see me. His power pushed hard; jackhammers beat against my walls.

"Show yourself!" he snarled. I stopped. That was the voice I recognized. The beastly snarl, the vicious rumble. That was the voice that had forever preceded the pain. Like Pavlov's dog, I froze.

Heavy hands landed on my shoulders. Warm fingertips gripped my neck. The moment Theo touched me, something inside me detonated. A blast of force burst out of me, blinding the hallway in white-yellow light.

Father flew backward over the dead guards and hit the far wall, crumbling the plaster behind him. He was on his feet again instantly. I gaped at him. Never had I lashed out so severely, even at the moments of my deaths. Theo pulled me back until I was in his arms, dragging me down the stairs. Father moved lightning-fast. In a blink, he stood in the fire exit doorway, no more than a few feet away from where Theo wrangled me down the stairs.

I looked up into Father's eyes and saw all the hatred and violence I'd known my entire life. Then I saw a shift. His brow wavered; his lips parted. His icy power paused its assault against my shields. He made a move to speak, but nothing came out. I pulled back against Theo's hold. What was he about to say?

"Ma-Marlena?" he whispered on a breath.

Marlena? I looked down and saw that I was flickering. Like a camera trying to focus, pieces of me could be made out. An image flashed in his mind, and I instantly remembered. The woman from the green corridor, the one he'd kept secret even from his brothers. Did he think I was her? I'd assumed she was dead.

Suddenly I was flung over Theo's shoulder. Holding me in a grip like a vise, he moved like I could—so fast we didn't need to be invisible not to be seen. He raced with me until we were outside and then kept going. Past the guard station, past the parking lot filled with police cars, past the entrance to the Capital One building. He raced until, literally, he couldn't move another step. We collapsed in a stretch of bushes behind the parking garage where Thirteen had set up his surveillance team earlier. But now everyone was gone.

"Where are the others?" I asked as I rolled off Theo and pulled his sagging body from the bushes.

"Moved on to the recon point," he said through heavy gasps. "Told them we'd catch up."

He'd kept his head while I'd faced off with my father, communicating with Thirteen to get Chang and the others to safety. We were visible now. As I picked leaves from his hair, I scanned his body. "Where are you hurt? What is broken?"

He choked on air, gasping for breath. His legs shook from the unnatural exertion.

"It's OK," I said softly. "You're OK. Just look at me. Breathe with me." Just like he had done for me on so many occasions, I held his gaze and forced him to follow my breaths. In and out. In and out. After a few moments, he inhaled deeply. I brushed his hair from his face. "Where does it hurt? I know the explosion hit you, and your legs are strained beyond what they should be. Where is the pain worse?"

He closed his eyes. With deep breaths he concentrated on settling his heart and lungs. "Explosion didn't hit," he managed. "Just knocked the wind out of me."

I let out a relieved breath. Muscle strain would be a quick heal. I caressed his face. "I did it," I murmured, more to myself than to him. "I faced my father again, and I survived."

In fact, I'd done more than survived. I'd impressed him. And hate it or not, that fact more than anything made the cowering little girl inside me shine.

"Yeah," Theo said, clearing his throat. "You survived. Congratulations. Now why the hell didn't you kill that son of a bitch when you had the chance?"

CHAPTER 26

Theo and I barely spoke on the drive over to the recon point. I'd healed his strained muscles, jacked a car from the Capital One garage, and called Thirteen from the car phone to let him know we were on the way. All the while, Theo's question hung heavily between us. Why hadn't I killed my father when I had the chance?

The rendezvous point was an empty parking lot behind a discount theater on the east side of the city. We passed a well-used putt-putt course, two liquor stores, and a cash-for-gold store before winding down the narrow alley to the back of the run-down theater. Broken streetlamps left the graffiti-ridden building in the shadows. As we pulled up, I saw a huge man in all black standing beside two souped-up BMWs.

Great idea, Thirteen. Let's see how many drug deals we can interrupt while we try to recon.

I pulled alongside Thirteen's SUV. Thirteen and Shane rushed over to us.

"Thank God! Are you OK?" Thirteen asked quickly. "Is anyone injured?"

"Not anymore," I murmured.

Theo slammed his door. "Where's Jon?" he asked.

"Jon was taken to the emergency room," Thirteen explained. "He was shot in the abdomen, but Heather reports that he's out of surgery and will be fine."

"What about Chang?" Theo asked, leaning against the car. "Did he get everything we needed?"

Theo's thoughts were cut off from me. I wanted to know what he was thinking, if he was really mad at me for leaving Father alive. But his mind was a complete blank. I ground my teeth in frustration and tried to listen to Thirteen.

"Chang's mission was a success," he answered. "He, Cordele, and the others are back at the offices downloading and sifting through the data. We are meeting in the morning at the farmhouse to plan next steps according to the sorted information."

"Where'd you get this car?" Shane asked.

I looked down at the late-model Corvette and shrugged. "It was in the Capital One parking lot."

"So you just stole it. Nice. Now we can add grand theft auto to our long list of felonies."

"It wasn't like we could go back to the reception and be like, oh hey, forgot our car."

His hands fisted so tightly, I waited for drops of blood to seep between his fingers. The two black cars pulled out of the lot, grabbing our attention as their tires spun on the icy pavement. The enormous man in black was still there, headed our way. I looked into his mind as Thirteen responded coolly, "We have ways of dealing with the authorities, Shane. You of all people should know that by now."

The man's thoughts were somehow blocked. After tonight, I was in no mood to be gentle. I pushed through his surprisingly strong mental walls. He stumbled. Calculation, focus, black-and-white thoughts without any of the colors of emotion gumming up the works. I recognized Jesse's mind at the same moment I recognized his enormous figure stepping into the moonlight.

"Your mind is like Father's guards," I blurted out. "It freaked me out the first time I met you because I thought I recognized the mental pattern. Those guards tonight had minds just like yours. Black and white, no emotion or stray thoughts. You don't feel drugged like they were. So what's the deal, FedEx? What are you?"

I'd stepped forward without realizing it. Thirteen, Theo, and Shane were all at my back now. Jesse had stopped a few feet away. I was still in his head, but there was nothing there I hadn't seen before. *Magnolia Kelch, Network agent under Red-Level Chief Thirteen, daughter of Magnus Kelch, blah, blah, blah.* It was like he was a robot or something.

He looked past me to Thirteen. "Surveillance disks have been confiscated and are awaiting your perusal. Local authorities have reported evidence of corporate espionage and possible infiltration into the Kelch Incorporated research line. Primary suspects include employees of Medco Rep, direct competitor to Kelch Inc. pharmaceuticals." He looked back down at me. "I'm sorry you had to face your father again, Magnolia." Then he turned, walked to the black pickup truck parked at the edge of the lot, climbed in, and drove away.

I turned to Thirteen. "What the hell was that?"

Thirteen glanced down at me briefly, then looked back to where Jesse had just pulled away. "We all have our roles, Magnolia," he said in a faraway voice. "Jesse is loyal to the Network.

That is all that matters." I wanted to ask more, but then he shook himself and said, "I'm heading into the office to join Chang on scanning the gathered data. If you want to rest until tomorrow's meeting, I have no problem with that."

Thank God. There was a lumpy queen-size mattress under ten layers of cheap quilts just waiting for me to fall into it.

"I'll follow you," Shane said, nodding to Thirteen. "I want to see if what we got was really worth all the shit we went through tonight." He turned to Theo. "What are you doing?"

I could feel the heat of Theo's gaze on the side of my face. He waited until I looked at him. "I'll see the team in the morning," he said, never taking his eyes off mine.

Shane huffed and stomped away. Thirteen cleared his throat. "Seven hundred hours, on the dot," he ordered.

Theo's lips twitched. "Won't be a problem."

My entire body flared with heat. Theo lifted one brow. "Ready?" he asked. A loaded question if ever there was one.

I swallowed. "Let's go."

CHAPTER 27

It was another silent drive, but not at all for the same reasons. My body hummed. I glanced at Theo from the corner of my eye. His head was back on the headrest, his eyes closed. I'd given up trying to get in his thoughts. Probably for the best. I didn't want to hear how he was still pissed off at me for leaving my father alive. Not with the way my skin tingled right now.

"I'm not mad at you," he said without opening his eyes.

"Don't get in my head." Especially since I couldn't get in his.

His eyebrows scrunched together. "I didn't realize I was. I thought you'd spoken out loud." He sighed heavily. "Look, Thirteen would love to get his hands on your father. He would like to hold him in one of the Network cells, get confessions out of him for every horrific thing he and your uncles have ever done. Most of all Thirteen would like to strip the man of as much power as possible—make him pay restitution for his crimes, bankrupt his empire, turn state's evidence against every illegal act his senator brother ever had a hand in. But personally, I think that outcome is nothing but a pipe dream. The only way to stop your father and uncles is to kill them." He turned to face me, his eyes glowing in the dashboard lights. "And I think that you, Mag, are the only one capable of doing it."

He brushed a piece of hair away from my face. "That's why I was so pissed when you didn't end the man tonight when you had the chance. You were face-to-face with him, alone in a camera-free hallway. You were invisible, and you were stronger than him on a level that terrified him. You could have killed him. But you didn't. Instead you stuck to the plan and walked away. It was the right thing to do—I know that. I also know that if I were the one with your powers and your past, I wouldn't have been strong enough to walk away." He looked me hard in the eye. "But no matter how I feel about Thirteen's priorities on this, I shouldn't have made you feel bad for doing exactly what needed to be done. I'm sorry."

I pulled into the farmhouse and parked. He caressed a strand of my hair, but I just stared out the windshield. He was right, of course, about Thirteen's ultimate plans. The Network goal had always been to gain legal evidence against my family, proof so strong that Father's or Uncle Max's powers couldn't dispel the ramification.

It would never happen.

But me killing my father? The idea churned uneasily inside me. No matter how strong I became, no matter how controlled, he was still my father.

Theo slipped a finger under my chin and turned my head to face him. Looking me in the eye, he said, "You are so much stronger than they are. It will take time to get where you need to be in your head, but I know that you can destroy them. You may be the only one capable of doing it."

I closed my eyes and let his hand cup the side of my face. The warmth of his touch spread quickly, speeding my pulse and tightening things low inside me. I didn't want to think about my father anymore. I wanted to go inside and shut out the rest of the world so that nothing existed except me and Theo. "Come on," I said—and didn't have to ask twice.

My wrap had been long forgotten back at the gala, and the night was absolutely freezing. We hurried around to the porch steps and didn't even bother with the keys. I unlocked the doors with my mind, rushed inside to the smell of burned furnace air, and instantly locked the door behind us. I was in Theo's arms before I could think.

My heartbeat thundered in my ears. He nuzzled the side of my face. "You are what I am supposed to have," he said. "When we're together, I am what I was meant to be."

As he spoke, he ran his fingers along a length of my hair that had fallen loose. The glow poured out of us, and I could feel it alive, growing inside us and through us. He lifted me at my waist, and my legs wrapped around him automatically. He pushed against me, and I gasped.

He captured my lips with his, and the next moment we were in the bedroom. Gently, he laid me on the bed. He held back my hands. Positioning me against the pillows, he tugged free the long folds of my silk gown. I wore only my strapless bra and panties now.

Holding my face between his hands, he kissed me. His tongue snuck past my lips, and suddenly I was dizzy. He tasted so good. So right. I felt his hands on my back, and my bra was gone. I shivered but only for a moment. His touch was so gentle. And I knew it now, knew what to expect here. There was no fear or panic. Not this time. I pushed his open shirt from his shoulders, kissing, licking his throat. His stubble teased my tongue. When his shirt was gone, I ran my hands over his back. So strong—feeling the dips and curves of his muscles made me squirm beneath him in anticipation. His mouth closed over my breast. I gasped again. Suddenly everything low in my body that had been clenching and aching went loose, ready. As if sensing the shift in my body, he looked up at me with my hard nipple between his teeth and grinned that cocky grin. *Oh yeah.* I was definitely ready.

With a long, slow lick, he rose from my breast to stare down at me once more. Watching my reaction, he slowly slid his fingers beneath the edge of my panties. The room started to spin. Still watching, he tiptoed his fingers lower, then deeper. I closed my eyes. Massaging, probing, he moved his hand in time with my gasps. I could feel the ecstasy building inside me. I grabbed on to him. Dug my fingers into his shoulders. Faster, deeper, two fingers now, maybe three. *More, more, more!*

The room shattered on my gasp. My eyes flew open. Radiant light everywhere. I feared I wouldn't be able to see him past the brilliance of the glow, but there he was. The dark, strong jaw, the wide, thin lips. Those chocolate eyes that anchored me. I cupped his cheek. He lowered his lids and inhaled a deep breath. The glow around us swelled with his lungs. I laughed. How could I have ever lived without this power? It was everything.

"More," I said, surprised by the huskiness of my voice. His eyes flashed, and that cocky grin returned. In a quick move, he removed my panties. Naked, I froze. He stopped, stared down at me. His expression was unreadable, but his thoughts suddenly opened to me. And warmed me nearly to tears. *Perfect.*

I reached out for the button of his pants. He blinked, and his thoughts vanished. I trusted him. He ran a hand over my hair, then kissed me as he laid me back down. Without a word, he took my hands and lifted them over my head. Then he removed his own pants, always watching my reaction. I smiled. The barriers between us were crumbling. I could feel his heartbeat now as if it were my own. I ached with the urge for more of him, but I couldn't tell if the need was mine or his. It didn't matter.

I spread my legs, and he moved his hips between me. *Don't want to hurt. Always hurts the first time. Don't want to be the cause of more pain.*

I touched his lips in a gentle kiss. *I know who you are, Theo. What we are together. No pain will change that. Only make us stronger.*

He kissed me back hard. I wrapped my arms around him. I felt his tension as my own. Slowly, he moved forward. *More, more,* I whispered through his thoughts. *Now.*

He pushed forward, and my lungs emptied on a moan. But this time, there was no deep breath of recovery. He stared down at me, his eyes wide, neither of us able to breathe as the warmth of the glow around us pulsed. The bond between us became our breath. I touched his face. Kissed him. Slowly he started to move.

I floated. No longer a person of flesh and bone, I was nothing but power now. An essential part to a glorious whole. He kept us joined as he pulled me from the bed to straddle him, on our knees. He guided our rhythm as the feeling built inside me once again. Only this time, it was so much more because I could feel it building in him as well. *Oh God!* Faster and faster we moved perfectly, as one. The light pouring out of us grew brighter, nearly blinding. I buried my face in his shoulder, held on for dear life.

Together we exploded.

CHAPTER 28

We lay in the bed, facing each other. I couldn't stop touching him. The sticky sweat on his skin. The hot feel of his chest. I couldn't remember how much time had passed since I'd last taken a breath. All our walls were down now, all our barriers vanquished. The burst of golden light had softened to a warm glow around us. Neither of us said a word. We didn't need to.

Staring into his eyes, I saw his entire life story play out like a captivating movie. What he remembered of his childhood on the streets of Chicago, the son of a teenage prostitute. The buildings they squatted in had been filthy, full of disease and feces. He'd been terrified when his mother's pimps went on a rampage. He'd taken the beatings and learned to cower whenever they approached. The hope he allowed himself during those fleeting days when his mother sobered enough to acknowledge him had been continually shattered when the drugs returned. When the social worker found him hiding in an alley, his distrust and fear had been instinctual. From group home to foster home, his life had been constant uncertainty. Then he'd been sent to school and found a savior in education. His resolve had been set. He'd make himself despite his beginnings, not because of them.

As a teen, he'd sought out his maternal grandparents. I knew this memory and winced, knowing what would happen. The luxury of the home set in a privileged suburban neighborhood had been like salt in his veins. The man he'd seen behind the etched paned windows—tall, sandy haired, with the distinct nose and eyes of his mother—spat in disgust when the housekeeper informed him of Theo's unexpected arrival. That was all Theo had needed to see. He hadn't waited for the housekeeper to return and dismiss him. He'd walked away with head held high, not even flinching when the iron-scrolled gates clanked shut behind him. He'd paused only a moment to memorize the ancient family crest—some distorted winged creature behind a decorated shield—an image he'd eventually have tattooed on his chest as a permanent reminder of who he would never be. The need to connect had shifted inside him that day. His family had refused him, but he would find that connection somewhere else. The search had begun.

I saw his high school years and was mesmerized by the athletics and normal high school trials that I'd missed out on in my captivity. He had entered Butler on scholarship, and it was there that the hand of fate had finally interfered. Jon Heldamo—Theo's designated roommate—had introduced himself that first day of classes. The years unfolded in a new light then. The two young men's companionship had grown into a camaraderie. The camaraderie had bloomed into a brotherhood. Never far from the other, they'd formed a bond that evolved into absolute devotion. It was fascinating. I'd always known that Theo was loyal to Jon, but this went beyond shared experiences. It was something that had always been inside Theo. I could see that now. Just as a piece of Theo had recognized a matching piece inside me, another part of him had recognized a counterpart in Jon.

But where had that part of Theo come from? Not from his mother; that was obvious. But somewhere. He'd been right when he'd said that this bond and power between us wasn't something I'd done to him. I could actually see it inside him, just as I could pinpoint the warm and welcoming place inside me.

The glow around us surged as I focused on this new piece of information. The new powers I'd developed since my escape— the transformative abilities, the increased strength in my control—had all happened after meeting Theo. Our connection had sparked something new inside me, just as it had sparked to life this piece inside him. Together we had created something new, and even more powerful than either one of us alone. Was this another kind of supernatural power? Was it love? As the room pulsed with golden light, I knew that trying to separate the two things would be as impossible as separating this connection between us. This was love, and it was more powerful than anything else in existence.

He ran his fingers over my face, touching, now learning my mind. We lay that way for hours, not breathing and not caring. Then when the need flared—always at the exact same moment for each of us—we'd reach for each other, come together again until the power swelled and exploded out of us, leaving us fuller and stronger than ever before. This must be what the poets meant by *bliss*.

His fingers paused under my eye, a small frown line formed between his brows. As I'd been visiting his past in his mind, he'd just walked through one of my memories, one where I'd hidden for hours in a cramped pantry cupboard, my knees to my chin and my eyes closed tight. Markus's tutor had caught me spying. I never had my own tutors and had to eavesdrop on my brothers' if I wanted any kind of education. Father had been incensed at my gall. I'd hidden in the cupboard for hours, waiting. Then he'd found me.

Theo closed his eyes. I knew he felt my terror, my pain. I wanted to take it away from him, so I pulled out one of his own memories. I wanted to know where this instinctual need in him to connect with others came from. So I drew a memory from where I'd felt the urge the strongest.

He stared down at a woman as he pounded himself into her. Lips parted, head thrown back, she'd cried out in pleasure as he continued to thrust his need inside her. As I watched, her face changed. Older, younger. Dark hair, blonde hair, red hair. Two at a time. In a closet, in a bed, in a car. Always the need to connect driving him, searching.

I pulled back, shocked. I stared at him and wasn't sure what I saw. The glow dimmed around his face. The frown darkening his face grew clearer. He reached out to touch my lips, and I pulled back. Suddenly, I gasped for air.

"No!" he growled, panting in his own breath. "Not yet! Don't end it yet!"

I closed my eyes as an unfamiliar hurt overwhelmed me. "All those women. My God, there must have been a hundred of them." I felt the glow slipping away. It was still inside me, but around us the air grew colder now. He tried to keep the power humming and connecting us on his own, but without me he wasn't strong enough. Would I be strong enough to control this power on my own? Or would I always be less without him? I covered my face.

He pried at my hands, but I held them in place. "Listen to me, Mag. Look at me."

I shook my head. It didn't matter. I knew it didn't matter. I'd known that he'd been with other women. And if I'd seen all that any other time, I probably wouldn't freak out this way. But, damn it, we'd just made love. A lot. I knew what it felt like for him when he was inside me—what he wanted and the powerful pleasure when he climaxed. And now I knew that he'd felt that while looking down on all those other faces.

"You know why I was with those other women, Mag. I had a hole inside me that needed to be filled, and I didn't know how to fill it. Not until you." His voice got hard. "Don't belittle what we just experienced by comparing it to everyone before you."

I took a deep breath. It felt odd and a little disappointing to need the air now. "I know why. But if there's one thing you've taught me more than any other, it's that I can't be held responsible for my reflexive thoughts and reactions." Slowly I lowered my hands. He narrowed his eyes.

"Touché," he said. "Now come here."

He pulled me in to his chest, and I let him. When I closed my eyes, all those faces came back again. *No.* He was right. I wouldn't let his past ruin this moment between us. Whatever he'd been looking for with them, he hadn't found it. Not until me. That's what I needed to focus on.

He sighed, and his muscles relaxed. "Feels weird to breathe again," he murmured. We sighed together. "I think we have about an hour or so before everyone shows up. Try and get some sleep, Mag." He kissed the top of my head.

I lay awake and listened to his breathing settle. The terrors of my past hadn't stopped him from finding what he needed inside me. The fact that he'd spent the past two decades being a manwhore wouldn't stop me from finding what I needed in him. I wouldn't let it.

CHAPTER 29

The alarm clock woke us an hour later. Theo slapped the thing off, rolled over onto his back, then settled back into that deep snore that had lulled me to sleep. The hint of morning sun peeked through the small frosted window. It was the first time since my return I hadn't woken with a chill. Warm, quiet, peaceful.

Anxiety seeped into the room quietly. I'd gotten a pretty good glimpse of how he typically handled the morning after. With the swell of our combined power still humming, I couldn't help but wonder if he would set a new land-speed record when he woke and decided to bolt. A little frown line puckered between his brows. Thick stubble on his jaw, hair tousled—God, he was beautiful.

"Stop thinking so much. You'll give me a headache." He stretched his arms over his head.

"Can you hear my thoughts?"

"Not really. More like I can sense your uncertainty." He stretched until his body shook, then fell slack beside me.

He brushed a finger over my bottom lip. "Worried about what happens now?"

"Maybe. Are you?"

"Nope." He swung me up and on top of him, flush tight against his body. He felt so good. A perfect fit. "We're supposed to be together. Last night proved that beyond a doubt."

I stared at his jaw, feeling oddly young. "So are we—I don't know—a couple now?"

He waited for me to look up. "You've never had a boyfriend before, have you?" he said softly.

I toyed with the hair on his chest, pissed off that I felt myself blush. "Not exactly a lot of dating opportunities on the estate unless you count my brothers. And believe me, I'd rather not."

His eyes flashed with danger before settling back to a cool calm. "Would you like to call me your boyfriend?"

"I don't know. I mean, it sounds kind of silly, considering you're so old and everything." In a flash I was on my back, pinned to the mattress with my hands over my head.

"Old?"

"Well, yeah. I mean, you're like what? Thirty-five? Forty?"

He nipped at my collarbone. "I'm thirty-four, and you know it."

I went still beneath him, waited until he stopped tickling my throat with his tongue. When he finally looked up at me again, I said seriously, "Thirty-four. The absolute perfect age for so much more than a boyfriend."

He kissed me then. And in the next moment, he was inside me again. This time there was only a soft glow when we came together, holding each other close. But the power was still there, still stronger than ever. There was no questioning the control we had over it now. Together we'd always be in control.

* * *

Thirteen arrived with Marie, Charles, and three boxes of dough-nuts. Shane and a barely awake Chang skulked in a few moments later. And right behind them, Tony and Luce arrived with bagels and coffee.

"What are you guys doing here?" I asked, snagging one of the coffees from Tony. He stood near the doorway, eyeing the others in the room.

"We were told to be here. So we're here." He glanced down at me. "How you doing?"

My heart warmed a little at his genuine concern. I shrugged. "I've been worse." He gave me a soft smile. Maybe some future coffee time with Tony wasn't out of the question, after all.

I heard the shower turn off in the back of the house and turned automatically, expecting to see Theo emerge from the bathroom. Marie stepped in front of me, blocking my view. *Bitch.*

"I left some of the readouts from last night's mission in the car," she said shortly. "Come with me to get them. Please." If it wasn't for the gritted-out *please* I would have laughed in her face. From the corner of my eye, I saw Thirteen watching us. *Great.*

"OK," I said and gestured for her to lead the way. I followed her out the front door. The cold made me cringe. It must have dropped twenty degrees last night. We stepped quickly to Charles's car. Over the roof of the car she said, "Get in," then crawled in the driver's seat and shut the door.

What the hell? I scanned her mind. Nothing stood out but an underlining aggravation that I assumed was her normal state of being. I climbed in the front seat and shivered while she started the car and blasted the heater. "Look, we don't have time for girl bonding, so just grab the readouts and let's get back inside."

She stared out the front window, her hands clenched tightly on the steering wheel. Suddenly she looked older. There were lines around her eyes that I hadn't noticed the past couple of times I'd seen her. But then again, she'd been absent at so many recent meetings I wasn't sure when the last time I saw her was. She closed her eyes. As if a long-bound book were opening, her mind slowly unfolded before me. Her thoughts became organized and clear, and I could see exactly what she needed from me, what she would never be able to say out loud. Against my will, my heart ached.

"I don't know if I could do that, Marie," I said softly. "When I healed Charles, his body had been broken. I don't know what endometriosis is exactly, but if it's part of the way your body was made, I may not be able to change it."

Her eyes stayed closed, but her lower lip began to tremble. "It's *not* the way my body was made. The cells are attacking me, and the laser treatments aren't working. I just..." She ran her hands over her face. "God, do you have any idea how humiliating this is? Talking to you. Asking you. Do you think I'd be here if it wasn't my absolute last resort?"

I cocked a brow at her.

She rolled her eyes at me. "You know how I feel about you. And I know how you feel about me. It's just..." Her lips pressed together again, and her thoughts explained what her pride wouldn't let her say. Three miscarriages. Two years of treatments. It was the only thing she'd ever wanted. More than being a part of the Network, more than the clothes and lifestyle she loved. She wanted a family of her own.

Her desperation left a lump stuck in my throat. I cleared it twice then said, "I can try. From what you've shown me, I don't think I can get rid of it forever. It will probably come back. But I might be able to clear it up enough for you to get pregnant and, you know, stay that way."

She released a long sigh. "That's all I wanted. Just for you to try." She looked me in the eye and forced herself not to curl her lip. "Thank you."

I had to smile. It would be nice if this moment was a new beginning for us, if her emotional turmoil over wanting a baby was the root of her bitchiness, and now that I was going to help her, she'd start treating me with some respect. But I saw the pettiness in her thoughts, the fact that it totally ate her alive to ask me for this. I was still prettier than her. And I was still a Kelch, with more money and power than she would ever have.

"Yeah," I said, grinding my teeth at that last thought. "Well, maybe your offspring won't harbor your bitch gene and will grow up to be a normal person." Now she glared full-out. I reached over the console to the backseat and grabbed whatever paper I could find. "Come on. People will probably think I've killed you out here if we don't get back in there soon."

"Oh right, like you could even," she snarled as we crawled out of the car. Once we were back on the path to the front porch, she flashed her sidearm at me.

I shot her a chiding look. "Don't be an idiot, Marie."

On the steps she pulled me to a stop. With an exaggerated eye roll, she said, "Fine. You're big and bad and powerful and can kill us all with your mind."

My eyebrows shot up. "How nice of you to notice."

She sighed. "So look. I'll be ovulating in ten days. Do you think…"

"Yeah. Why don't you come over this weekend, and I'll see what I can do."

Her face relaxed again, the lines around her eyes smoothing on their own. She nodded, and even though she didn't say it, the gratitude and hope that poured out of her was palpable. Not that I was eager for Charles and Marie to pass on their winning character traits, but still. I did want to help her.

Marie walked into the house, and for a moment I just stood on the front porch. I'd never considered using my power to heal something like this. Was it even possible? And God, a baby. To be a part of creating some new life. A chill ran up my spine, and I knew it wasn't from the cold.

I shook my head. I'd had enough moments of deep contemplation lately. Now wasn't the time for another. I pushed open the front door that Marie had so thoughtfully closed in my face and paused. I was glowing. Not a lot, but there was a nice golden shimmer over my skin that stood out against the early-morning darkness.

Jon's SUV pulled up the drive behind me. I waited on the porch as he and Heather stomped through the snow to the house. Heather smiled up at me. "Hey! Are we the last ones here?"

"Yeah, everyone else is inside. And some of Colin's team is here too."

Jon frowned. "Why?"

I just shrugged. When they got to the porch, I held open the door for them. When I looked down at my hand again, the glow was gone.

"You OK?" Heather asked as she stepped by me into the house. I smiled back at her.

"I'm good. Just need another drink."

I followed her into the house and closed the door on the cold outside.

CHAPTER 30

"Baby, we are rolling in the intel."

Chang didn't bother sitting. He'd downed three coffees and was in high-energy report mode. "I got it all—names, dates, places. Of course, it was easy since I'd already done all the groundwork. Man, Magnus's system was the bomb! If I hadn't gotten as far as I did before we went in—oooh, it would have been a close one. But I recognized the file right off. I got in, I got out, got it clean, and got it good."

I watched him bounce around the room from my seat on one of the giant ottomans. Theo was on the sofa behind me again, this time with Jon and Heather. His leg brushed against me every time he shifted, sending little waves of warmth through my body.

"Chang!" Jon shouted, sitting forward. "We get it. You did awesome. Way to go. Now, the data."

"Right." Chang scurried across the great room to where Thirteen sat in his usual big chair by the fireplace.

"From what Cordele and I got through last night, we have the brothers' first meeting with Russian Federal Assembly member Spielrien and Deputy Prime Minister Fedorov back in October."

"I thought only Senator Kelch met with Spielrien," Charles said.

Chang shrugged. "The meeting's listed on Magnus's calendar."

"Where's Cordele?" Marie interjected. "And why are there nonmission agents here?" She sneered toward Luce and Tony over on the far love seat. Ah yes, the Marie we all knew and loved.

"Cordele had a call from an informant and will join us when she can," Thirteen explained. "And your fellow Network agents are here because I asked them to come. Chang, continue, please."

Marie sat back in a huff. I smiled into my glass. I loved it when Thirteen put her in her place.

Chang cleared his throat. "Right. So anyway, the next meeting was with Belarusian foreign secretary Alton Preshenko. This was a week after the Russian meetings. There were three consecutive meetings with Preshenko over the next ten days. Then they headed to Ukraine, where they met with Deputy Andriy Boyko. Now, I don't know much about this Preshenko guy, but Boyko is old-school—like he was around way back when all of this was Russia."

"Oh yes," Thirteen said wryly. "Obviously Mr. Boyko is an ancient."

"I know, right?" Chang was so clueless. "So the bros had four meetings with Boyko, then moved on to Bohlren. Here's where it gets weird. In Bohlren they met with two fellas: Councilman Okhotnikov and somebody named A. Fahran." He looked at me. "If I got your research data right, Okhot—whatever—is one of the four council members who run the little island city and deal with whatever country is in charge of them at the time."

"Five councilmen," I said smoothly. Thank God for supernatural recall. "The city is run by the two port overseers who handle the limited export business the city manages. Then there's the mainland liaison, the head of tourism, and the city deputy."

"Yeah, from what I got from Magnus's notes, Okhot-ness is most likely the mainland liaison or the deputy guy. But there's nothing on Fahran."

Everyone in the room had been scribbling furiously, taking down every word Chang had said. I frowned into my whiskey. I'd have to do research again; I just knew it.

Shane started in on some questions about meeting agendas, and Theo leaned forward in his seat behind me. Resting his forearms on his knees, his fingers brushed back and forth in my hair. Warmth tingled inside me.

Mental fury hit me out of nowhere. *What the hell?* Someone was suddenly totally pissed off. I looked to Shane out of habit. He'd barely acknowledged me since our elevator disaster last night, and right now he was busy focusing on Chang and Thirteen. Marie wasn't shooting mental darts at me either. She was taking notes and thinking through a timeline for how Thirteen might move forward. Then who in the world...

I met Luce's gaze. Her glare was lethal and aimed right for me. She breathed hard through her nostrils, her teeth grinding together. I got in her head instantly and froze. I should have known.

She had been one of the hundreds.

Pink hues tinted the room as a new kind of anger spiked inside me. I saw her jealousy, her lust. I bared my teeth. Somewhere in the back of my mind, I knew that Theo's past meant nothing. He was with me completely now. But I didn't care. How dare she want what was mine? Theo's hand tightened on my shoulder. I hissed as the dimly lit room grew brighter. Pressure at my back stopped me from rising out of my seat. I felt the warmth of our joined power, pushing against that bloody place of mine just straining to lash out. The pink receded quickly, but the room remained bright—as if our joined power was feeling just as possessive as I was. My hiss turned to a growl. Luce scrambled to her feet. *Coming for what's mine, Luce? I'd like to see you try.*

Strong arms held me. The pressure at my back grew. Deep murmurs at my ear turned my gasps to steady breathing. My focus never left Luce's face. "*Mine*," I growled.

Voices around me spoke quickly. Someone pulled Luce from the room. The moment she was gone, my vision returned to normal. I blinked the room back into focus. I wasn't on the ottoman anymore but on the sofa, sitting on Theo's lap. His arms were tight around me. In my ear I could hear him whisper, "Just breathe, Mag. She's gone. Just breathe with me."

Everyone in the room was on their feet, staring down at me. Their shock, their fear, it filled the room.

"Magnolia?" Heather knelt in front of me, her eyes full of concern. She placed a hand on my knee, and instant calm washed over me. My muscles nearly fell slack.

"You're getting stronger," I said softly. She blushed and pulled her hand away.

"Are you OK?" she asked. "Did Lucinda do something or think something that we should know about?"

Theo loosened his grip on my waist. It certainly would have been less embarrassing if Luce had been plotting against the team, maybe seeking some payback for Colin's frustrations. That would have been a much easier explanation than my jealous rage.

"No, she didn't do anything. I just...saw something in her thoughts that I didn't like. It was, you know, personal."

Heather's eyes went to Theo. I ran my hands over my face. God, could we just once have a meeting without my fucked-up emotions ruining everything?

"I'm sorry. I didn't mean to disrupt the meeting, Thirteen. I'm sorry."

"At least we didn't all come in our pants this time," Shane murmured. I shot him a glare.

"Can you tell us what happened?" Thirteen asked gently.

I glanced over my shoulder to Theo. He released me enough to let me scoot off his lap. I didn't want to talk to Thirteen with him wrapped around me.

"It had nothing to do with the mission or anything else. It was just stupid. Her thoughts took me by surprise, and I overreacted a little. I'm sorry."

"Overreacted a little?" Tony asked from the doorway. He'd taken Luce outside but had peeked back in to see what was happening. "Damn, girl, remind me to keep a pocketful of downers whenever we're in the same room. Properly prescribed downers, of course." He grinned at Thirteen.

Thirteen sat on the sofa beside me. He took my hand, and his massive palms dwarfed my small fingers. *I worry so much for you.* His thoughts floated through my head. I smiled up at him, but it was a shaky thing.

His next words carried around the room. "You have your assignments. Tony, if you will bring in the documents your team procured from Dr. Everett, you may all be dismissed to your work. I will contact you for the next follow-up meeting."

He glanced at Theo, who rose to join Jon and Shane in the kitchen. I didn't miss how his eyes turned cold when he looked Theo's way. I touched Thirteen's arm. "Don't. It's not his fault."

He narrowed his eyes at me. "We will have to disagree on that."

Tony brought a thin file folder to Thirteen. "Thank you. I know how much you enjoyed your research assignment, Magnolia," Thirteen said with a raised brow. "But we have to dig a bit deeper now. This is the information Colin's team gathered from Dr. Everett. I'd like you to scan through the information for any connections with Chang's data."

I took the file and laid it on the ottoman. It was a cop-out assignment, and we both knew it. Father and Uncle Max building a weapon's facility in Eastern Europe wouldn't have anything to do with a South African art smuggler. But at least I wouldn't have to stare at screen after screen of random data.

"I'll go through it. And Thirteen, I really am sorry."

He smiled now—my smile. "You are growing, Magnolia. Don't ever apologize for that." Then he leaned over and kissed my forehead. Unwilling tears burned at the back of my eyes. His unconditional love for me never seemed to waver.

He got to his feet. "I will be in touch." Then he strolled from the room to meet the others waiting outside.

CHAPTER 31

I listened as the cars drove from the gravel drive to the county road. It was snowing again, and a couple of the smaller cars spun a little on the ice. God, poor Luce. I'd have to call or text her—texting would probably be easier—and apologize. That's what Heather was thinking I should do when she left.

I rubbed my hands over my face, then jerked my head up. Theo leaned against the wall to the kitchen. Our connection felt so natural now; I hadn't even noticed it hadn't faded as he left.

He cocked a brow at me. "You thought I'd leave with the others?"

"Well, yeah."

He shook his head and came over to the sofa. "That's not how the whole boyfriend thing works."

"I thought we agreed you were too old to be a boyfriend."

He didn't smile like I thought he would. Instead, he sat beside me and clasped his hands between his knees. "You know she didn't mean anything. None of them did."

"I know. Somewhere inside me, I know that. It's just…I can't be sure I won't lash out at her again the next time she thinks of you like that."

"Sure you can. You know what to expect now."

"What about that whole not being responsible for our instincts and reactions? I can't help that it pisses me off that you were with her."

He ran a hand over my hair. "You can't help when you instinctually feel something, but you can recognize the feeling inside you before it boils over. You can temper your power in reaction. It's what I do every time that asshole Shane starts undressing you in his mind. You don't see me ripping out his throat every other minute, do you?"

"I don't know. That moment in the elevator was a little touch and go for a few minutes."

His eyes turned dark. "He's lucky he walked away that night."

I considered him for a moment. "This possessive streak inside me, it isn't part of the evil stuff in me. It's part of the normal, human stuff."

"There is nothing evil inside you."

I waved that off. "Semantics of being one of the damned."

It was a revelation. I was so sure that every negative reaction I had was specific to my supernatural side that it had never occurred to me my reactions might be normal. OK, maybe the blood-colored haze and beastly transformations weren't everyone's regular, but the feelings were just like everyone else's. *Look at me, all normal!*

He must have sensed the change in me because he smiled and shook his head. "You will never be normal, Mag, and you shouldn't want to be."

We'd have to disagree on that one for now. I leaned over and planted a quick kiss on his cheek. "I think I like this not-a-boyfriend thing."

His eyes grew dark again. "Yeah, there are all kinds of benefits to a not-a-boyfriend."

The energy between us simmered. Things low in my tummy started to heat. "You mean other than making me feel better when I freak out?"

He leaned into me, brushed our noses. "There are all kinds of ways to make you feel better." Then he lay me down on the sofa and spent the rest of the day showing me just how much better I could feel.

* * *

My laptop beeped from the table in the kitchen. I slid on my jeans and grabbed a piece of the pizza we'd had delivered a couple of hours ago. It was cold, but I sure as hell wasn't complaining.

"You've been getting a lot of e-mails," Theo commented as he followed me into the kitchen. His jeans were unbuttoned and he pulled on his tight T-shirt as he walked. I looked him up and down and couldn't help but lick my lips. "Hopefully people are finding info on those meetings Chang found." He glanced at me and paused. "Seriously? Babe, I'm not a machine."

"Sorry." My face flushed, and I poured a quick drink. When I looked back up, his expression had grown sober. "What?"

"Jon and I need to leave for Kiev to try and nail down Boyko and Fahran, but we should be back by Sunday. You have any plans that night? With Thirteen or anyone?"

"Why would I have plans with Thirteen?"

His sad grin actually reminded me of Thirteen. "Sunday's Christmas Eve, Mag. I wasn't sure if you were doing anything with Thirteen or not."

Christmas? I'd never even thought of it. "He hasn't mentioned anything."

"Good. I was thinking when I get in, that night we could go downtown. See the monument lights, grab some hot chocolate. Then you could come back to my place. I don't have a tree or anything, but we could probably pick one up. A small one or something."

I gaped at him, my mind frozen. *A Christmas tree? Downtown to see the lights?*

He leaned forward and brushed the hair from my face. "I never had a Christmas until Jon's family invited me to theirs. This being Jon and Heather's first in their new house, I figured it was time they started their own holiday traditions. And maybe I could start some of my own. Our own."

His fingers brushed over my cheek again. "Don't cry, Mag." But I couldn't help it. He wanted Christmas with me. A tree, traditions. Together. It was so much more than a supernatural connection. It was all the things I'd never thought to hope for.

"So is that a yes?"

I nodded so hard I thought I'd pull something in my neck. And when he smiled and opened his arms, I went to him and cried some more while he held me. I probably looked like an idiot, but the way he ran his hands down my back and kissed my hair, I didn't feel stupid at all.

By the time the sun set behind the frosty trees, it was time for him to go meet Jon for the red-eye to London. I walked him to the door.

"I can go get a tree tomorrow. Keep it here, and then when you get back we can move it to your place."

"Or we can just do Christmas here if you want."

"No, I've never been to your house. I want to do it there."

He tapped a finger on my chin. "Then that's what we'll do." I practically bounced as we walked to his car. "And I'll get presents," I said. "For everybody. On Christmas we can go around and give presents to people like Thirteen and Jon and Heather and Cordele."

He chuckled. "I think that sounds just about perfect." He took my face in his hands, turned serious again. "I'll be back in a few days. Be careful. Don't go on any other team's missions."

I rolled my eyes.

"Take care of what's mine, Mag."

I gripped his wrists. Everything inside me fluttered. The power between us swelled so that the falling snow around us melted before it touched our skin. "And you take care of what's mine."

He kissed me, and our shimmer grew to a steady glow. I watched him climb into his car. As he drove down the icy path, disappearing behind the tree line, I held tight to the warmth of him inside me.

* * *

The giant trees had been brought in from the forests of Washington and stretched to the ceiling of the main ballroom. One at each end of the long room, they were expertly decorated with white-and-silver lights and glistening ornaments. Garlands had been strung along the balconies; wreaths hung in each of the enormous windows, showcasing the perfect view of the snow-covered landscape.

I lifted a hand to touch the chilled window but pulled back quickly when I saw how bloody my fingers still were. Even at five years old, I knew the rules well. No blood in the house, especially when there were guests there.

Through the glass, I saw the wide double doors that led into the room open as people made their way inside. Their smiles were so wide, their eyes so bright. Looking into their minds, I saw how much they envied my family and the beauty we lived with. They saw the decorated trees and just knew that in the morning, presents would fill the space beneath them, overflowing with so much more than any of them could ever provide their own children. But there was something more in their thoughts as well. There was an excitement and joy that I didn't understand. A hope. Their laughter was louder than it had been at any of Father's other parties. The sound of it warmed me in an unfamiliar way.

Uncle Max entered the room, and instantly I flinched away. No one was allowed to see me. Ever. If Uncle Max or Father found me staring in from outside, I'd have to go back to the barn. The deep cuts on my legs and stomach ached enough from making the long trek from the northern acres back to the main house, and my shoeless feet were so frozen now they'd turned purple. Another trip to the barn, and I wouldn't make it back for at least another day.

Tsk, tsk, tsk. The deep voice slithered through my thoughts. I spun around and instantly cowered. Uncle Mallroy stood several feet away on the stone path that led from the gardens to the ballroom's patio. He stared in my direction with his dull gray eyes. There is a trail of blood. Right across the stones. Anyone who comes out to the patio will see.

I looked at the snow-covered ground I'd just trodden on. Sure enough, blood had dripped from my slowly healing wounds in a long, obvious trail. I'd been healing faster lately, but the long walk must have reopened some of the gashes on my legs. It looked as if some animal had been gutted and dragged through the yard.

I looked to Uncle Mallroy, fearful. His face was as indifferent as ever. He had the same thick hair and prominent brow as Father and Uncle Max, but his eyes were always focused on something no one else could see. He was dressed to work in the horses' stable. He never attended these parties. He hated all the strange people. As I looked at him, his eyes changed shape and color, going from gray and round to blue and oval, then brown and narrow. It always made me nervous when he did things like that.

Don't tell. The thought came unwillingly and surprised me. I'd never asked for anything from anyone, especially one of my relatives. Why I did now, I had no clue. Maybe it was seeing all the hope and joy in the minds of Father's guests, maybe it was because I was still in so much pain and couldn't think clearly. Whatever the reason, my child's mind had let the request slip, and now I held my breath, waiting for his response.

Uncle Mallroy cocked his head and looked at me. His eyes focused on me—one green and round, one black and narrow—and he seemed almost surprised. As if this was the first time he'd actually seen me. With a frown he opened his mouth and said, "Magnolia." I gasped at the soft rumble. It was the first time I'd ever heard his spoken voice. "Magnolia," he said again. "We already know."

No sooner had he spoken the words than three of Father's guards appeared from a side doorway farther down the house. Automatically, I ran. My legs ached, but it didn't matter. Instinct always took over when they came for me. Even injured, I moved in a blur. I'd made it all the way to the south side of the house when three more guards were suddenly there, blocking my path. My powers lashed out on their own, cutting the guards, making them curse in pain. The distraction had given the first group time enough to catch up. Thick arms wrapped around me, pinning my arms to my sides. I kicked out and felt the sharp pain of my already-injured legs making contact. Another guard grabbed my legs and immediately bound them with the leather straps they always carried on them. I wanted to scream but knew better than to try. If Father's guests heard my cries, he'd kill me—then wait until I came back and hurt me again.

The first guard shoved another leather strap so far into my mouth I choked. Then he tossed me over his shoulder. "Cover the blood," he ordered, then began walking. The other guards moved automa-

tically, the drugs in their systems ridding them of any thought of not complying.

Bouncing on the guard's back, I knew I wouldn't be going back to the barn tonight—there was no time, and the guards had other duties while the guests were there. Instead, he'd take me to the farthest garage, where I'd be locked away until Father was ready to deal with me. I almost preferred the barn.

As we entered the garage, the guard didn't bother turning on the lights, but the darkness didn't keep me from seeing the two small forms standing in the shadow of the doorway that led from the garage to the house. Both wearing warm flannel pajamas, Malcolm and Markus watched. They weren't old enough to attend Father's parties, so they usually spied on the guests from their hiding places nearby. Apparently, tonight, I was more entertaining.

The guard carried me past the lines of parked cars and stopped at a wall of stacked shelves. He dropped me on the hard cement floor and pulled down one of the medium-size steel trunks Father kept in there to store old documents and business papers. As the guard worked the lock on the trunk, I heard Malcolm's excited whisper. "See, Markus. It looks like we'll be getting a decent Christmas present, after all. Just think how fun it will be to watch Father with her in the morning after we open all of our other gifts. And I have the perfect hiding spot to get the best view. We'll even get one of the cooks to give us hot chocolate before we sneak out."

They high-fived, then turned and closed the door behind them. The next moment, the guard lifted me into the metal box. He had to bend my legs to get me to fit, and the searing pain of my reopened injuries made my head spin.

Good, *I thought as agony leached away my consciousness.* I'll pass out for a little while and get some actual rest. See, Malcolm, I'm getting a Christmas present too.

* * *

The memory had come unwillingly, but I was glad that it had. It made the Christmas to come that much more important. I had seen the trees and decorations, heard the music, and smelled the treats. But this year, for the first time, I would experience the feeling—the one I had only ever caught from Father's guests. I felt joy and hope, an excited anticipation that made me not want to sleep even though Christmas morning was still a few days away.

My cell phone vibrated, and I snagged it from my nightstand.

SLEEP SWEET, MAG.

My smile grew so wide it hurt my cheeks as the feeling inside me swelled even more.

CHAPTER 32

Endometriosis: a condition in which bits of the tissue similar to the lining of the uterus grow in other parts of the body.

I shut down Wikipedia. *OK,* I thought, *I pretty much got it.* I ought to be able to get rid of the scar tissue enough for Marie to get pregnant and stay that way until the baby was born. But it sounded like no matter what I did, this stuff would come back again. And that just sucked.

I looked at the love seat under the wide front window. Bags of *stuff* were piled atop the cushions. Christmas shopping had been much more work than I'd ever expected. I mean, how the hell was I supposed to know what size bathrobe Thirteen wore? And Jon or Cordele or Marie and Charles…you'd think being able to hear someone's thoughts would give a person some insight into what they might want as a gift.

Yeah, right.

Thank God for the Nordstrom girl. The personal shopper had walked me through the store, top to bottom, pointing out all the traditional presents that people bought for one another. Of course, once she realized that money was no object, my options became much broader. I'd never actually seen Heather carry a purse, but the girl had insisted that the Stuart Weitzman tote was *the* must-have of the season, and that Heather would absolutely die if she didn't have it. Whatever.

An icy breeze shook the storm windows in the great room. The furnace moaned in protest. I reached over to snag another blanket off the ottoman and took another swig from my bottle of Beam. As I pulled on the blanket, papers fell to the floor.

What the—? A thin file of photos and papers lay scattered on the hardwood floor. Oh, crap—Colin's file. I'd completely forgotten to look over the stuff he and his team had gotten from Dr. Everett. Thirteen had called that afternoon about meeting again on Tuesday after Jon and Theo got back. He'd probably expect me to have at least opened the thing.

I shuffled the papers back together, settled under my mound of blankets, and used my mind to flick on another light. I glanced at the clock: 5:30 p.m. Night fell fast these days, and it was already growing dark outside. Still, it would be another few hours before Theo called to wish me sweet dreams and get me all excited with his phone talk—another not-a-boyfriend perk I'd discovered since he left. I might as well go through this stuff now and get it over with. Throwing back another gulp of whiskey, I began.

The first photo I saw stopped my heart. The second sent it plummeting to the floor. How had I not seen these? My mind flew as I flipped furiously through the rest of the photos, each page sending my stomach further into a free fall. Finally, I found the inventory list. The photos were of every confiscated artifact that Everett had smuggled into the country. Colin's handwritten notes pointed out those items that Everett's partner had indicated as holding particular interest for their prospective client.

No shit, they held interest for their prospective client. These were my father's tools. The ones that had left deep, burning impressions every time they'd been used. The tools in the pictures were cleaner, maybe a little newer, but they had the same hand-crafted style. The same deadly purposes.

My God, I had had these things used on me. I even knew their proper names. The A-frame Sweeper's Daughter—kind of a rack in reverse that locked the head, wrists, and ankles together in a compressed knot. Strappado cuffs and weights that hung victims by their locked hands behind their back and pulled them down with varying weights. My shoulders ached in memory of dislocation at just the sight of that one. Handsaws, awls, pliers— each one imprinted with the blackened double-X trademark that decorated everything Grandmother had passed down to her sons.

I dropped the file and raced to the bathroom. My stomach unloaded again and again. I closed my eyes, knowing that when I opened them again, everything would be red. I could feel the blood boiling inside me. Father had loved those tools. The humiliation of them, the pain they caused. Each time he pulled them out, a special gleam had shone in his eye. He hadn't used them every day; he'd liked to test his powers and the more modern instruments during his daily experiments. But if he suspected I'd developed a new ability, or if he and Uncle Max wanted to elicit a specific kind of fear in me, they'd roll out those ancient relics. And I'd known the pain would be unlike anything else.

The tools themselves were important. Things to be locked away and protected. I remembered Uncle Max had been livid the times he'd found out Father had used them on me without telling him beforehand. Uncle Max would rant and rave about how unworthy I was of their attention. As if the tools cared who they bled out.

I gripped the sides of the sink and focused on calming the throbbing in my head. When only a light-pink haze fuzzed my vision, I walked back to the living room. The file lay on the floor, the scattered images facedown on the rug.

Dragging my feet, I returned to my seat on the couch and stared down at the file. On the ottoman lay another paper. I could tell by the texture that it wasn't a photograph. Hand shaking, I took it and laid it in my lap.

With a deep breath, I scanned Colin's report. He'd first listed the details his team knew going into the mission. It wasn't much, especially now that I knew how a real mission was supposed to work. Then he outlined what they'd learned after interrogating the pyro smuggler.

Dr. Everett had worked within different branches of the Aunre Institute for the past seven years. According to Colin's notes, the Aunre Institute was a privately funded global foundation whose mission was to preserve the world's most valuable historical resources and provide a cultural outlet to those nations who might not otherwise experience the joys of being creative.

You know, just in case the starving kids in some war-torn third-world nation wanted to express themselves with acrylics instead of killing insurgents to protect their families.

Initially, Everett had insisted that he was the only supernatural at the institute. Why advertise you're a freak to your employer, he'd argued. After some time, however, and a little taste of Cordele's new truth serum, he'd corrected that statement. Turned out that Everett's partner, Ken Ward, as well as his direct supervisor at the institute, Dr. Mikel Grabowski, were both Network-known telekinetics. Once that little tidbit was revealed, Everett insisted that it was Ken Ward who'd set up the client meeting.

Everett had had no clue he was there to meet Senator Kelch. It was the only statement he never reneged on.

I skimmed through the rest of the interview notes and was about to toss the sheet back on the floor when the list of institute locations caught my eye. Among various other nations, Moldova, Ukraine, and Belarus came up. All three nations were listed as having Aunre Institute facilities.

OK, wait a minute. Hadn't Shane argued weeks ago that Father and Uncle Max would be stupid to build plants in all three nations because none of them had the money to support the industry? No way these countries had enough money to support some lame-ass cultural awareness program. Or to smuggle medieval torture tools across borders.

Unless…of course. They wouldn't need to put a facility in all three countries. They could just put it in one location and have access to all three nations' artifacts.

Bohlren.

I flipped open my laptop and accessed one of the sites that Heather had shown me how to use. Jon had homed in on the museums, but I'd thought he was just being a pain in my ass, interrupting my report. I pulled up the city's statistics, and there it was, like a flashing neon light: YAKIVIY i AUNRE МУЗЕЙ ГІСТОРЬІІ (THE YAKIVIY AND AUNRE MUSEUM OF HISTORY).

I threw back a long swig of whiskey and stared at the computer screen. I couldn't imagine how in the world Everett's connection to Bohlren and my father's ancient tools fit in with Kelch Inc. manufacturing facilities and whatever Jon and Theo were doing in Europe, but surely this was a coincidence Thirteen would want to know about.

An image of my twin flashed in my mind. Her soft, pretty face frowning in the bloody reflection of the lake. She'd wanted me to see the emblem burned onto her palm. The tools were important.

I didn't know why, but she'd needed me to recognize that symbol. And since she was a part of me, *I* needed me to make this connection.

A strange urgency churned in my stomach. I needed to go. Now. I wouldn't wait for Thirteen's call in the morning. I needed to get this new information to him right now.

Without looking at the photos again, I swept them back into the file folder, then quickly shoved my feet in my boots. Keys in one hand and file folder in the other, I'd just reached for the front door when the quiet alarm announced a car turning into my drive. My power went on vibrate. I reached out to the driver, and even though I recognized her, my instincts still screamed at me that something wasn't right.

CHAPTER 33

I stepped out onto the front porch and waited while Cordele parked along the side of the house. Engine off, she sat behind the wheel and gave herself a serious pep talk. She had to convince me, get me to understand. It was the only way. With a deep breath, she heaved herself from the car. As she moved around the house with purpose, she focused her thoughts. Over and over, she recited some silly poem about Henry the Eighth. *Second verse, same as the first.*

Power lit at my fingertips, my instincts on full defense mode. I had to stay calm. Cordele wasn't a threat. She was my teammate. Whatever had my power flaring, I had to stay in control.

I hadn't bothered turning on the porch light. Clouds hid the bright moon, but the fresh snow lit up the yard. I didn't make a sound. No breath, no shift of weight. When Cordele reached the porch, she skipped the first two cement steps and nearly ran right into me. Like a stone wall, I didn't budge.

"Oh!" she yelped. "I didn't see you, Magnolia." She stumbled backward into the yard.

My instincts had been raw the night of the gala, but I couldn't remember the last time they were ever this loud. Everything inside me screamed for me to attack. Right now, before it was too late. But I had absolutely no idea why.

"Why are you here, Cordele?"

Her eyes looked to the tree line, to the sky, to the ground—anywhere but me. "I, er, haven't seen you forever. Not since the night of the gala. I just wanted to stop by and see how you were doing."

Right.

"I—well." She cleared her throat. "Chang and I have been working hard to find connections between the data we got from your father's PC and the stuff we already had. You know, the flight information from Captain Bennett and all that. I thought maybe you'd want to know everything we'd found out."

"We already had that update meeting. You weren't there." And why was that? Thirteen had said she was meeting with an informant. Informing her of what?

"Yeah, I had another meeting…another Network team…"

"Thirteen said it was an informant."

"It was. An informant with information for another team's mission."

I felt the burn behind my eyes as my vision began turning red. My fingers itched, and I could feel the pull of my nails wanting to grow longer. Something was causing my powers to react just as they had when I'd first arrived at the gala. *Stay calm, just stay calm.* I couldn't control my instincts, but I could control my reactions. Isn't that what Theo had said?

"I was just about to leave," I replied coolly. "If you're just looking to visit, why don't you come with me and we can catch up in the car."

She didn't move. I narrowed my eyes.

"I'm going to ask you one more time, Cordele. What are you doing here?"

Her face went pale behind the haze of red clouding my vision. Her mouth opened and shut, but no noise came out. For the first time since she'd arrived, I really looked at her. She didn't wear a coat or even a jacket. She wore a bow-neck sweater that showed her shoulders. Her hair was down, her makeup applied perfectly, lips outlined in a full, pouty look. Tight jeans, heeled boots—she was dressed for going out.

"Where's the party?" I asked drily and moved forward down the steps. She stepped back.

"What? There's no party." She laughed humorlessly. Her hand moved toward the gun at her back—her own instincts kicking in.

"You know I'm going to find out why you're here, Cordele. You might as well just tell me. I really don't want to hurt you."

Her jaw lifted as her resolve set. Her lips thinned into a tight line. I'd warned her.

With a quick, sudden burst, I pushed my power into her mind. I tried to be gentle, but she cried out and fell to her knees, her fists clasped against either side of her head. In her mind, the last hours played out for me like a rewinding movie. She'd spent hours getting ready for tonight. Eager to come here, to get me on her side. She'd discovered something, something no one else would ever believe. She knew the real reason why the Kelches were so interested in Eastern Europe—and she had known for weeks. But she had to be careful. Play her cards right, or no one would ever take her seriously again. They'd call her a traitor, probably lock her up. But that was bullshit. After all, they believed in me, right? And I was a Kelch myself. Why shouldn't they believe her too?

The images in her mind shifted to an earlier date. Instead of jeans and boots, she wore capri pants and a lightweight cardigan sweater. In her hand, she examined one of the tools confiscated from Everett. Turning it side to side, she examined the trademark imprint burned into the steel.

But wait a minute. We'd just gotten those tools. How was she studying them in a memory? I focused more closely on the blade she held. Ancient in style with jagged, razor-sharp teeth on both sides, the foot-long knife weighed heavily in her hand. It was different from the tools I'd seen in Colin's file. The weapons Dr. Everett brought over had glistened with polish—the edges sharp, the handles clean. The one Cordele examined was covered in a thick coat of dried blood. The metal of the blade was rusted in some places, and cleaned at the hinges for continued use.

Bile churned inside me. This wasn't some smuggled artifact. This was one of Father's actual tools. She was holding one of the torture devices that had been used on me. That was *my* blood she brushed her fingertips over.

The shock made me pause, pull back enough from her mind that she fell forward, catching herself with her hands. She looked up at me, and I remembered just how strong she really was. I knew the mindsweep had sent pain coursing through her, but she refused to betray any sign of her hurt. She really was one of the strongest agents on Thirteen's team.

"It's not what you think, Magnolia," she said, her words a struggle. "You have to listen to me."

"There's only one way you could have gotten your hands on those tools. You've been to my family's estate."

"No. Magnolia, listen—"

I tore into her again. I had to know. This time she writhed on the ground, her body contorting as she screamed out in anguish. In her mind I saw the tools again, laid out on a kitchen table I didn't recognize. She lifted a set of needle-nose pliers, her hands shaking. Tears pooled in her eyes as she examined the tool under a fluorescent light. Another moment and she dropped it back on

NO LOVE FOR THE WICKED

the table. She turned away, disgust plain on her face. A deep voice spoke softly from behind her. Pinpricks needled over my flesh. In her memory, her horror instantly faded. Peace, serenity, and hope washed over her as that deep rumble continued murmuring close by. When she finally looked up, her face and mind had been completely transformed. Gone was the disgust of an intelligent, strong agent. In her place was a malleable, devoted woman whose eyes shone with complete and utter adoration.

She'd turned in to the chest of the man behind her, eager to take comfort in the warm, strong hands that pulled her close. His deep voice continued lulling her with mumbled explanations about stolen tools that had only ever caused pain. A pain that she needed to help him put to an end.

When she finally pulled back, her eyes moved slowly toward the man's face. My body coiled to attack. Ice ran through my veins, painful against the heat of my fiery power.

No, it was impossible. This was Cordele. One of the most loyal, intelligent agents Thirteen had. We'd been in explosions together, shopped together. She was awkwardly trying to be my friend. Hell, I'd saved her life, like, three times already. There had to be an explanation. If I could just hold my instincts in check, let her explain…

Reluctantly, I returned to her memory. She drew out the vision of the man before her. The silk fabric of a custom-made designer shirt, the thick tendons of an olive-toned throat. Cordele licked her lips at the smooth jawline, the full, perfect mouth so similar to my own.

By the time she reached his eyes, my hands were fully changed. Claws stretched and curled into fists at my sides. My jaw ached as my teeth fought to sharpen in my mouth. In her mind, she sighed as the monster cradling her came into sight.

Malcolm. My older brother.

"Oh, Cordele. What have you done?"

CHAPTER 34

Snow looked like drops of blood falling softly on Cordele's weeping body. When I'd pulled out of her mind completely, she'd collapsed against the pain. I'd gone too deep and torn too harshly for her to bounce back anytime soon. Damn it, now I felt guilty.

When she finally found the strength to lift her head and attempt to glare at me, one look at my face had her falling back in a weak crab-walk, scurrying away from me in a horrified cower. I rolled my stinging eyes.

"What did you expect, Cordele? You've been at my family's estate. You're all cuddled up with my brother. Did you think I'd be happy about that? Jesus Christ, what are you thinking?"

"Magnolia," she said, her voice both overly reasonable and trembling with urgency. "Just listen. You remember when I was taken to your family's estate last year. When I was tortured by your brother Markus until you courageously broke through your family's security and rescued me and the others."

"Don't even think about kissing my ass right now, Cordele."

She started over. "That experience changed me. I never really trusted you until that moment. When you killed your brother and Banks to save Thirteen and the rest of us, it was like a light going off for me. You really weren't some double agent for your family, like Marie and Charles always thought. You were a part of our team. A real agent trying to destroy your family, just like the rest of us."

My fingers flexed at my sides, the leathery skin pulling taut. Where was she going with this?

"You were an inspiration to me…"

A snarl vibrated from my chest. "You're kissing ass again."

She shook her head quickly. "I mean it. Being at the estate like that—it confirmed for me that everything you'd said about your family was true. They really had tortured you. Heck, while I was captured, Markus even talked about some of the things he'd watched your father and uncle do to you." She swallowed hard. I raised my eyebrows impatiently.

"I barely survived what Markus and his guards did to me. But you, you not only walked away—you joined the Network to keep them from doing it to other people. I respect you, Magnolia. You have to know that."

OK, I wasn't nearly the humanitarian she was making me out to be. Hell, if Thirteen hadn't been the one Markus had captured, no way I would have returned to the estate just to rescue her and some other agents. But her sincerity rang true. I didn't sense any feelings of guilt or disloyalty from her—only anxiety mixed with varying degrees of fear.

"What I know is that you are a liar." She cringed as if I'd slapped her. "All this time you've been blocking your thoughts from me, I left you alone about it because Heather thought you wanted to be my friend. But I can't trust someone if I can't see inside them. It never occurred to me that you were betraying not only me but the entire Network. God, Cordele. Working with my brother? How could you even do that?"

Her lower lip quivered. The tears in her eyes weren't from the lingering pain of my mindsweep. After a moment, she swallowed hard and lifted her chin. "I've never betrayed my team or my mission. I'm the most dedicated agent Thirteen has. You *can* trust me."

"Bullshit! I saw your memories. I saw you curled up with Malcolm. God, I don't even want to think about all the Network information you've passed on to him."

"I never passed on anything! Not about our team and certainly not about you. I would never betray our mission like that. Malcolm has been helping *me*. He's the one passing information on to me."

Jesus Christ, she really believed that. It was plain as day all over her mind. She truly believed she'd found the perfect inside informant in my brother. And Thirteen had thought *I* was naive when it came to relationship shit.

She pushed herself to standing, holding herself up on unsteady legs. With a swipe of her hand, she pushed the snow and tears from her face. "Think about it, Magnolia. Everything your father and uncles did to you—the torture, the degradation. You had to escape the only home you've ever known just to get away from the daily persecution. Malcolm is the same way. He's just not as strong as you are. He has to fight them in secret. If he ever tried to escape—"

"Wait. What?"

"Your brother Malcolm." She took a deep breath to steel herself. "You were right. I have met with him. Not at the estate," she said quickly, "but at secured locations." She sighed. "He found me right after that whole thing with Markus. While the

FBI questioned your father and uncles, he snuck out and went to the hospital to see if any of Markus's prisoners had survived. Your family knew we were all with the Network, and Malcolm figured this was his best chance to get in with us, to help stop your family. He saw me leave the hospital and followed me home. When he surprised me on the front steps of my house, at first I was terrified. I knew who he was, and I tried to shoot him right then and there. But then we looked into each other's eyes, and it was just…" Her voice turned dreamy, and I wanted to vomit.

Yeah, I bet everything changed the moment she'd looked into his eyes. His mental manipulation powers weren't nearly as strong as mine or Uncle Max's. He had to look his victims in the eyes to turn their minds to his will.

"He's the one who gave me the formula to develop the truth serum we use," she continued eagerly. "He's the one who got us the invitations to the gala. He wants out of your family as much as you did, but he can't escape the way you did. He can't fake his death and run away. His father and the senator would come looking for him. They need him, Magnolia."

My chest burned, and I realized I'd stopped breathing. This was so bad. The lies she was remembering him telling her, the stories she believed so completely. *Oh God.* Malcolm had completely scrambled her logic.

"Cordele, listen to me very carefully." My eyes were still red, and my hands were still claws, but maybe if I kept the sincerity in my voice, she'd see past all that and actually hear me. "You are the smartest person on our team, and I need you to use that big brain of yours to understand what I am saying. Cordele, Malcolm has used his powers on you. He's lied to you. He has never helped you or anyone else. Ever. Whatever information he's passed on to you, he did with his own agenda."

She shook her head. "No, Magnolia, you're wrong. I know him now. I know what he's been through. He hates your family as much as you do for what they did to you and him."

"They never did anything to him!" And if her mind wasn't totally twisted right now, she'd remember that.

Cordele flinched again. I took a deep breath. "Cordele, Malcolm has never been tortured a day in his life. He tortured me. And I'm not talking about him just sitting there and watching while Father did his thing—I can see that's what you're thinking right now. He participated, Cordele, in nearly all the stuff that Father did to me. Hell, he'd seek me out so he could hurt me on his own."

Still she shook her head. In her thoughts she replayed all the tales he'd told her: how Father had forced him to watch my punishments, how he himself had been used in Father's experiments, cut and beaten. I tasted blood as my teeth fought to turn into fangs.

"Lies!" I hissed. Cordele pulled out her gun. Holding it in both hands, she aimed it at the ground in front of me. Fortunately, I was too pissed off to care. "Father never laid a hand on that bastard. Never bled him, never beat him. Nothing. If Father had even attempted to do half the shit to him that was done to me, Malcolm would have been dead years ago. Instead, Malcolm cut me and gutted me—and the prick got off on it! My God, you are not this fucking stupid. He's the one who killed me, for Christ's sake!"

"Apparently not."

The clear satisfaction in his deep voice came from behind me and froze me in place. *Motherfucker.* I'd been so wrapped up in my shock and anger at Cordele that I hadn't even felt his energy in the air. But I felt it now. Cold, arrogant, calculating. This was the reason my powers were acting up right now. Malcolm was here.

Son of a bitch.

Chapter 35

Slowly I turned. Cordele and I had moved farther into the yard than I'd realized. Malcolm stood right in front of the porch steps, a good twenty feet away from me. My breath caught as a slew of memories crashed into me: the cracking laughter of an adolescent as Father showed him how to bind me with chains in the old horse barn; his tireless whining at dinners, while I hid motionless behind the draperies, begging to be given a chance to bleed me on his own; the sick, endless games of hide-and-seek where his lust-filled thoughts always preceded his painful gropes.

It had been over a year since he and Markus decapitated me and buried me under Uncle Mallroy's shed. Weak-ass morons had had to shoot me in the back with a tranq dart to get me down. Neither was powerful enough to take me out on his own. Standing before me now, the bastard was more handsome than ever. Taller than me by a good couple of inches, dark-blond hair waving in the snowy breeze. Polo cologne wafted all around him, so thick I had to swallow back my gag reflex. Thick eyebrows over deep-set eyes, a jaw so similar to Father's it should be broken on principle. Only his nose disrupted an otherwise flawless set of features—I'd shattered his face too many times defending myself for it to have been set perfectly.

Malcolm's thoughts were churning. A raw smugness warred with a remembered hesitancy. My family thought I was dead and that he had killed me. He'd seen vague images of a Network agent with supernatural powers when he intruded on Cordele's thoughts—a flash of hair, a shot of speed—but nothing concrete about who I really was. She'd protected my identity, after all, just like she said.

So then why wasn't he surprised to see me?

My eyes flared, and my claws curled. He took a step back. His thoughts narrowed with a steady stream of *Ohshitohshit-ohshitohshit!* I smiled. Of all my family, only Markus had ever seen my beastly transformation, and that was right before I'd ripped out his throat. Malcolm, the piece of shit, should be scared.

His fear only lasted a moment, though, before he masked it with that arrogant look I knew so well. He tugged on his heavy black trench coat and squared his shoulders.

"Magnolia," he said with an annoying air of satisfaction. "I knew it was you. When we found Markus in that barn, his throat shredded like that, I knew it had to be you. No matter what Uncle Max said about not sensing your powers anymore."

He raked his gaze over me, and my stomach clenched in revulsion. How many times had he scanned me like that, his thoughts eager to start touching me?

"I have to admit, though," he continued, "this new look isn't the most attractive I've seen you."

I hissed, my teeth straining. Malcolm flinched before he could help it, then forced himself to stand his ground. A new calculation gleamed in his eyes. *Still alive and with more powers. Father's going to shit himself.*

Before I knew what I was doing, I picked up Cordele's car with my mind and threw it at him. A few feet away, Cordele screamed. Malcolm stepped out of the way, using the same supernatural speed I had. But when he did, the car hit the ground hard, skidding in the snow, straight toward Cordele. She'd inched her way to the side of the yard, moving toward the house.

Shit! I diverted the car into a small tree to keep it from crashing into her.

"Temper, temper, Magnolia." I felt the chill of Malcolm's power slide along my thoughts. "You don't want to hurt our lovely Cordele, do you?" he purred. "Your teammate? Your friend?" He twisted his mouth in a way that told me just how little he really thought of her. "And you don't really want to kill me either. Not when I'm here to help you."

A whip of power slashed across his chest, tearing a nice, satisfying hole through his cashmere sweater. He countered instantly; a smack of power slapped across my face, leaving my cheek throbbing. *Shit!* I'd forgotten how much stronger he was than Markus. I balled my clawed hands and forced myself not to attack. I needed Cordele out of there. Malcolm and I were going to battle it out—right here, right now. If she hung around while we went at it, there was no way she'd get away without being hurt.

With a not-so-subtle push, I directed her thoughts. Get in her banged-up car and leave. Drive to Thirteen, head to Charles and Marie's, whatever—just go.

She didn't move. I pushed again.

Nothing.

As if sensing what I was doing, Malcolm smiled. *You can't touch her mind,* his thoughts slithered through my head. *She's mine now.*

I tried again. Sure enough, there was a block there. I could read her thoughts but not direct them. *Damn it!* How did he do that?

"Cordele," I growled out. My teeth were painful to speak around now. "You have to get out of here."

She stood several feet away, gun in hand, watching as Malcolm and I squared off. At my words, she moved quickly. But not to her newly dented car. She moved to stand directly in front of Malcolm, blocking him from me.

"You have to listen to us, Magnolia," she pleaded. "Malcolm isn't the same person you remember him to be."

The utter adoration that I'd seen in her memories was back. It was as if the brainy Network agent I'd known for the past year was gone.

"Jesus Christ, Malcolm, what have you done to her?"

From inside the farmhouse, the shrill sound of Alannah Myles's "Black Velvet" rang out. I'd just customized the song as Theo's ringer in my cell phone yesterday. Instantly a surge of warmth shot through me, swelling my power like a pulse. Malcolm's eyes went wide. I slammed down my mental walls, but the flashed thought of my connection to Theo had been too strong in my mind.

Malcolm moved behind Cordele, snaking his arm around her waist. The new calculation shining in his eyes made me want to scream.

"It's not what I've done to her, Magnolia. It's what she's done to me. We have a connection, you see, Cordele and I. She strengthens me, gives me purpose. Surely *you* can understand that, can't you?"

How dare he make up a lie based on what I had with Theo! A hard growl erupted from my chest. Cordele's mind swirled. She remembered image after image of me and Theo: the noticeable strength that Theo now had as a result of our being closer; the energy that had poured over the entire team that first time we'd been reunited after my return. Did she give that same power to Malcolm? The very idea of it had her snuggling into him, holding his arms around her.

Malcolm smiled at me, content that his lie had sealed her even closer to his side.

Fuck! Now how was I going to kill him without hurting her?

"He knows what your father and uncle are doing, Magnolia," Cordele pleaded. "He wants to help us stop them."

Over her shoulder, Malcolm smirked. I ground my teeth and tasted blood as my fangs finally broke through. "God damn it, Cordele, wake up! It's all a lie. You have no connection with him. He couldn't care less about you. You have to leave before you get hurt."

She held tighter to his arm. "Just listen. What your father and Senator Kelch are doing in Russia and those other countries has nothing to do with manufacturing facilities. They're trying to grow their power—their *real* power, not just their political and economical foothold. This is so much more than what Thirteen and Jon think."

Behind her Malcolm suddenly grew serious. "She's right, Magnolia. This isn't about Kelch Incorporated. This is about us." In his mind I saw Father's tools again. "You remember the tools, don't you?"

I curled my lip. "Are you kidding me? You used one of Father's blades to cut off my head!"

Cordele straightened. She hadn't known that. Malcolm just waved it off. "I was a different person then." She instantly calmed. *Moron.* "It's the symbol on them that's important, Magnolia. Do you have any idea what those tools are?"

Something inside me hesitated, and the man from my dreams flashed in my mind. "They came from Grandmother," I said slowly. "She used them to punish Father, Uncle Max, and Uncle Mallroy when they were young. Then she gave them to Father to use on me before she died."

Malcolm frowned. Whereas my ability to crawl through people's minds had been there at birth, his had developed over time. He hadn't gotten all the background stories that had played through Father's head over the years. He'd never realized that Grandmother—the sick bitch that she was—had used the same torture tools on Father that he'd used on me. And to show just how twisted a fuck my older brother really was, he actually felt a twinge of jealousy that the tools hadn't been used on him. Like he'd missed out on some family tradition or something.

"God, what the hell is wrong with you?"

He cleared his head and glared. "The point is: Where did Grandmother get them? They're family heirlooms. They had to come from somewhere, and it sure as hell wasn't her side of the family." For a moment all arrogance fled Malcolm's face. "I'm not enough for them anymore, Magnolia. They need more."

It took me a minute, but I finally understood what he was saying. It was all about the bloodline, the way our powers grew stronger when we were near one another. Separate, Father and our uncles were each a force to be reckoned with, but when the three of them were together, they were virtually unstoppable. Father's telekinesis jumped from car battery to nuclear power plant. Uncle Max's telepathy could create an entire city of zombies if he wanted. Uncle Mallroy could shape-shift into anything—at least, I think he could; his powers were always hard to figure out. But whatever their strongest ability, they needed the power of their family to keep themselves at their strongest. It was why Father had had children in the first place, and why he had experimented with other supernaturals. Like his Marlena.

Uncle Max had been completely against any of them procreating, terrified that they'd inadvertently create a child more powerful than even them. But Father's need for more had ultimately won out.

Of course, in the end, Uncle Max had been right. I was more powerful than any of them combined. And according to Malcolm's thoughts, when I died—or rather, escaped—their power levels had taken a bigger hit than they expected. And then I'd killed Markus. All that was left now was Malcolm. If what he said was true—and judging by the anger and fear pouring out of him, I had a feeling it was—his presence wasn't providing enough juice to keep their power at the level they were used to. They wanted more.

I remembered facing off with Father during the gala, the eagerness he'd felt when he'd realized I could strengthen him. All those years of torturing me and trying to kill me—it had never occurred to them just how much the presence of my power had been affecting them.

My cell phone rang out again. The urge to run in there and hear Theo's voice was nearly too tremendous to suppress. But I had other things to deal with at the moment.

"What does that have to do with the tools?" My voice was almost normal. My teeth had receded a bit. I curled my fists. *Yep, still claws. Good.*

"It's what they're doing in Bohlren and those other places," Cordele explained. "They are looking for more of those tools because they think they will yield them more power."

I cocked a brow at my brother. He rolled his eyes behind Cordele's back. *Father doesn't think the tools will make them stronger*, he whispered with his thoughts. *He knows our power doesn't come from inanimate objects. The man's not an idiot.* We'd have to disagree on that one. *It's the symbol. They're searching for the maker of the tools.*

A new fluttering began to brew inside me. Were they really thinking what I thought they were thinking?

Grandfather, his thoughts said. *They're trying to find where we came from, Magnolia.*

Against my will, the pounding of my heart went into overdrive. A tempered excitement seeped into my chest. It was something I'd never thought about while I lived on the estate. My life was nothing but pain there. It had never mattered who I was or where my powers came from. But now everything had changed.

"What have they found? Tell me, Malcolm."

He paused. His arm around Cordele's waist tightened as he brought his free hand up to caress her collarbone. She turned her head in to him, nuzzling against his touch.

"Unfortunately, you know as much as I do. I really have been helping your team, Magnolia. I want to know where we came from just as much as you do."

I narrowed my eyes. "Why? Father never hurt you. No one did. You've always gotten everything you ever wanted. Hell, you even work for Kelch Inc."

"From home, you idiot. I work from home where they can keep me on their tight, short leash. I'm thirty-two years old, and the only time I ever get to leave the estate is when they are out of the country. I'm as much a prisoner to their powers as you were."

"That is such fucking bullshit, and you know it."

He stepped back and took Cordele with him. She squeaked as his grip turned tight. Damn it, he was going to seriously hurt her. She might not believe it, but I sure as hell did. I took a deep breath, tempered my powers again.

"I want them dead, Magnolia," he said, surprising me with his boldness. "You don't know what it's been like since Markus died. They never let us leave before, not even to go to college. But now they're fanatical about it. Their guards lock me in my wing every fucking night. I work for Kelch Inc., but I barely get to speak to anyone. I'm a senior vice president, for Christ's sake, and I've only ever met my staff via video conference. Hell, I didn't even get to go to the Winter Gala!"

His jaw dropped open as his mind suddenly connected the dots. "You were there. With Cordele and her other teammates. Oh my God—you were the one with the power that Father felt. It was all he talked about when he got home that night. He and Uncle Max spent the entire next day locked in their offices, trying to figure out who you were." His face was suddenly transformed with renewed anger. "Fuck them! You got to go to the gala, and I was stuck in that fucking house? They have to die, Magnolia. All of them."

Maybe he and Cordele really would make a good couple, after all. They were both completely delusional.

"You do not honestly expect me to feel sorry for you? Oh, poor baby. Daddy locks him in his two-thousand-square-foot wing every night. He wasn't allowed to go to the fancy party and get drunk and laid."

"It's more than that, and you know it."

"Do I?" My teeth were growing again. "How many times were you hung from one of Mallroy's barns and bled out, Malcolm? How many times were you stripped naked and beaten and left for dead, only to be ignored by the groundskeepers because Father told them if they helped you, they'd be gutted too?" I stepped forward, flexed my claws again, and enjoyed the stretch of their leathery pull. "How many times did you have to hide from your brothers because they wanted to tie you down and rape you?"

Cordele gasped.

"I never raped you," Malcolm said quickly.

"Only because I was too powerful and beat you back every time you tried."

"But don't you see, all of that is just more reason to kill them. They turned us into what we are." He looked pointedly at my claws. "You can't honestly tell me you enjoy being what you are."

"*Fuck you!*" It came out as a harsh snarl. Cordele cowered into Malcolm's chest, but this time he didn't flinch.

"No, Magnolia, fuck them. They are this close to finding out where we came from. They've tracked down those tools and are almost there. I've given Cordele all the information I have on where they're going, but I can get more. Think about it. If they find where we came from—the source of our powers—they can figure out how to use it. They'll be able to make themselves stronger than ever. They'll be invincible. But if *we* find the source first…"

His eyes filled with that glassy, hopeful gleam you see in mental patients when they think they've found a sympathetic ear.

"We can do it if we work together, Magnolia. They're looking for the maker of those tools, the man they believe will lead them to Grandfather. Our powers came from him. We always knew that. But now they are really going to find him. All we have to do is find him first. Neither of us is strong enough to kill them on our own. But if we work together, we can finally end this nightmare of our lives. Forever."

CHAPTER 36

For a moment, I almost fell for it. So many strange and incredible things had happened to me since my escape: becoming a real member of Thirteen's Network team, my teammates accepting me—hell, even Marie had come to me for help. Most of all, Theo had happened. That the connection with him had turned into a real relationship made almost anything seem possible—even the idea of fighting alongside my brother to defeat Father and Uncle Max once and for all.

As we stood across from each other, the icy trees glistening under the peaking moonlight and my little farmhouse covered in the softly falling snow, so precious in the background, I could almost see it.

"We could keep Mallroy alive," he said, finalizing the plans in his head. "He's nothing but a retard anyway. And we could use him just like Father and Uncle Max have always used us: to fuel our power with his proximity. Hell, he probably wouldn't even care anyway, as long as we let him keep his stupid pets."

As he spoke, he pictured it all in his mind. First he'd use Cordele's Network team to find the toolmaker and Grandfather. Then he'd manipulate Grandfather into strengthening his power. I wouldn't really need to have my power strengthened because, well, look at me. With those claws and eyes, I was already more powerful than anyone in the family knew. After that, he'd have me kill Grandfather. There was no chance of me dying, after all, and even with Grandfather's powers to boost his own, Malcolm couldn't be sure that his own immortality would be guaranteed. Then he'd turn on Uncle Max. Malcolm would rip out our uncle's throat himself, just like Markus's throat had been ripped out. God, the power I must have felt in that moment!

As his mind raced, he let out the barest of slips. As Theo had pointed out so many times, people can't control their errant thoughts and reactions. And Malcolm, with all his power growing stronger by the minute, was still just a person like the rest of us.

For the briefest moment, his mind went to Father. Father and son, together. Conquering the world with their powers. Father would be so proud of him. Malcolm's power, his initiative, his ability to finally destroy the one thing Father had never been able to destroy: me.

He met my eyes. The vision left his mind instantly, shifting to what he'd originally said about the two of us destroying Father and Uncle Max together. But it was too late. I saw. And he knew it.

We moved at the exact same moment. I lunged forward, claws out and mouth suddenly full of fangs. Just as fast, he pushed Cordele toward me. I swerved at the last second to keep my outstretched claws from digging into her. She fell to the ground, and I kept going.

Malcolm moved with lightning speed, retreating to the side yard. When I came around the house, he ambushed me. With a solid punch to the gut, he sent me flying into the nearby woods. Ice and limbs tore into me as I plowed into the thick woods. I was back on my feet instantly. Jaw open, claws ready, I flew into him. Arms around his waist, I dug my claws into his back. He screamed as we slammed into Cordele's car. As we banged into the windshield, my grip was knocked loose, just enough for him to get both feet between us and kick me back into the air. I landed hard against the wall of the house, tearing into the siding and denting the brick underneath.

"That's my house, you piece of shit!"

He stood glaring at me, fists tight at his sides. "It's the house that's a piece of shit."

The night I'd fought Markus flashed in my mind. The crazed look on his scarred face, the maniacal tremor in his voice. Malcolm had none of that. His mind was just as calm and shrewd as ever. *Damn it.*

I jumped to my feet and met his glare. In a move so fast I couldn't track it, he picked up Cordele's car and threw it at me. It slammed into the house, shattering the remaining windows on that side. I moved out of the way just in time for Malcolm to body slam me into the car. He pinned my arms to my side so I couldn't use my claws. But his face was right in front of mine. I felt my jaw stretch as I leaned into him and clamped down hard. My fangs dug into his cheeks and chin. I felt the bones break as his blood filled my mouth. My already-red vision went dark with his screams; his blood slid thickly down my throat. God, it tasted so good. The bloody place inside me roared.

Pain bit into the side of my head. Once, twice, three times in quick bursts until I had no choice but to release Malcolm's shredded and shattered face. I turned with a snarl to find Cordele no more than ten feet away, gun in hand, aimed right at me. Malcolm dropped to the ground. Cordele shouted, but even this close I couldn't understand her. She pulled the trigger. Pain sliced my throat. I stumbled back against the car and heard the pop of her gun explode again.

Heat washed over me. I was flying. High in the air for a long moment before crashing to the ground several feet into the woods. I shook myself, ears ringing, and blinked until I could see again. I turned on my back and winced at the raw, overwhelming pain. I was shot. And burned. Badly. Would have been nice to land in the snow rather than the hard, dirty woods floor.

Slowly I got to my feet. As I moved, I realized the entire back side of me—legs, back, shoulders—was completely scorched. As if I'd somehow been set on fire.

When a boom from my farmhouse shook the air, I realized that's exactly what had happened. *Son of a bitch!* That piece of shit had set my house on fire! Markus had developed a type of pyrotechnic ability before he'd died; I should have suspected that Malcolm would grow a similar power.

Stumbling quickly through the trees, I got to the clearing just in time to see Cordele's car shoot into the air as the fire that had encompassed my home hit the gas furnace inside.

I scanned the area, but through the smoke and soot I couldn't see Malcolm anywhere. Movement by the trees near the back of the house caught my eye. Instantly I appeared across the lawn, ready to continue my fight. "You piece of shit! I'm going to tear you to shreds…"

But it wasn't Malcolm.

"Oh my God! Cordele!"

Skin black and bleeding, hair singed to the scalp, she could barely lift her hand as I knelt down beside her. "Just keep breathing, Cordele. I can heal you, just keep breathing." She grabbed my wrist. A gurgle escaped her throat, but her injuries were too great. She couldn't speak. "It's OK. It'll be OK."

I put my hand against the charred flesh of her chest. Heat and smoke filled the air around us, making it hard to take a deep breath. I'd just started to concentrate my powers into the worst of her injuries when her thoughts stopped me.

I'm so sorry, Magnolia. I'm so sorry.

"Stop it. This isn't your fault. Malcolm's the one who tricked you into thinking you should trust him. He's the one who destroyed my house."

No, it was me. I—I couldn't let you kill him. I couldn't let you...I love him, Magnolia.

Then I saw how she'd shot me in the head while I bit down on Malcolm's face. How she had continued shooting at me after I let go until one of the stray bullets had hit her car, exploding the wreckage against my house.

For a long moment I just stared at her. She'd helped Malcolm escape. After everything she'd heard between us—the things I'd accused him of that he hadn't even bothered denying—she still chose to save him over me. She gurgled again.

I pushed my elongated palm to her chest again and started to send my power into her wounds.

You're still going to heal me? she asked.

"I'm a Network agent, Cordele. And I'm not answering to Thirteen or Heather or anyone else about why I let another agent die when I had the chance to save her. Even if that agent is a backstabbing traitor like you."

She stopped me again.

No, Magnolia. It's too late.

"Not for me, it's not." I kept pushing. She winced as the heat of my energy seeped into her. I knew it was painful, but damn it, she deserved a little pain right now.

Magnolia, stop! I paused. *I don't want you to save me. It's too late. You'll tell Thirteen what I did. I'll be kicked out of the Network.* She lifted her head, just barely, and darted her eyes about. They filled up, and her watery gaze met my eyes. The glistening anguish I saw there made my own chest ache. *He didn't come back for me,* she thought. *I thought for sure he'd come back for me.*

That's when I realized it was more than being kicked out of the Network or labeled a traitor. She didn't want to live, knowing that Malcolm would leave her there to die—that he didn't really love her the way she loved him. In that instant, her heart was broken as badly as her body. But I didn't have any powers to heal that.

Wincing, she took the hand I had on her chest and held it in her own. She looked at me as tears streamed down her blackened cheeks. *I'm so sorry.*

With my precious home burning behind us, snow falling among the ash and smoke, Cordele died holding my hand.

CHAPTER 37

The fire trucks arrived in a caravan with the police and ambulance. By the time Thirteen and my team showed up, nothing was left of my little farmhouse but the cement porch and charred fireplace.

I sat on the bumper of the ambulance, totally numb. I had healed my gunshot wounds—there was nothing left but some tender spots in my head and neck. I couldn't explain to the EMTs why I didn't need any treatment for the slow-healing burns on my back, so I accepted some topical ointment and bandages.

Thirteen jogged up to me with Shane, Heather, and Marie right on his heels. Charles went over to talk to the police, anxious to get as many details as possible. Apparently luck was on our side for the moment. Detective Pryor, a Network operative as well as a decorated member of the IPD, had been the first on the scene and knew exactly how to report the unexplainable to his superiors.

Thirteen waited until the medics were out of earshot. "What happened? Are you OK?"

"It was Malcolm. He was Cordele's informant."

Thirteen straightened. His mind, full of worry when he'd first arrived, slammed shut behind mental walls. "Your brother was here? He did this to your home?"

I shrugged. "Actually, Cordele started the fire when she tried to shoot me and hit her car's gas tank instead."

"Why would Cord try to shoot you?" Shane asked. The accusation in his voice made my fists curl. I winced and relaxed my hands again. Nice normal hands now, although the stretched-out skin was still painfully sore.

"She did shoot me, several times actually." I brushed a finger over the tender spots at my temple. "And she was trying to shoot me again because I was about to kill Malcolm. He tricked her into thinking she loved him. She didn't know what she was doing. I tried to heal her, but—"

"Or maybe she knew exactly what she was doing," Shane interrupted. "Maybe she shot you because she realized just how much of a threat you really are. The only body the firemen found was Cordele's. If your brother was here, why isn't he burned to a crisp somewhere nearby? You always said you were the only one with the power to heal yourself. Was that a lie too, Magnolia?"

Power spiked under my skin. But before I could do anything, Thirteen had Shane by the collar and hauled him out of my line of sight. *Good.* I'd had enough of delusional team members for one night.

"He's upset, Magnolia," Heather explained softly, holding my hand. "His emotions are so confused right now. He's upset about Cordele, but at the same time he's so happy you're OK. For some reason that pisses him off more than anything else. Just ignore him."

I looked at Marie. She leaned against the ambulance door, arms folded over her chest, silent.

"What about you? You think everything I said was a lie? That maybe I'm the one who's been working with Malcolm and just decided on a whim that it was time to end Cordele's life? It would certainly go along with everything else you've ever thought about me."

She narrowed her eyes. Her soft leather coat wrinkled against the lingering heat of the explosion. After a long moment, she said, "No, I don't think you're lying. Cordele's been acting strange for weeks now. And I know for a fact she had a new boyfriend that she didn't want any of us to meet. No, I believe you, Magnolia." *I have to.* She didn't say the last out loud, but it was clear in her mind.

Guess I could understand that. I had promised to do what I could right before her next ovulation cycle, and she needed to believe that deep down I wasn't a killer who would betray our team.

I leaned back and closed my eyes, exhaustion sweeping over me.

My brother was still out there. Was he nearby? Watching? I doubted it. I couldn't sense him anywhere. Anyway, he would have run home with his tail between his legs, ready to nurse his wounds in the comfortable luxury of the estate. Did he even care that Cordele had died saving his life? I doubted that too. Whatever moment of delusion I'd experienced, thinking that maybe he and I could work together to bring down Father and Uncle Max, I'd seen past to the heart of who he really was. Caring for someone like Cordele just wasn't in his blood.

And yet, somehow, it was in mine.

After what seemed like years, Detective Pryor took my statement. Since I refused to go to the hospital, the medics finally released me. Or rather, they released Miss Maggie Alvin. Couldn't have any records of a dead Kelch daughter running around, now could we.

"You're staying with me," Heather announced. "Jon and Theo won't be back until Sunday night, so I have the whole house to myself."

I nodded until I met Thirteen's gaze.

"It might be easier for her to come back with me," he said earnestly. "She'll need somewhere to stay for longer than a couple nights. Might as well get settled now, Magnolia, until you figure out whether or not you want to rebuild or do something else with the land."

Heather shuffled her feet. She had felt what was happening between Theo and me, and Jon had told her just how official we were now. She had no doubt where I'd be staying once they returned from Bohlren.

I touched Thirteen's arm. "Thank you, but I'll stay with Heather for the weekend. After that, I already have someplace to stay longer term."

He stared down at me. The moment he realized where I planned on staying, his jaw tightened. An image of his daughter flashed in his mind but then quickly disappeared, as if he'd suddenly realized the memory didn't apply anymore. "You should rebuild this place," he said shortly. "The land is still yours. It would be a shame to waste the property."

I smiled. "I plan to rebuild. And if you have the time, maybe you could help me find some contractors."

He visibly relaxed. "I have a couple people I've used in the past."

"I'd appreciate the help."

He placed his hand on mine and gave me a light squeeze. As the fire trucks drove away, we stared at the remains of the little farmhouse. Cordele's face was in everyone's mind. Her sharp eyes, her dark roots. She'd shot me to save my brother. Now she was dead, and I hadn't done anything to stop it. How was I supposed to feel about that? Because right then, I just felt numb.

Since my car had been destroyed in the explosion along with everything else, I climbed into Heather's passenger seat and stared out the window as we drove the long length of my driveway. For the second time in my life, I was leaving my home in shredded clothes with absolutely nothing to call my own.

Heather reached over and squeezed my hand where it lay on my leg. She didn't say a word, but she didn't really need to. I might not have any possessions left to my name, but I guess this time I couldn't really say I had absolutely nothing.

CHAPTER 38

I sat on the floor in front of the L-shaped couch, Theo's legs on either side of me. He leaned forward in his seat, arms on knees, playing with the tips of my hair. Jon and Heather's Christmas tree glowed with twinkling white lights, Christmas-card perfect.

Since all the presents I'd bought had burned up along with all my clothes, Heather and I had spent most of yesterday at the mall. I'd tried to buy all the same things I had before, but when Heather saw how much my presents had cost, she'd nearly choked.

"You don't have to buy the most expensive of everything," she'd said, aghast.

"Why not? Look, the only conversation I ever had with my mother was her telling me about an anonymous bank account with all her family's money. I'll never be able to spend it all in this lifetime, even if I build ten houses where the farmhouse used to be. Father doesn't know about any of it, so seriously, why not?"

She hadn't really been able to come up with an argument for that one. Especially when she'd spotted the display of the new line of Birkin bags the store was carrying for a limited time only.

Theo's fingers brushed against my neck, making the butterflies in my tummy sing. I looked back at him and smiled. He tried to smile back, but just like every other time since he'd come charging into Heather and Jon's house last night, the smile got stuck halfway, never quite reaching his eyes.

I should have been here, he thought for the thousandth time.

It wouldn't have changed anything, I reminded him again.

You would have been stronger. You wouldn't have been burned and shot. You'd still have your home.

No, the only difference would have been that you would have gotten hurt too.

He ran a hand over my hair. *I felt you. All the way on the other side of the world, I felt your anger and hurt.*

And I felt you when you called.

Thirteen entered from the entry hallway, cutting off our silent conversation. We were all there now. I looked around the room. Heather and Jon were in the kitchen, stacking plates and gathering utensils for the mouthwatering spread on the dining room table. Shane sat in the corner, every now and then responding to something Charles or Marie said from their seats nearby.

On the floor by the TV, Chang and Tony dug through Jon's video game collection. Heather had warned me last night that Thirteen had permanently assigned Tony and Luce to our team, even though Luce was out of town visiting family for the holiday. Apparently Colin was reconsidering his role within the Network, leaving his team available for new assignments. It would be a test of my emotional control to work with Luce.

"Let's make this fast," Jon said, wiping powdered sugar off his pant legs as he took a seat on the sofa. "The roast is keeping warm in the oven, but the casserole will dry out if we don't serve it soon."

"Listen to Betty Crocker over there," Theo teased.

"You know it," Jon replied, swinging his arm around Heather as she took her seat beside him. "My spinach and cheese casserole is the bomb."

"All right," Chang said and gave him a thumbs-up in approval.

Thirteen stood in front of the TV. "In that case, if there are no objections, I'll simply summarize each update rather than going around the room."

Jon waved a hand. "Summarize away."

"The trip to Ukraine was a success in that Jon and Theo were able to confirm the meeting between Boyko and both Senator and Magnus Kelch. They obtained meeting minutes from Boyko's assistant on all four meetings with the brothers. Their trip to Bohlren was equally successful, if not more so. In addition to confirming the meeting between the Kelch brothers and Councilman Okhotnikov, Theo was also able to track down Dr. A. Fahran, curator of the Yakiviy and Aunre Museum of History."

He turned to me. "Minutes from all three meetings confirm what Magnolia discovered not only from Colin's team's information, but also from what Cordele was able to relay before her demise." A wave of ache washed over him, making my heart clench. I wasn't the only one he'd held paternal feelings for—he loved every member of this team.

He cleared his throat. "Kelch Inc. may very well establish facilities in the nations of Ukraine, Belarus, Moldova, and western Russia, but their primary objective is to locate the manufacturer of a certain type of ancient tool. If I understand correctly, they believe the maker of these artifacts will lead them to discover the source of their supernatural bloodline, a fact currently unknown to all Kelches. Is that correct, Magnolia?"

My throat was dry, but I managed to swallow. "Yes. We've never known where our powers came from. Grandmother never revealed Grandfather's identity, but it's always been assumed it was from him that we drew our abilities."

"And by identifying this toolmaker, the senator and Magnus hope to locate their birth father, thereby devising a way to increase their current supernatural strength."

"Exactly." I sat forward. "But you have to keep in mind that Malcolm is after this guy too. He wants to break out on his own, and he wants to kill my uncle Max. Badly. Cordele had a strong mind. She managed to keep my identity secret whenever she was with him. But I don't know if he picked up anything about the rest of the team. Whatever he learned, though, you can guarantee that he will be passing at least some of it on to Father and Uncle Max. The rest he'll use to find this toolmaker first. Especially now that he knows I'm helping you."

"Then it's a race," Jon said, completely serious. "If Magnus and the senator are searching for their father, and Malcolm is playing double agent right on their heels, then we'll just have to find this guy first." He looked at me. "Are you up for that? Going on the hunt for Grandpa?"

My heart picked up the pace as a new excitement suddenly sprouted inside me. I was a proven Network agent now, one who had been in on more than one successful mission. I wasn't a normal agent, but I was a powerful one. And they truly trusted me. They trusted me not only to have their backs and to pull my weight, but to put the needs of the team first, even when going against my family.

"You bet your ass I am," I said, and I knew exactly where to start.

CHAPTER 39

I went home with Theo after the update meeting and Christmas meal at Jon and Heather's house. He drove the long way through downtown, passing by the monument lights, which were even better than I'd imagined.

It turned out that Theo's house was an oversize Cape Cod on a side street just south of the city, not even two blocks from the safe house Thirteen had kept me in when I'd first escaped. He'd been refurbishing the home for the past five years. Right now, the basement and upstairs were closed off to conserve heat. A red-and-black pool table in the dining room announced the place as a bachelor pad, even though the updated kitchen boasted stainless steel appliances, a granite-top island, and a pet betta fish standing guard against the stack of unopened mail. The downstairs bedroom, currently being used as the master bedroom, sat just off the kitchen. With twelve-foot ceilings, a wide-mantel fireplace, and a king-size bed with a thick brown comforter, the room was absolutely perfect.

Theo had helped me carry in my shopping bags of clothes, poured me a glass of whiskey, then led me to the bed. As I drifted off, his musky scent surrounded me. I couldn't remember ever feeling that safe.

In my dream, my golden island was a continent now. The bloody lake, a full ocean. I lay on the long, sandy beach with my fingers in the water, playing softly over my smiling twin as small waves lapped from the subtle red sea on the shore.

I pulled my fingers from the bloody sea and sat up when I felt the dream man approach. Looking over my shoulder, I saw him standing a few feet away, hands in pockets again, a hesitant smile on his face. "Hello, Magnolia."

I'd been thinking about him when I'd fallen asleep, hoping he would show himself again. He'd left so quickly last time; I took a moment to study him. In his features, I saw the different pieces of my family: my father, my uncles, my brothers. He didn't even look as old as Father, and certainly not old enough to be my grandfather, but he had always felt like just another part of me. I realized now that's exactly who he was.

"You're my grandfather, aren't you?"

He smiled. "Yes, Magnolia. I am." My dream grew a little brighter as he strolled closer. "When I began visiting you here in your dreams, it was because I'd felt a sudden spike of new power in my bloodline, one that I'd never felt in someone other than myself. This golden power that's inside you now—no one else in my lineage has ever managed to develop it. Until that moment when it revealed itself inside you, I didn't even know you existed."

"You mean you didn't know about me before?" It was the question that burned inside me more than any other: had this man, who had only ever shown interest in me and had never once tried to hurt or intimidate me, known about my life of hell all those years on the estate?

"No, I didn't know. I can feel the power of my bloodline as it grows. I felt when each of my sons was born, even though I wasn't present at their births. And I felt when they had children of their own, so in that sense I knew grandchildren existed. My own power grew stronger with each new offspring. But I never followed the events of their lives. There never seemed to be a reason to. Until you."

So he didn't need proximity to his bloodline to feel the strength of it. He could just feel the growing power of his family wherever he was. That must be nice.

"Why weren't you there when your sons were born?"

"Their human mother was enough to raise them. There was no need for me to be there as they matured. After all, it was their power that mattered. Their existence was enough to fuel me. What they did or didn't do with their lives was of no consequence." He said it with such nonchalance that I couldn't help but cringe. As different as this man seemed from the rest of my family, when it came to paternal responsibility, he was exactly the same.

"So the only reason you had children was to grow your power?"

He looked down on me with subtle confusion. "Power is everything."

And there it was. The very heart of where I came from. I couldn't argue with him—I'd had that very thought on more than one occasion. Most recently while lying in bed with Theo, letting the power around us become our life force, sustaining us as it grew. It was the start of that power with Theo that had brought Grandfather to me in the first place.

"But you were right, Magnolia," he said with an excited gleam in his eye. "There is more inside you than in your father or siblings. You have found the means not only to hone the darkness, but to embrace and fuel the light as well."

He looked out over the bloody sea. "Hatred, pain, rage—the power of these things will always flow through you, crashing in their violence and making you stronger." As if responding to his words, the blood of my dream ocean instantly boiled to life, rising high in tsunami-like waves. Just as quickly it settled back down. He turned to the golden shoreline, the long stretch of land behind us. "But it is the love you have discovered yourself capable of and the love you have accepted from others that has become your foundation. With the balance of the two, your powers have the potential to be truly limitless."

I looked back out over the sea, then down at the reflection of my twin. Grandfather watched me. Questions suddenly raced through my mind. What was he? Where had he come from? Was he evil? Where was he located outside this dream? I had so many questions…

"And I will answer them all," he said, addressing my unspoken thoughts. "I never meant to deceive you. I've enjoyed our visits, enjoyed getting to know you. I hope our conversations will continue in the future."

I thought over our many dreamed talks, the interest he'd always shown in me. He'd said on his last visit that he wanted me to trust him. Now I knew I really wanted that too.

"I'd like to keep visiting with you like this," I said. "Visiting in my dreams." Then I studied him closer. "You didn't love my grandmother or your sons—you were only interested in the power they gave you. How is it, then, that you can recognize this golden energy inside me?"

He shrugged. "Your grandmother approached me with a proposition of power, one that would best serve us both. She wanted the most powerful offspring possible, and I wanted to strengthen my bloodline. Though completely human, she had a deep darkness inside her, and I recognized the potential of strengthening that side of me through her. It was never about any emotion."

"So your dark powers are your strongest because we came from her?"

"Not at all. Just because I never felt those things for her or her sons, it doesn't mean those feelings aren't a large part of me. Just like you, the vastness of my darkness is very much shared by the vastness of my light. Power is power, Magnolia. And now that you have unlocked the light inside you, you will have the ability to wield both as you see fit." He smiled warmly. "It has been a very long while since I have spent time with another who shared my powers so closely. I would very much enjoy helping you to grow in your abilities."

There was such sincerity in his gaze, I couldn't help but smile back. Then he sighed and stepped away. "Unfortunately, at the moment, I haven't the time for much more of a visit. I only came here tonight to make sure you would be open to more visits in the future."

A breeze whipped my hair as I frowned. "You can't stay? But there's so much I want to know."

He knelt down and patted my hand. It was such a grandfatherly gesture, the landscape of my dream glowed brighter.

"I will be back, Magnolia. And we will talk, and you will learn. Although, I have to admit, you seem to be doing very well on your own. Your control is astounding. Your power, magnificent."

The glow around me was nearly blinding as the pride he so obviously felt in me shone in his eyes. My grandfather, the source of my everything, was proud of me. Even in my dream, my smile was so wide it ached. He got to his feet, and my smile vanished. How long would I have to wait to see him again and start getting some of my answers?

"Not long," he answered. "I just have a few matters that require my attention right now."

Suddenly his eyes flashed red, just as mine did whenever I transformed. He smiled, and his mouth had grown wide, full of sharp, razor-like teeth. It was exactly the way I looked when I transformed. But instead of being horrifying or monstrous like I always pictured myself after the change, he was beautiful. Ethereal and radiant.

His voice didn't fit the appearance, though. He sounded as eloquent as ever as he said, "Apparently my sons have taken it upon themselves to become involved in matters that don't concern them. The tools they are tracking won't lead them to me, of course, but their efforts may very well become a problem that I don't wish to deal with. You see, even if they discovered the origin of their gifts, they would never be able to realize its fullest potential, not without the ability to realize the light side of our powers. In their quest to do so, however, they may very well get themselves killed."

"You'll kill them?" I asked, not sure if I was hopeful or frightened by the idea.

"Of course not," he replied, waving away the idea with a clawed hand. "But there are others that will. As powerful as your family is, there are always more powerful creatures out there—creatures that your Network hasn't even discovered yet. I'm not willing to lessen my bloodline's power just because my greedy offspring poke around those who don't wish to be disturbed."

Creatures more powerful than my family. Thirteen would most definitely be interested in that. I was trying to imagine how this new information might change the direction of our current assignment when a horrible thought occurred to me.

The golden sky darkened as I asked, "What if someone from the Network kills my father or uncles? Would you kill my team?" My vision turned red as I had a quick fantasy of Theo taking on my father, overpowering him with the abilities our connection had given him. No way I'd let Grandfather retaliate against Theo just for weakening his bloodline.

Grandfather's lips twitched like he was holding back a laugh. "Your Network serves its purpose policing those supernaturals arrogant enough to reveal themselves and their powers to the human world. If your father or uncles are so inept as to get themselves killed by a human agency like that, then their power wasn't worth the blood in their veins anyway." I relaxed. "Now, my dear Magnolia," he said with a slight tilt of his head. "Until next time."

His smile changed then, turned violent in a way that made everything in my dream go still. The sea, the breeze, my twin, everything stopped as I stared at this most powerful, most dangerous being.

Then just like that, he was gone. The breeze picked back up as movement returned to the sea.

For a long moment I sat there, absorbing the revelations Grandfather had left me with. How incredibly ironic that in Father and Uncle Max's quest for greater power, they had turned away from what apparently could give more than anything imaginable. Love. I thought of Father's Marlena. Things would have been so different if he'd just been able to love her like I loved Theo.

I'd never shared these dreams with anyone else before, but tomorrow, I'd talk to Theo, tell him everything about this place, about my twin and my grandfather. After all, the foundation of my power was love now. Sharing could only strengthen it.

I'd also tell Thirteen what Grandfather had said about more powerful beings existing that the Network wasn't yet aware of. I couldn't imagine him actually doing anything about it—I mean, if these beings were a real threat, he would have already known about them.

But all that would happen tomorrow. Tonight, I slept warmly in the arms of the man I loved, a man whose love for me grew my powers to a level that changed who I was for the better. I had a team of friends who accepted me and trusted me. And now I had a real member of my family who was truly interested in me. He would continue to talk to me, answer my many questions, and visit me again in this safe place. Our paths would cross in real life one day, either through a Network assignment or through some other means, but I had a feeling that wouldn't happen until both of us were ready.

I reached out to touch my fingertips back to my twin's and returned her smile. I wasn't evil and I wasn't good. I was powerful, with the potential to do so much with both. Glancing around the crimson-and-gold landscape, I felt surer of myself than ever before.

And for once, I was much too at peace not to lie back and simply smile.

ACKNOWLEDGMENTS

First and foremost, I'd like to thank you, the reader. Thank you for spending some time with Magnolia in all her beautiful, dysfunctional glory. She is very dear to my heart, and as she continues to grow, I can't thank you enough for coming along for the ride.

I would also like to thank Amazon Publishing, 47North, and the many people who worked so hard to bring *No Love for the Wicked* to life. Most especially, I'd like to thank Maria, Jayne, and Patrick—your constant communication and support are more than I could have ever hoped for in a publishing team.

Speaking of teams, my eternal gratitude will forever be sent to the incredible people at New Leaf Literary. Kathleen, Suzie, Danielle, and the miracle worker herself, Jo—I hit the jackpot, won the lotto, and found a pot of gold at the end of the rainbow the day I signed with this incredible agency. I thank my lucky stars every time I send in another round of edits that they are still willing to work with me.

I'd also like to send a special thank-you to my dad's crazy old roommate—your encouragement and insight is more appreciated than you know.

Finally, I'd like to send my loving thanks to those who are always with me, whether it be in my created worlds or my real one: Molly, my always reader. Mark, my always inspiration. Sarah and Cathy, my always supporters. Stephanie and Amy, my always cheerleaders. J and R, my always foundation. And Brian...my always. Thank you.

ABOUT THE AUTHOR

Megan Powell was born and raised in the Midwest, where she developed a strange affinity for state fairs and basketball humor. Her debut novel, *No Peace for the Damned*, was the first book in her Magnolia Kelch series. When not writing, Powell can be found feeding her paranormal romance addiction.